D0775536

GET LOST

BOOK TWO
THE GABE MCKENNA SERIES

ROBERT D. KIDERA

Robert D. Kidera

SUSPENSE PUBLISHING

GET LOST
By
Robert D. Kidera

PAPERBACK EDITION
* * * * *
PUBLISHED BY:
Suspense Publishing

Robert D. Kidera
COPYRIGHT
2016 Robert D. Kidera
www.robertkiderabooks.com

PUBLISHING HISTORY:
Suspense Publishing, Paperback and Digital Copy, March 2016

Cover Design: Shannon Raab
Cover Photographer: iStockphoto.com/Stevanovicigor
Cover Photographer: iStockphoto.com/Jamie Farrant

ISBN-13: 978-0692645277 (Suspense Publishing)
ISBN-10: 0692645276

To my daughters and grandchildren, Anne Elizabeth, Jeanne Marie, Liam, and Bridget Grace.

PRAISE FOR "GET LOST"

"Robert Kidera is an absolute master of mystery! He grabs you with irresistible intrigue and fresh, seductive writing and refuses to let go while he pummels you with twist after delicious twist. I highly recommend this book and this writer!"
—*NY Times* Bestselling Author **Darynda Jones**

"Follow Gabe McKenna on an emotional journey full of unexpected twists and discoveries. 'Get Lost' is a delightfully exciting New Mexico mystery. I highly recommend it!"
—**S.H. Baker**, Author of the *Dassas Cormier Mystery* Series

" 'Get Lost' is a seasoned hybrid of a first class thriller and modern day western that effortlessly layers Native American concerns in the blood-soaked fabric of murder and conspiracy. Robert D. Kidera handles this difficult mix with a skill and aplomb worthy of the late, great Tony Hillerman and his latest is a modern marvel of both form and function. As riveting as it is thought-provoking, 'Get Lost' is reading entertainment of the highest order."
—**Jon Land**, *USA Today* Bestselling Author of "Strong Light of Day"

"The spirit of Raymond Chandler hovers over Robert D. Kidera's mystery writing. His gift for telling atmosphere and sharp dialogue and his continually surprising plotting make him an effortlessly skillful storyteller. His flawed but noble protagonist, Gabe McKenna, is a worthy modern successor to Chander's Philip Marlowe."
—**Joseph McBride**, Biographer of Frank Capra, John Ford, and Steven Spielberg

GET LOST

BOOK TWO
THE GABE MCKENNA SERIES

ROBERT D. KIDERA

CHAPTER ONE

I cradled a 12th Century Anasazi duck-shaped pot in my hands. One large crack ringed most of its neck, but nearly all of the head and sienna ochre markings remained intact. Red Mesa, I figured. And priceless. It felt good to be back in the game.

That's when everything fell apart.

Frantic pounding on my back door—a crash of broken glass—a cry from an obviously terrified man.

"*Señor* McKenna! Professor! *Por favor!*" Work crew foreman Ernesto Acosta should have been leveling the ground in my barn and pouring a concrete floor, not yelling through my door.

"What's wrong?" I placed the artifact back into its protective case. His pounding and yelling continued. I rushed through the kitchen, careful to avoid the shards of window glass beneath my feet, and unlocked the door.

Acosta burst into the room, knocked over the cat's water bowl and came to a stop against the edge of the counter. Fear bled from his eyes.

"*Encontramos huesos!*" He gasped and waved a frantic arm toward the barn.

"Bones?" I said. "You found bones?"

"*Si, en el granero.*" He crossed himself and offered his hands to Heaven.

Bones in my barn? I caught my breath. "Ernesto, get a grip. And try English, *por favor.*"

He grabbed my sleeve and pulled me toward the now-open door. "*Pronto.* Come!"

"What kind of bones?"

"*Un esquelito.*"

Damn, too many years since Spanish III. "A skeleton?" Adrenaline surged through me, just like the old days. I'd forgotten how much I loved the feeling.

"*Sí,* skeleton." Jockey-size Ernesto scrambled toward the barn as fast as his stumpy legs permitted.

I followed, stepping on the back of his shoe in my excitement. "Was there anything else?"

"*Que?*"

"Pots? Clothes? Jewelry?" I grabbed his shirt.

"Clothes...metal."

Sweet music. A find—right under my garage! In New Mexico, these things happen. I warned Ernesto with my eyes. "You didn't disturb anything?"

"No, *señor.*" Ernesto shook his head twice. Then he shook it a couple more times.

"Okay. Just stand back." I maneuvered around a stack of sheet metal that up until yesterday had served as the barn's huge front door.

Five other workmen stood inside, hugging the right-hand wall. Large, leathery, muscular, ready to bolt. "Hold it, guys—*estar*! Ernesto, you stay here by the door. Don't let anyone else in."

He let his breath out like he'd just been told his teenage daughter *wasn't* pregnant. He aimed a quivering finger toward a mini-excavator twenty feet inside. "Behind there."

Small mounds of fresh dirt surrounded the machine. I swung to the rear of the digging arm and stopped. John Deere, surrounded by bones. Lots of bones. Human bones.

I'd seen my share during a thirty-year career in archeology. Pre-Puebloan maybe, the people I'd written and taught so much about. I knelt beside the remains, hoping to see an artifact, potsherd, some datable object, anything that might hold a clue.

Something sparkled amid the bones. I bent down for a closer look.

An oxidized, crusted pocket watch. Fragments of vintage 1970's polyester. A dulled onyx ring that circled what appeared to be a finger bone. And a skull.

Nothing for an historical archaeologist here. Plenty for the cops. "Everybody outside." I pointed toward the open door.

The workers didn't wait for a translation.

I stood outside the barn and watched the minutes tick off on my cellphone. At ten minutes past noon, two squad cars and a third Bernalillo County vehicle veered into my driveway. Detective Lieutenant Sam Archuleta led the landing party up the incline toward my barn.

I gave the lieutenant a wave when he reached the top of the rise. "Been a while, Sam."

"Everything beautiful comes to an end," he shot back. Not one warm note in his voice. Not one.

"Love you too. Got a body for you."

"What is it with you and dead bodies?" His voice straddled the line between a question and an accusation. He sucked on his cigarette and blew the smoke in my face.

I swatted away the fumes and offered my hand instead to a woman by his side.

"Doctor Rachel Holtzmann, Bernalillo County Medical Investigator." Robotic, but informative.

We shook, and I laid my academic credentials at her feet. That got me nowhere. The fortyish Holtzmann nearly matched my six feet in height. Her thin, beak-like nose and large eyes suggested a hungry bird of prey.

"Where's the body?" She looked past me into the barn and cocked her head.

"This way." I led her to the far side of the excavator and pointed down at the remains. "I'd say they've been here for fifty years. Maybe more. Think you ought to call in a forensic archeologist?"

She recoiled like I'd just stepped on her open-toed shoes. "Don't be ridiculous." She knelt close enough to the bones to hear them whisper. One crank of her neck and she was peering up at me. "These bones aren't *that* old, Professor."

I walked back to Sam. He looked happier now that I'd been put in my place.

Holtzmann called back to him. "I'm going to need several hours here. Have the area roped off."

"Right away." Archuleta motioned to a young officer a few feet off, an angelic muscle mass with a blonde buzz cut. "Jackson, secure the area. Then question the workers. Names. Contact info. Then get them out of here. Any of them you think are illegals, pull them aside."

"I'm on it, Lieutenant." He bounded off like the only one interested in being here.

"Rookies." Sam grabbed my elbow and dragged me out and away from the barn. "Now, suppose you tell me what the fuck is going on here."

"I'm having a new concrete floor poured. More space for my cars. The workmen uncovered human remains, alerted me, and I called you right away."

"Nice of you to follow the rules for a change." Sam had two hobbies: smoking and sarcasm. He looked toward the driveway when a fourth vehicle pulled up. Another cop car. "Well, look who's here."

I turned in time to see Detective Sergeant Harold Crawford rumble out of the vehicle.

An ungentle giant who never missed a clue or a chance to inflict some untraceable pain, Crawford hustled his two hundred and fifty pounds of malevolence up the hill. When his eyes settled on me, he sidled up close and bowed overdramatically. Near enough to spit closer to my shoes.

Sam stepped in. "That'll do, Sergeant."

Crawford and I had a history, kind of like the Thirty Years' War. "McKenna. I should have known. Stay out of our way and leave this to the pros." He hadn't changed. I looked at Sam. Sam looked away.

Crawford emitted a guttural sound. His eyes swept the inside of my barn.

I decided to try nice. "See anything?"

"Nothing I care to share with you."

I raised my hands and backed away.

Sam turned to his sergeant. "Go over and see how Jackson is doing with those workers."

"Is that an order?"

Archuleta took a step toward his hulking subordinate. "That's an order."

"Yessir." Crawford's elbow stabbed my ribs as he brushed past me.

Holtzmann stood and walked to Sam's side, two Baggies in her left hand. "Lieutenant, you better cancel any dinner plans. This one's a puzzle."

Archuleta looked at his watch the way a condemned man stares at the prison wall clock. "Second night this week. And it's only Monday."

"What?" I said. Sam usually wasn't one to complain.

"We had a homicide last night at that new Pueblo-66 Casino. Some guy bit the biscuit in the owner's office. The secretary is missing. Nobody saw nothing. Now this." He peeled a fresh roll of antacids, took the cigarette out of his mouth, and popped a couple of lozenges.

He wanted answers. I wanted lunch. "If you don't require my presence—" I pointed toward the house with my head.

"Did I say that?"

"Come on, Lieutenant. Curtis Jester is getting out of the hospital today. We're throwing him a Welcome Home party at his restaurant. Rebecca and I are due there in half an hour."

"Rebecca Turner's here?" Just like that, the lieutenant was full of sugar.

"Inside the house."

"I see." His voice flashed like he'd heard the first interesting news of the day.

"She's my secretary now."

He gave me a knowing look. "Uh-huh."

"Lieutenant, for a happily married man, you sure have a dirty mind."

He let that pass, flicked his half-smoked cigarette to the ground and re-lit.

I headed for my house, but not before a final parting salvo. "Why don't you concentrate on the body *inside* the barn?"

"Don't leave town."

"Any more clichés before I go?"

Sam's third finger added a spring to my step all the way down to the house.

15

Rebecca Turner held the curtain aside and looked out the library window. She turned when I reached my desk. "What's the story, Gabe?"

"No idea. That body's been buried out there for decades. It's a police problem, not ours. Don't worry about it."

"Okay. I left the mail on your desk. There's a royalty check from your publisher. I slit it open for you." She appeared delighted about something.

There it was—my quarterly envelope from Dumbarton Press, publishers of *Mystery of the Anasazi*, my one and only academic work, now in its thirtieth year. My ego traveled to my right hand. I slid the check out like it was Christmas morning.

Two dollars and forty-three cents. Some fool clicked the wrong button again on Amazon. I sighed and tossed the check onto my desk. "Great literature never dies. Ready for C.J.'s?"

"Give me five minutes." Rebecca swung down the hall toward the bathroom. She didn't need five *seconds* to stun a crowd. Twenty-five, blonde, slim, athletic, so improbably innocent. I knew Rebecca's truth: orphaned, enslaved, abused. And then she saved my life.

I loved Rebecca. The way a father loves his daughter.

CHAPTER TWO

Happy people filled every seat at every table in C.J.'s Barbecue Restaurant. Smoke from a smoldering pit in the center of its large single room rose, danced and disappeared into the soft blue ceiling light. Youthful servers zigzagged through the crowd with platters of smoking meat, bowls of green chile stew and pitchers of beer. Extra napkins, too.

Rebecca and I sat at the head table, waiting with those assembled for the Man-of-the-Hour to arrive. She sipped a Diet-Pepsi; I did my best with a club soda and lemon.

The front door opened. House lights dimmed. A zydeco band struck up a funky, off-center version of the opening riff from Curtis Mayfield's *Super Fly*.

A stoop-shouldered silhouette of a man filled the doorway, clutching a microphone in his right hand. "In the far corner—from Bed-Stuy in Brooklyn, New York—weighing considerably more than his former one hundred and sixty pounds…" Curtis Jester didn't get any farther. He broke into his trademark laugh. And laughter spread through the room faster than the sweet smell of baby-back ribs.

His laugh faded as he took in the size of the crowd. He swapped the microphone for a cane and his smile for a look of grim determination.

His first step was tentative and showed visible pain. No one spoke. There was nothing to hear except for meat sizzling on the grill.

C.J.'s wife Charmaine held his left arm above the elbow for the first couple of steps. He shook her off and two steps later handed her the cane. The smile crept back across his face. He paused, steadied himself, and slow-walked toward the head table, unaided.

Charmaine gasped at first, then wept, one hand finding her mouth. The band played louder. I found it hard to swallow. That's when the applause started, slowly, haltingly, until it grew to a mighty wave of tears and cheers.

C.J. reached the head table and hobbled over to the seat on my left. I grabbed his hand and held it above our heads.

A shattered leg, two cracked vertebrae, a ruptured spleen, and a concussion—C.J.'s bitter reward for helping me recover a couple million dollars in gold. I'd used much of it to cover his medical bills, but…

Charmaine rarely spoke to me, even now. I was trouble. That's all I'd been to her since the day I rediscovered my former sparring partner two thousand miles away from Gleason's gym back in New York. I felt thankful she'd let me come to welcome her husband home from five months in the hospital.

C.J. insisted I sit at the head table, despite his wife's feelings. During a lull in the stream of friends who came up to shake his hand and offer congratulations, I leaned toward my old pal.

"I'm sorry for all that happened to you."

He bent back like he was avoiding a too-slow left hook. "Dog, how many rounds did you go as my sparring partner?"

"I lost count a long time ago."

"Right. And how many times did I make you bleed?"

I shook my neck and shoulders as those painful memories returned.

"I figure you and me are about even. Maybe you owe me a couple of Cuban cigars." He laughed again and lifted a rib from his plate to his open mouth.

I plopped my right elbow on the table and leaned forward until my head rested on my raised hand. My middle finger slid along the scar tissue beneath my eyebrow. Nothing bonds you to a guy like spending a hundred hours in the ring trying to beat the snot out of him.

C.J. looked down at my empty plate. "Can I hit you again?"

"I never could stop you."

He waved at a waitress who slid over and dumped another half rack in front of me. "Where's your lady?" C.J. said, once the first bit of sauce touched my lips.

I leaned back from the table so he could see Rebecca, two seats down. She'd attracted a crowd of her own. "Right there."

"No, man. Where's your *lady*? Where's Nai'ya?"

I glanced at my watch. Almost two o'clock. Nai'ya Alonso-Riley told me she'd stop by at one-thirty after teaching her last morning class at University of New Mexico. I'd been saving her the seat to my right.

Nai'ya and I first met more than twenty-five summers ago. She was a grad student. I was a full-of-myself academic with a grant to excavate Ancestral Puebloan ruins. We'd been close for those short summer weeks. Re-discovering her was the best thing that had happened since my return to New Mexico six months ago.

My cellphone rang. I smiled at the caller ID. "Hi, sweetie!"

"I can't make it to the luncheon. Say hi to C.J. for me." The tone of Nai'ya's voice raised an alarm.

"What's wrong?"

"Can't talk now. Something's come up."

"Nai'ya, what's the matter?" My cellphone began beeping. Another call.

"I have to go." She hung up.

"Nai'ya?" The phone flashed Sam Archuleta's number. I punched it in.

"How soon can you get back here?"

"Can't it wait 'til tomorrow?"

"Let's just say I'd appreciate it if you made every effort to get here. *Pronto*."

I didn't need this. "You're a hard man. Give me ten minutes."

"I'm a cupcake. Take fifteen. Bye."

C.J. cut in. "Something wrong?"

"Some trouble back at the house. I'm having work done on my barn. Be back as soon as I can."

"Don't take too long. Charmaine made sweet potato pies for dessert. They won't last."

I motioned to Rebecca. She met me outside the front door. We climbed into the 1948 Hudson coupe I'd inherited as part of my great-aunt's estate and sped north along Fourth Street.

"What did Nai'ya say?" Rebecca asked.

"It's what she didn't say. There was fear in her voice. Something's wrong. She hung up without telling me."

Now I had Rebecca worried. "I'll deal with the cops," she said. "Just drop me off. Go to her."

We pulled up to the curb in front of my house. Two more vehicles had just slowed to a stop in my driveway. That made six. Three men carried a portable light kit out of the first car and rushed around to the barn. The other vehicle was an ambulance.

CHAPTER THREE

Archuleta leaned against his car door and waved. He said something to Crawford who shrugged and slouched off toward the barn.

Rebecca held onto my arm as we hurried up the walkway to my house. The considerate lieutenant flicked his cigarette butt on the ground and followed us inside.

"More room in the library." I led the way and sat down at my desk.

Rebecca tossed her blonde hair over a shoulder. "Care for a drink, Lieutenant? We stock just about everything."

"I'm on duty. Thanks anyway." His hands fidgeted. He checked out the furniture and the standing clock in the corner.

"Would you get me a club soda with a twist, please?" I asked Rebecca.

Sam's eyebrows shot up so fast he should have gotten a speeding ticket. "Club soda?"

"One day at a time. Tomorrow will be three months of sobriety. Now, why did you call us away from C.J.'s? This better be important. We've got someplace to be." I checked my watch in case he wasn't in listening mode.

A few more lines creased the lieutenant's face than two hours before. And he needed a shave. "Dead bodies are always important," he said. "May I?" He took a pack of Camels from his jacket and waved it at me.

I picked up an empty candy dish from the end table and handed it over. "Puff away."

Sam stood by the door and blew the first lungful of smoke into the hall. "We need some answers about this property."

"Shoot."

"How long has it been in your family?"

"As I recall, great-aunt Nellie bought the place around 1990."

Rebecca returned with my drink and I held it in my right hand. "Before you sit down, there's a folder labeled 'Real Estate' in the second drawer of my file cabinet. Could you please bring it out for the lieutenant?"

"Sure."

Sam studied her curves, his hand fumbling with what might charitably be called his tie.

I cleared my throat. "To our health, Lieutenant." I slugged down a mouthful of club soda.

He inhaled and coughed into his sleeve. A thin strand of smoke seeped through the fabric into the air. "Was that barn here when your great-aunt bought this place?"

"The mortgage and title should tell us that." *What kinds of questions were these?* "Where the hell are you going with this, Sam? Those bones have been here for a long, long time. I've done enough digging to see that. Ask Holtzmann if you don't believe me."

Sam raised a finger. "Just because the corpse is old doesn't mean it's been in the ground *here* that long. Could've been moved."

"Don't you think Aunt Nellie would've noticed?" I put my drink down on the desk. "Or are you suggesting she might have had something to do with this?"

Rebecca closed the file cabinet with a bang. She crossed to the desk, handed the folder to me and sat down to my right. I put down my drink, located the title deed and Nellie's original mortgage and slid them from the folder.

Sam leaned forward, his hand outstretched.

I held out the two documents and made him come over to me. He looked like he needed the exercise.

He paged through the contents and carried the papers with him to the bay window. "So, the barn pre-dated the sale. The previous owner is listed as William Klein Associates. We'll check them out."

I drummed my fingers on the desktop. "That answer your questions? May we leave now?"

Sergeant Crawford and Medical Investigator Holtzmann charged into the library without knocking. She carried a clipboard, Crawford carried his scowl. They got Sam's full attention. "What have you got for me?"

Holtzmann did the talking. "Pelvic structure and height would indicate male, approximately six foot one or two. My estimate, subject to confirmation at the lab, is that he died at least fifty years ago. Somewhere between forty and seventy years old at the time of death."

"Cause of death?" Sam said.

"Homicide."

"Marvelous. Details?"

"His skull is virtually intact."

Sam's eyebrows rose once more. "Odd, for a body loose in the ground that long. You sure it's a homicide?"

"There's a clear bullet hole in the back of the head," Holtzmann continued. "Likely an entry wound from the size of the aperture. No exit wound visible."

"Find a bullet?"

Holtzmann shook her head. "The shot may have gone out through an eye socket. That's my guess."

"I'm betting this guy was shot somewhere else and dumped." Archuleta popped another antacid.

The medical investigator checked her watch. "We have a few more hours' work here before we can safely move the remains to the morgue. The skeleton, what there is of it, is fragile. We don't want to miss anything that might be in the fine sand."

Sam stubbed his cigarette in the candy dish and let out a tired sigh. "Okay...anything else?"

"Bits of fabric among the bones," Holtzmann said. "We'll do microscopic textile analysis tomorrow to see if there are any hairs present for DNA testing. Don't expect anything."

"I never do."

"There's more." She flipped the page on her clipboard. "At one time the victim suffered fractures to both the radius and ulna bones of his left forearm. Could have been in childhood. They didn't set properly. He might have had limited use of that arm."

Sam rubbed the back of his neck. "Is that it?"

"No. Our man didn't have any teeth."

"None?" I asked.

Crawford eyes burned into me.

"None." Holtzmann's glasses slid far enough down her narrow nose that she pushed them back up with the eraser end of her pencil. "No gum tissue left after all these years, of course. The jawbone was worn down. The teeth may have been gone a long time. No sign of dentures. If he had them, either they weren't in when he was killed, or they were left behind when his body was moved."

"Any personal articles with the body?" Sam said.

Holtzmann turned to Crawford. "Show him the ring."

Crawford handed a plastic bag to Archuleta. As he held it up for a closer look, I stood and moved forward for a better view. The bag held the black onyx ring I'd seen on the finger bone of the corpse. The large gold icon on its surface glistened as it caught the ceiling light.

"Let me see that." I peered through the plastic as Archuleta held the bag between his thumb and forefinger. A profile figure of an Indian chief in full headdress. Gold on black. "That's Chief Tammany, Sam."

"Who?" Sam returned the bag to Holtzmann. She brought it closer to her eyes and adjusted her glasses.

"A legendary figure from early-to-mid nineteenth century American folklore. The symbol of Tammany Hall—you know, the old New York political machine. I'd bet this guy was a member of that organization. A 'Son of Tammany' as they called themselves. The banner here below the figure—" I slid my finger along the bag in the Doctor's hand.

"Don't touch that!" Crawford moved toward me.

I pulled my hand back. "Sorry. Just trying to help, Sergeant. Can I offer you something cold?"

Veins stood out on Crawford's forehead. "I got no use for you, McKenna. None. You always think you're the smartest guy in the room."

"That's enough, Crawford!" Sam stared down the taller sergeant. "Outside." Crawford held his ground for a moment until his boss pointed to the door. "Wait by the car. Do it *now*."

Crawford spun on his heel and disappeared into the hallway. The front door slammed.

Sam waved toward the door. "Forget Crawford. He's a hard-ass with a bad marriage and a sick kid."

"Life is tough." I turned to Rebecca. "Ready to go?" She nodded but seemed to look at Sam for approval.

"All right," he said. His cellphone rang. He raised a hand toward us. "Wait a minute. Okay…right, boss. About two more hours, according to Holtzmann. Good." Then his face brightened and he bobbed up and down, like he wanted to do a little jig before thinking better of it. "Excellent. I'll get on it first thing in the morning. What about this one? He'll be glad to hear that. Bye."

"Well?" I said.

"You're both free to leave. Give my best to C.J. I know he hates cops, but tell him just the same."

"I will. Mind if I lock up the house before we go?"

"Not at all. My guys can always pee in your flowerbed. We won't be seeing each other for a while, anyway."

"Why not?"

"That was my boss. I'm now leading the investigation into last night's casino shooting. That's more of a priority than any fifty-year-old cold case."

"Congratulations," I said. "So who will I have to deal with on this mess?"

Sam smiled. "Crawford." He patted my sleeve and left the house with Holtzmann.

Rebecca huffed out to my car. I cursed under my breath and locked the door behind me. Cleaning up the broken glass could wait.

Most of the guests had left by the time we returned to C.J.'s. The zydeco band played on with no loss of energy, like they'd just been re-wound. Decorations still fluttered in time with the rotation of the ceiling fans. C.J. looked like he needed a nap, but he'd saved us two slices of sweet potato pie. Rebecca and I washed them down with fresh cups of coffee.

"So what's up, Gabe?" C.J. took a cigar from his breast pocket and peeled off the cellophane.

"The crew working on my barn unearthed a body. An old one. The cops are all over it."

He looked around. "Don't let Charmaine hear about this, okay? I called in all my chips just to get her to invite you today."

Before I could respond, somebody switched on the restaurant's big screen TV. A local channel flashed its top story: the killing at Pueblo-66 Casino. The sound was muted, but the screen showed a bloodstained cloth over what must have been the body of the victim.

Sam appeared onscreen, a microphone nearly stuck up his nose. At least he didn't look so short up there on the big screen. The story's final image was of a young woman. Under her face it read: *Missing and wanted for questioning.*

I'd seen her before—in a framed photograph on the mantel in Nai'ya's living room.

CHAPTER FOUR

Rebecca's car was in for repairs and I was her ride home. She anticipated me. "Listen Gabe, I'll take a cab. You go to Nai'ya. If there's anything I can do, call me."

So typical of her. I called a taxi and gave Rebecca enough for the fare and a generous tip. I rode the accelerator and brake down Fourth Street and then east on Lomas until I reached the area near UNM called Collegetown.

Nai'ya's dark blue Mini Cooper Countryman sat in her driveway. The living room blinds were closed, the front patio dark. I pressed the doorbell. Its ring echoed inside. There was no other sound, no movement, only the slow, steady sinking of my stomach.

I looked through the peephole and laid a couple of hard raps on the door. "Nai'ya? It's Gabe."

The patio light switched on. A dead bolt clicked and the door edged open a couple of inches. A feminine hand slid the chain behind the key slot. The door opened halfway.

Nai'ya's eyes looked red and puffy. "Come in." She backed up and allowed me to wedge past her. A .45 dangled from her right hand. I closed the door and threw the dead bolt.

Her face was little more than a foot from mine, but I don't think she saw me. I glanced down. Her gun hand twitched. A tremor passed from her right hand to her arm. Her body swayed, her knees buckled. I caught her just before she fell.

The gun slipped from her grasp and rattled on the hardwood floor. I reflexively shielded her, but the gun clattered to a harmless stop. The thumb safety was on.

Nai'ya sagged into me. I helped her to the couch and propped her head on an end pillow. Her eyelids fluttered. I stroked her now-pale cheeks and rubbed her wrists.

"Water. Let me get you a glass of water."

I hurried to the kitchen and back, but I couldn't outrun her tears.

"Here." I held the glass as she sipped, then set it on the coffee table. Her head eased back against the pillow.

The missing young woman I'd seen on C.J.'s wall-TV watched all of this from a picture frame on the mantelpiece.

Nai'ya closed her eyes. I walked over and studied the photograph. Familiar, somehow. Mid-to-late twenties, dark brown shoulder length hair, widely separated dark eyes, strong cheekbones. A turquoise necklace, just like the one Nai'ya often wore. Native, probably. Beautiful, definitely.

"Angelina." Nai'ya whispered from behind me.

"She's lovely. Don't think I ever met her, but she looks *so* familiar. What's her full name?"

"Angelina Harper."

I swung around. "A relative?"

Nai'ya nodded.

"I saw her picture half an hour ago on the TV at C.J.'s. Thought I'd seen her picture here. That's why I came over." I eased across the room and sat on the edge of the couch. "You need my help, don't you?"

"She's gone." Nai'ya raised her hands to her face and sobbed into them. "Gone!"

I fumbled for something to say. "Talk to me."

She took a steadying breath. I helped her to a sitting position and guided her head to my chest. My left arm held her as close as I dared.

Nai'ya lost it. She trembled. Her whole body grew rigid. She let out a wail the neighbors must have heard.

I tried to rock her, but she resisted. "Tell me what to do," I said.

She gripped my leg and pushed herself out to an arm's length. "There's more to this than you realize."

I pulled a tissue from the box on the coffee table and handed it to her. "I'm here. I'm not leaving. Whatever this is about, you don't have to face it alone."

Nai'ya clasped the water glass from the table and drank it dry. I handed her a couple more tissues. Her face disappeared into a fistful of white and then re-emerged, lips quivering, eyes unfocused. She paused. "Angelina is my daughter."

I froze, the way a guy does when his world is suddenly no longer the same. I lifted the wad of tissues from Nai'ya's hand and crushed it in my own. "I had no idea."

Nai'ya dug her nails into my wrist. "I don't know where she is."

I rested my hand on top of hers. "Can her father help find her? Is he around somewhere?"

"He is." She drew away a few inches and clutched her arms over her breasts.

"Good. I'll contact him. Where is he?"

She looked at the floor. There was a pause. "Sitting next to me."

I sank back against the couch, my lungs trying hard to breathe. The wadded up tissues dropped to my lap. I turned to stare at the back of Nai'ya's still-lowered head.

"Are you sure she's mine?" I spoke each word with care, afraid that any one of them might explode.

Her voice crackled with defiance. "There was no one else."

She jumped from the couch before I could say another word. Without looking at me, she ran along the hall and into the bedroom. The door sounded like a jail cell when it slammed shut.

CHAPTER FIVE

I hurried after her down the hall and stood outside the closed door. My mind flew back to a single August night a quarter century before. Our project team had completed a dig at Chaco Canyon. We celebrated with a wrap-up party back at UNM in Albuquerque.

Booze flowed freely and pot filled everyone's lungs, even a non-smoker like me who has always preferred to drink himself into oblivion.

Nai'ya and I left early for my motel room, I think. The rest of the night…I was too far gone by then to remember what happened.

My hand slid down the door to the knob. "May I come in?" I didn't hear a "no," so I took that as a "yes" and opened the door.

Nai'ya lay on the bed with a pillow clutched against her body. Two tearful eyes blinked at me over the top of the white linen case. "Forgive me?" Her voice barely reached me.

I entered the room and sat at the bottom of her bed, figuring she might need the distance. "What's to forgive? I'm sure you did what you had to do."

She sounded far away. "You'd gone back to New York by the time I found out. I was afraid, all alone on the Pueblo except for my family. My mother and grandmother told me to let you go. That you lived in your own world." Her hands clenched the pillow so tight I thought I heard it scream.

"I could have been a part of your lives. If—"

"Would you have turned away from your wife and come back to us?" The pillow slid down. The pain on her face came into full view.

Dear god. "Yes, Nai'ya, I would have. That was three years before Holly and I met."

"Oh." She looked away. "I never expected to see you again. Then you showed up last April. I thought about telling you. I wanted to. I couldn't. You'd been left all that money. You might have misunderstood."

"Have a little faith in me."

"I was afraid if I told you, I would lose you again."

"Then you don't know me." I stood and walked to the window and looked into the darkness. "What does Angelina think of me?"

"She thinks her father died before she was born."

I struggled to hold in all the emotions I felt like letting out. My hands trembled. I put them in my pockets. I couldn't swallow. My stomach flipped. I leaned against the wall.

Neither of us spoke. Minutes must have passed before I turned around and looked at her lying there on the bed.

I actually think she expected me to hit her. "Please, don't judge me," she said. "Or Angelina."

"I don't want to judge anyone. I want to know the truth."

She didn't say anything, just drew farther away. I guess that was all the truth for tonight.

"Try to get some rest," I said. "We can talk some more in the morning. Should I cover you up?"

Nai'ya's head bobbed up and down just one time. I pulled the sheet over her and turned out the light on my way out of the room. I left the door open a crack.

The living room couch seemed the best place to come up with a plan. All I had to do was find a daughter I'd never met who didn't know I existed.

I slumped forward and spotted the .45 on the bare floor near the edge of the carpet. I'd forgotten about it. Could the gun tie Angelina to the casino killing? I glanced across the room at her picture on the mantel and walked over. I studied her face and wondered what she might have looked like as a little girl. And wondered what I'd say to her if we ever met.

The picture frame was cheap and I gripped it too tightly in my hands. The wood sections in the upper right hand corner came apart. Everything was coming apart.

I didn't see the envelope until I reached to put the damaged frame back on the mantel. No address on the front, just a hand-written *Mom*. I took out the single sheet of paper it held.

I have to go away for a while. I saw a man murdered in Mr. Klein's office at the casino. They may come after me. Whatever you do, don't go to the cops. I took a lot of money when I left. I'll pick up Matty and disappear for a while. We'll be back when it's safe. Don't you try to find me either. You might be followed. I can do this on my own.

I love you.

Angelina

I knocked softly on the bedroom door and pushed it open. "Who's Matty?"

Nai'ya looked at me and then looked away. "Our grandson."

"Of course." I sat back down at the bottom of the bed.

"He's six years old. So handsome. He has your eyes."

"Don't." I ran my hand along the bed sheet. "So where is my son-in-law? And don't tell me he's some college professor from back east." *Shit, why did I say that?*

Nai'ya let my cruel remark pass. "Angelina's husband John was military. He's MIA in Afghanistan. It's been more than four years now."

Her words shamed me. The Old Gabe would look to kill a bottle right about now. Instead, I leaned forward and placed the letter on Nai'ya's pillow. "You need to turn this over to the police."

"No!" She grabbed the envelope and stuffed it beneath her pillow.

"It's evidence in a murder investigation. The police need it to understand Angelina had nothing to do with any murder. Right now, all they know is a man's been killed and she's run away. And before too long they'll find out about the money she took."

She stubbornly shook her head. "Angelina said not to go to the cops."

"They can protect her. Matty too. If you keep that letter from Archuleta and he finds out, there'll be hell to pay."

"Sam Archuleta?"

"He's in charge of this case."

She nodded and let out a deep breath. "Good. Sam would understand why I'm keeping the letter."

"Don't bet on it. He's a cop first, last, and always. Let the police know. Let them help find Angelina and Matty."

"I won't betray my daughter." Her demeanor recalled the words of my great-grand uncle James A. McKenna: *Don't ever mess with a mama bear.*

This was useless. I gave up and moved away from her. "I'll come to bed later."

Nai'ya's bleary red eyes pleaded with me. "I know you won't let us down."

I could have uttered some empty words of reassurance. Instead, I grabbed my bathrobe from the closet and shut the bedroom door behind me.

In the half-bath off the kitchen, I filled the sink with cold water that I splashed over my head. My anxiety didn't wash away.

I changed into the bathrobe and walked through fog to the living room. I picked up the .45 and stuffed it into my pocket. I had lots to say, but it would keep until morning.

Nai'ya stored her liquor on the bottom shelf of a credenza next to the television. I gave both of the little guys on my shoulders equal time. I really did.

Then I got up and fetched a clean glass from the kitchen. Just one small whiskey. One.

CHAPTER SIX

An overturned glass lay on the coffee table less than a foot from my head. An empty whiskey bottle stood accusingly nearby. A dead fly lay on his back next to the bottle, both feet in the air, its wings spread wide and still. I wondered if anyone had notified his family.

The walls pulsed and contracted like an old respiratory bellow behind a dying patient's hospital bed. No. That's my head. Sunlight oozed around the edges of the front window blinds and abused my eyes. The doorbell rang.

"Nai'ya?" I lifted my head and called her name a second time. She didn't respond.

I dragged my body off the couch and staggered to the front door. Once the dead bolt and chain were off, I peered out into a brightness that hurt.

Lieutenant Sam Archuleta looked me up and down. "Jeezus. Gabe McKenna, Man of Many Surprises." He crushed his cigarette butt into the porch's concrete floor.

I moved forward until my body filled as much of the doorway as it could. "Sam Archuleta, the cop who doesn't like surprises."

"Not when I'm working. May I come in?" He pointed past me into Nai'ya's living room.

"The lady of the house is still asleep. Can we talk out here?"

"She's the one I came to see." He pointed inside again.

"Knock yourself out." I backed off and let him brush past me.

He cast a policeman's eye around the room, walked to the couch and gazed down at the coffee table. "Where's your club soda?"

No use pretending. I picked up the empty glass and whiskey bottle and headed for the kitchen. "Coffee?" I asked in a loud over-the-shoulder whisper.

"I've had mine, thanks."

I set the empty glass in the sink, the bottle on the counter, and looked back over my shoulder. Archuletta stood in the living room facing away from me. I slipped the .45 from my bathrobe pocket and stuffed it toward the back of the utensil drawer. Then I strolled with affected nonchalance back to the lieutenant.

He stood by the fireplace mantel, one finger tracing the framed photo of my daughter.

"Lovely girl."

"Angelina."

"Got any idea where she is? I have a few questions."

"No."

"Then you'd better wake up your sweetheart. Angelina is her daughter." He paused. A look of surprise came over his face. "Or didn't you know?"

"I know. She's my daughter, too. Anything you want to ask Nai'ya, you ask me."

By now Sam's eyebrows had merged with his widow's peak. He reached into his pocket for a Camel and sighed. "That's another surprise, Gabe."

"Life is so full of them."

He lit up. "So how come you never told me about your family?" He paced a Great Circle Route around the living room and ended up back at the fireplace. "Been supporting them all these years? Good for you."

A faint rustling sound came from the kitchen. Sam's gaze darted in that direction.

"Let me get you an ashtray. Be right back." I hustled out of the room.

The kitchen was empty. I had no idea if Nai'ya had any ashtrays or where she might keep them. I checked the cupboards.

Sam appeared in the kitchen doorway. He watched me fumble

through the rest of the cabinets. "Maybe in one of these drawers?" He opened and shut the one closest to him. "Nope." His hand moved to the utensil drawer and slid it open.

"Sam—"

"Nothing here either." He flicked his ash into the sink. "I'm sorry. What were you going to say?"

I loosened my grip on the countertop. "What do you want to know about Angelina?"

"I want to speak to Nai'ya. And I don't have all morning. Wake her up."

I shuffled down the hall to the bedroom. The door was shut. "Nai'ya?"

Still no response.

I opened the door. Sam peered around me. The light was off, but enough sunlight made it through the blinds to give us a dim view of the room.

The bed was empty, the door to the master bath ajar. The fluorescent ceiling light above the sink flickered a bit, the way it often does on cold days. I edged past the bed to the bathroom door. A dark green towel lay crumpled on the floor. The medicine cabinet was open.

Sam called from behind me. "You got a problem in there, Gabe?"

"You might say that."

He walked into the bedroom and flicked on the overhead light.

"She's not here," I said. "I have no idea where she could have gone, or when."

Maybe he saw the fear in my eyes. In any case, his tone softened. "Look, I didn't come here to pry into your personal life. You and I, we've been on the square most of the time. But I have to talk to Nai'ya if we're going to find your daughter. Now where is she?"

"I have no idea. Honest."

"Let's start again. When was the last time you saw her?"

"About nine-thirty last night."

He looked confused. "Not this morning?"

"I'm telling you, she was asleep. Right there." I pointed to the bed.

"Okay, okay. Then when did *you* last see or speak with your daughter?"

I cringed inside. "I've never seen or spoken to her. Not even once."

He glanced at the empty bed and then back down the hallway toward the living room. "You just found out. You didn't know about her until last night."

I slumped down onto the bed.

"I saw the bottle—"

"Yeah."

"Jeez, I'm sorry, Gabe." He scratched the back of his neck. "Listen, I'm going to break the rules here. Tell you what we know so far. You have a right to that much."

He stepped into the bathroom. A cigarette hissed under running water and the toilet flushed. He came back to the bedroom empty handed. "How about we go back to the living room?"

I wanted to get rid of him and look for Nai'ya. But I knew Sam. The harder I tried to get him to leave, the longer he would stay. "Sure you don't want a cup of coffee?"

"Some water maybe?"

I moved into the kitchen and filled a glass from the tap. I glanced at the utensil drawer on my way to the living room. Closed.

Sam sipped the water and paced the room as I sat on the edge of the couch. He told me what he could.

"Two nights ago, a man was shot and killed inside the owner's office at the Pueblo-66 Casino. A .45 slug to his brain."

I didn't want to give anything away so I kept my head down. "Saw that on the news."

"Your daughter's desk is in an office one door down the hallway."

I nodded like I knew.

"Surveillance cameras caught Angelina Harper running out of the owner's office moments after the shooting. We also have video of her removing money from the office safe a few minutes later. The outdoor cameras show her running to her car carrying a dark bag and then driving off at a high rate of speed. This is shortly after midnight. Night before last."

"That doesn't mean she had anything to do with the killing."

"Maybe. Maybe not. But you see why I have to question her. There's an APB out. She hasn't been seen or heard from since."

Angelina was in deeper than I'd figured.

"This is murder, Gabe. If you hear from Nai'ya or Angelina, I expect you to contact me."

I stared at the floor. Sam put a hand on my shoulder. "I have a daughter myself. And I have some idea what must be going through your head right now. Just don't get any crazy ideas about getting involved. Promise me you'll let the police handle this."

"I can't."

He took out another cigarette and slipped it unlit between his lips. "Gabe, you've been told. Keep in touch. I'll do the same."

I followed him to the door and stood there until he got into his car. He spoke to somebody on the police radio and lit up. He started the engine and drove away with smoke billowing from his exhaust and the driver's side window.

Pigeons scuttled on the metal roof of Nai'ya's front porch. A young girl rode by on her bicycle. I closed the door and dashed back to the kitchen to see how Sam could have missed the .45 in the utensil drawer. The gun wasn't there.

CHAPTER SEVEN

I checked everywhere. The closets, under the bed, even the crawl spaces. Nai'ya wasn't there.

Outside, I checked the patio, the yard, the area behind the garage, and the adjoining lots. Nothing. I ran to the front yard. The little girl on her bike rode past again. She pointed at my bathrobe and laughed.

Nai'ya's car remained in the driveway. I punched in the code numbers on the garage door keypad. The door lifted and sunlight spilled inside. Her Diamondback mountain bike was gone and the far-side door left ajar.

I sagged against the wall. *Think, man, think.* I charged back into the house. My cellphone was in the pocket of my jacket on a living room chair. Nothing in my call log. I speed-dialed Nai'ya's UNM office. No answer. The phone system connected me to the office secretary.

"Professor Alonso-Riley's office."

"Mary, this is Gabe McKenna. I need to reach Nai'ya. It's important."

"She called in ten minutes ago, all upset. She canceled all her classes for the rest of the week."

"Did she say where she was?"

"No. She said a family emergency had come up. Professor McKenna, what's wrong?"

"That's what I'm trying to find out. Call me back if you hear from her." I gave Mary my cell and home numbers.

"Will do. And—"

"What?" I said.

"I'm worried about her. Please call me if there's anything I can do. I'll pray for her."

Good old Mary.

Nai'ya's other office was at the Laguna Pueblo Education Center, a forty-five-minute drive. I left a message:

"It's Gabe. Call me when you get this. Everything's going to be all right. We can do this without the cops. I love you."

Nine-thirty. Rebecca would be at the house by now.

She answered my call right away. "No, Nai'ya hasn't called. Was she supposed to?"

"She's disappeared."

"What?"

"I'll tell you about it when I get there. I'm coming right over."

"Please. We have a problem with Sergeant Crawford."

"Shit. Did the work crew show up?"

"They did, but Crawford sent them all home."

"He had no right to do that!"

"He's out in the barn with a bunch of other cops. Said he needs to speak to you as soon as you get here."

"Give me half an hour."

"The coffee's on."

"Add a shot of whiskey to mine."

"Gabe?"

"Bye."

I took a one-minute shower and put on clean clothes from the hall closet Nai'ya let me use.

One of the cop cars in my driveway sounded its horn when I drove up. Crawford had them watching for me. He bulled his way across the front lawn and intercepted me before I got to the front porch.

"McKenna, what's the big idea putting those men back to work? This is a crime scene."

"This is my home."

"Figured you might see it that way." He poked me in the chest. "Listen smart guy, I have authorization to dig up every foot of your barn."

"Says who?"

"Deputy Chief Cornejo. You got a beef, you take it up with him." He spat on the ground again.

"What's the point of digging everything up?"

"The *point* is, we found a body yesterday. Maybe you got others. And we got probable cause to find out." He took a folded document out of his coat pocket. He waved it in my face and stuffed it into my hand. "That's a court order. Go ahead. Take it to that lawyer of yours. Waste your money. See if I care."

"I will. And if you go one step beyond what's authorized, I'll report you." I jammed the paper into my jacket pocket.

Crawford parked his bulk in front of my nose and blocked my exit. "You're nothing to me, McKenna. Get in my way and I'll bust you good."

For a split-second I weighed the cost of assaulting a police officer against the immense satisfaction of landing a straight right to one of his chins. But I swallowed that, turned around and stomped into my house instead.

"Coffee's ready." Rebecca nodded toward the drip percolator on the counter. "Mail's over there, too."

"Thanks." I took a sip. No whiskey. I sat at my desk and brought out the fifth of Black Bush from the bottom drawer. "Sorry."

"Don't." Rebecca frowned. "Please."

I poured a generous amount of the amber into my mug, and slumped back in my chair. The coffee and whiskey burned my throat by turns. My cat Otis lay curled under the desk lamp. Without rustling his jet-black fur, he opened his eyes a slit and closed them again.

Rebecca marched over and put the cork back in the whiskey bottle. "Tell me what's wrong."

"The short version? Like I said, Nai'ya's gone. I'm the father of her daughter. I'm a grandfather." I grabbed a couple of aspirins from the bottle in the middle drawer and washed them down. I looked up at her. "Okay?"

Tears welled in her eyes. Rebecca had lost both parents as a teenager, and since the death of her brother, I'd been her surrogate father. She gripped the edge of my desk. "You must be overwhelmed.

41

I'm sorry."

"I tried to drink it away last night." I rubbed my temples with both hands. Even fast-acting aspirin is too damn slow.

"All those months of sobriety." She clasped her hands together and raised them to her lips.

I waved off her concern. "I need to find Nai'ya before the cops or anyone else does. Maybe drive out to Laguna, see if she shows there. You stay by the phone. Call me the minute you hear from her. Or if Crawford causes any more trouble."

My phone rang. Caller ID read "C.J."

"Gabe, Nai'ya called—"

"On my way."

Charmaine met me at the restaurant door. "Don't you be causing him any more problems." Charmaine's tone and sharply pointed finger said she wasn't joking. Thirty years of her life were invested in C.J. "I'm watching you."

"Promise." I forced a pained smile.

She led me through the main room. Half an hour before the lunch crowd. The aroma of ribs and barbecued chicken might have seduced me on an ordinary day.

We entered C.J.'s office together. My friend sat behind his desk, working on what I assumed was his first cigar of the morning.

Charmaine shot me a narrow-eyed look and closed the door on her way out.

"So what did Nai'ya say?"

"Sit down." C.J. motioned me to the chair in front of his desk. "She said she heard from Angelina."

"And?" I bent forward.

"Who's Angelina?"

"Our daughter."

C.J.'s cigar dropped onto his desk. "Say what?" He brushed away the ashes.

I leaned against the desk. "Go on. What else?"

"Hand me that ashtray." He pointed to a crystal piece in the shape of a boxing ring that sat on my side of the desk.

I slid it over to him.

"She says Angelina had nothing to do with the killing." C.J. leaned forward. "Gabe, *what* killing?"

"The one at the casino two nights ago."

"Shit." He stared at the ceiling until I prompted him with a keep-it-coming gesture. "Okay," he sighed. "Angelina's not running from the cops. She's running for her life. Nai'ya says she's going to try to meet up with her. Someplace up north. Says it's better you don't know where just yet. She'll call again when they're safe."

"What else?"

"She said to watch out for a guy named Klein and don't trust nobody."

I tried to connect C.J.'s words with what little I knew. Klein. Same name as a previous owner of my house. Too much coincidence.

C.J. shifted in his seat. "Your turn."

I told him about the previous night and what Nai'ya had revealed about our family. I mentioned that Archuleta showed up in the morning and how Nai'ya had fled. I left out the booze.

"Not often a man gets blessed with a daughter and a grandson at the same time." He put down his cigar. "You thirsty?"

"Coke, if you have it. Anything, really."

C.J. swiveled his chair around to a small refrigerator and popped a couple cans of soda. He's the kind of a guy who wouldn't drink beer in front of me.

"I have to find them before anyone else does."

"The cops must be scouring the state by now," he said.

"I don't mean the cops. I need to get to them before whoever pulled the trigger at the casino does."

C.J. put his soda on the desk and looked at me. "How?"

"Start at the beginning, I suppose. At the scene of the crime."

"Be careful."

I chugged the last of my soda and promised to keep in touch. Charmaine stared me through the restaurant and I gave her a wave on my way out.

I shielded my eyes from the brilliant morning sun on the way to my car. Over on the far side of the parking lot, a gray SUV squealed its tires around the corner and sped toward me.

Sunlight caught a glimmer of metal from a rolled down rear

window of the vehicle. I dropped to the ground. Three shots exploded. One whistled past my ear. I hit the asphalt with a thump. One shot tore into the pavement inches from my face. A chip of concrete grazed my cheek. A sharp crack sounded behind me. Air hissed from a front tire on a blue Chevy Camaro parked next to my Hudson.

I hugged the ground until the SUV sped away. By the time I struggled to my feet, there was no sign of my assailants. I paced around the Hudson. No visible damage. I wiped some wetness from my cheek. Blood. I checked the shot-up tire on the Camaro and took out my wallet, rolled a couple of fifty-dollar bills together and stuffed them into the driver's door handle.

Charmaine stood at the restaurant entrance, her one hand on hip, the other screening her eyes. "What's going on out there?"

"It's okay," I lied. "A couple kids on a joyride. They're gone."

She shook her head all the way back inside. I crawled into the Hudson and drove home to get my gun.

CHAPTER EIGHT

Rebecca looked up from her desk when I walked into the library. "What happened to you?"

"I'm okay. Heard from Nai'ya?"

"No, sorry. Crawford left about half an hour ago, so the police haven't been a problem." She stared at my cheek. "You're bleeding!"

"It's nothing, just a scratch."

She came over and dabbed at the wound with a tissue.

I shook her off. "Don't fuss." I walked to the big desk and took my .38 from the middle drawer, checked to make sure it was loaded and turned toward the door.

Rebecca moved to block my path. "I'll let the wound on your cheek go, but why do you need a gun?"

I raised my hand to protest, thought better of that and let it rest on her shoulder. "Relax. I have to run out to Pueblo-66 to talk to a guy. My mother taught me never to go visiting empty-handed."

"Let me come with you."

I studied the worry in her eyes and shook my head. "I've lost one daughter already." I touched her cheek and left without looking back.

People tend to notice my Hudson, so I took the Land Cruiser instead. On my way up the access road, Sam Archuleta passed me going in the opposite direction. My driver's side visor was down. And the sun was shining into his eyes as he drove past. I didn't think he noticed me.

Pueblo-66 Casino is one of those sad places where people who can't afford it get separated from their money. It had been opened for six months now, against the will of Duke City politicos who'd lobbied for a downtown casino run by their friends. The money behind Pueblo-66 came from some East Coast "tribal" organization of questionable pedigree. Whoever owned it enjoyed solid connections up in Santa Fe.

I passed on valet parking and pulled into the free lot. A short walk to the casino gave me time to enjoy a sudden fall breeze and figure out what I'd do once inside.

The building was an overdone mix of neon and silver chrome, like a diner on steroids. Two massive electric warriors guarded the front entrance and cast ghastly orange light on the steps. I removed my sunglasses and walked inside.

The recent murder hadn't dampened business. Mid-week, mid-day, yet the place was crowded. The dissonant sounds of a hundred slots assaulted my ears. Thick carpeting that reeked with six months of stale tobacco made my nose a liability.

I bumped through the crowd, past the gaming rooms, and followed the "Main Office" signs. Yellow crime scene tape crisscrossed a stairway to an upper floor. A thick rope stretched between heavy silver stanchions in front of the stairs. A small metal sign read: "Authorized Personnel Only."

One step over the rope, a quick bob-and-weave under the police tape, and I was on my way.

Two suits of young muscle appeared at the top of the stairs and descended toward me in tandem. I tried to glide past them. They parted like the Red Sea, each grabbing one of my upper arms.

"Nope." The unibrowed hulk to my left held my arm in a vice-like grip. His partner roughed up my jacket and patted me down to my knees. Neither of these bright boys thought to check my right pants leg above the ankle. They missed my strapped-on .38.

"Tell Mr. Klein that Angelina Harper's father wants to see him."

That got their attention. They froze and gazed at one another, two minds challenged to make a decision.

"Are we going to stand here until the cops come back?" I said. "Let go of my arms and take me to Klein. I got information he needs to hear."

This they seemed to understand. They bracketed me and marched me up the stairs.

The sign above the open door read: *Joseph Klein, Manager.* Crime scene tape blocked the entrance. My escorts paused in front long enough for me to glance inside. I'd seen the décor before, in a Motel 6 somewhere south of the civilized world. But the motel didn't have such a large, dark stain on its rug.

"Move." Unibrow pulled me away. "Nobody goes in there." We moved two doors down to another open office.

"Sorry to interrupt, Mr. Klein. This guy insists on seeing you. Says he's Angelina's father."

Only at the mention of her name did Klein look up from whatever he was reading to stare at me. I'd seen his type before, back in my boxing days. His sour, unshaven face and ill-fitting suit recalled the lowlifes that populated the seamier fringes of the New York fight game. Judging from Klein's girth, the most exercise he got was hoisting a fork to his mouth. That, and maybe lifting the five pounds of jewels that kept the sunlight off his fingers.

The muscle boys prodded me into a chair across the desk from their boss, who scowled at the guy on my right. "Let's get something straight. The only person who *insists* around here is *me.*"

"Sorry, Mr. Klein." Unibrow bowed his regret. The other guy checked his reflection on the top of his shoes.

Klein rubbed his nose. His hand sparkled in the light. "Who are you?"

"McKenna. Gabe McKenna."

"You have two minutes."

"I'm trying to find my daughter. I thought you might be able to help."

"Angelina's a sweet kid, but why come to me?"

"Figured I'd start where she was last seen. That's here. On the night of the shooting."

"So you heard about that unpleasantness." He sounded like maybe a glass of spilled wine had stained the carpet instead of a man's blood. "McKenna, I haven't seen her since I left for the opening of the Sun Mountain Art Gallery in Santa Fe. That was a couple of hours before the unfortunate incident occurred."

"Did anyone else see her? Speak to her?"

"I wouldn't know. I didn't get back until yesterday morning. I'm afraid I can't help you. But if you do see Angelina, tell her we all miss her and to hurry back soon."

I squeezed the armrests on my chair and stared him down. "Can anybody verify you were in Santa Fe when the killing took place?"

Klein leaned toward me. Each word unfolded carefully. "Who the hell do you think you are?" He looked at his boys and made a quick, circling motion with his hand. "In case you get any ideas, my two associates here will vouch for me."

"That's right, Mr. Klein." Two voices responded as one.

"I may have even shaken hands with the governor there. What do you think about that?"

I leaned toward him. "Too many convenient details, that's what I think."

Klein held his right fist an inch from my face. The muscle boys moved in close on either side. I didn't flinch.

"I've had people hurt for saying less than you just did," Klein snarled.

"I'm sure you have."

He nodded toward the door. "Get him out of here."

With a strong arm on either elbow, my feet barely touched the floor all the way to the casino door.

Unibrow bid me farewell. "Fuckin' wise guy. Show your face here again and I'll rip it off your skull."

They stopped at the front door like dogs at an invisible fence and pushed me down the few steps. I kept my balance and most of my dignity. I shook out my shoulders and waved before fast-walking to my car.

I started the engine and leaned back against the driver's seat. So that was Joseph Klein. Crude. Dangerous. A by-the-book, unimaginative guy. If he was in charge of the casino, he had to be fronting it for somebody else.

The only distinctive thing about Klein was his taste in jewelry. Especially the ring he wore on the fourth finger of his right hand—a large, black onyx number, with a raised golden figure of Chief

Tammany.

CHAPTER NINE

Rebecca held the front door open as I walked inside. "How'd it go?"

"Too early to say." I strode into the library, unstrapped my gun and slipped it into the center desk drawer. "I need you to check a few things for me. Online."

"Such as?" She grabbed a pen and yellow pad and sat at her desk.

"Guy named Joseph Klein. With a K. Joseph Klein Associates. Anything you can find. See if the Joseph Klein who runs the casino is the same guy who once owned this house. Any personal or business information that's out there. Any indications of criminal activity—"

"Slow down!" Rebecca flipped a page on her yellow pad.

"While you're doing that, I'm going to check something else. If I get back early enough, how about dinner?"

"Sure." Rebecca's gaze followed me as I moved toward the door. "Now where're you going?"

"Santa Fe. To look at Southwestern art."

I left her shaking her head. It was time to change cars. Love to see my Hudson turning heads in the state capital.

A chilling wind blew through my half opened side window. The City Different—as appreciative Santa Fe residents often call their town— burned bright with autumn. Aspens spread a palette of yellow gold on the Sangre de Christo Mountains. The late September sun peeked around swift-moving clouds.

I followed Cerrillos Road into town and suffered slow traffic to Canyon Road. I lucked into a rare parking spot in front of my destination.

Yellow, red, and blue Grand Opening banners fluttered in the courtyard of the Sun Mountain Art Gallery. Three outdoor metal figures—an eagle in flight, a Native warrior and a mounted cowboy—defined the artistic theme. A sign above a newly renovated door proclaimed "The Finest in Historical Southwestern Art."

The front door of the single-story adobe building was itself a work of art. I paused to admire its arched, Old World style, inlaid stone and weathered warmth. I pressed the metal door lever and walked inside.

In contrast to such a distinctive door, the gallery interior was white bread all the way. Granite islands of pottery and small sculptures dotted a hardwood floor. Track lighting illuminated paintings along each exposed brick wall. It could have been any gallery in any town.

Thanks to my background in archeology and pre-Columbian America, I know quality historical art. I didn't see any here. Still, with the exterior decoration and extensive collection inside, whoever was behind the gallery sunk a significant amount of money into it.

I gazed at a washed-out watercolor labeled *Mesa at Sunset*. A polite throat cleared itself behind me. I turned around to a smiling countenance on a man about four inches shy of my six feet. His pinstriped gray suit was neatly tailored, his half-glasses looked comfortable on the end of his nose. The light streaks of gray at his temples could have been applied with an artist's brush. This gentleman spent serious time in front of a mirror.

"Lovely piece, don't you think?" He touched my shoulder and peered around it. He let out a muted purr.

"Hmmm. You the owner?"

"I am." He extended his hand and gave me half a squeeze. "Reginald Addison. Is there some way I might assist you?"

I returned a squeeze and a half. "As a matter of fact, there is. I'm here to buy a painting for my friend's new office." I strolled down the line of wall-to-wall art. Addison followed me like a puppy.

"How large a space do you wish to cover?"

I turned. "I beg your pardon?" Maybe this guy sold paintings by the square yard.

"We could narrow things down if you'd tell me what size space you need to fill."

"Okay." I rubbed my chin and pretended deep thought. After a mannered sigh, I took a shot in the dark. "You know the painting *Summer Rain* by Fritz Scholder?"

"Of course. Wonderful study."

"About that size."

Addison put a delicate finger to his lips and tapped like he was taking inventory of his front teeth. "Perhaps if you could describe your friend's office décor I might have a suggestion or two." He cocked his head and waited.

"Sure. In fact, you may even know the guy. I think he attended your recent opening. Name's Klein. Joe Klein. Runs the new casino down in Albuq–"

"How do you know Mr. Klein?" From the tone of his voice, this puppy was now a guard dog.

"Joe and I go way back."

"I see. Perhaps he mentioned you the other night?"

"Calder. Alexander Calder. Mobile Communications." I fumbled around in my pockets. "Fresh out of business cards, I'm afraid. Anyway, I was thinking a western scene, watercolor or oil, but muted, you know? The dominant color in his office now is red." I glanced at my watch and pursed my lips.

The gallery phone rang. "One moment, Mr. Calder." Addison huffed and hurried to a cluttered desk by the front window.

I edged toward the door and called back over my shoulder. "Gotta go. I'll check back in a couple of days, okay? Nice to meet you, Reg."

The man was deep into the call. I don't think he saw me leave.

My Hudson was down to a quarter of a tank, so I stopped for gas on the way out of town. I held the pump hose steady and considered Mr. Reginald Addison. Any reputable Southwestern art dealer would have known that *Summer Rain* is a signature work by Gustave Baumann, not Fritz Scholder. He'd also have caught my lousy Alexander Calder joke.

Addison and the art gallery didn't add up.

I settled in behind the wheel and checked my cellphone. Three missed calls from Rebecca, less than ten minutes apart. Maybe word from Nai'ya? I dialed my office number.

"Sorry, Gabe, she hasn't called."

"So why were you trying to reach me?"

"You won't believe this. The cops just dug up another body in your barn."

"Shit." I rested my left arm against the window and braced my forehead.

"This body's not as old as the first one. Sergeant Crawford has an idea who it might be. Some guy I never heard of. A guy named Hoffa."

CHAPTER TEN

Word that the latest dead body might be Jimmy Hoffa, the Teamster boss who disappeared in 1975, spread like a mutant virus. The Albuquerque office of the FBI intruded a trailer into my back yard and took control. Cable news networks ran with the story. The media locusts swarmed.

The Feds had a thousand questions. The press had even more. When the networks realized I was the same guy who'd discovered the Lost Adams gold back in April, they came at me with full fury. My dinner plans with Rebecca would have to wait.

Groups of reporters clustered in my driveway. I walked outside and faced them. "Guys, you're missing the latest development. Better hustle back to the barn before the Feds rope it off."

A few reporters bolted from the pack and raced to the barn. The others, the more experienced ones, stayed put.

"You gonna let the young bucks scoop you?" I stared back at the lot of them. "I have nothing for you—nothing at all."

I gazed at the sky, glanced at my watch, and ignored every question they threw in my face. After several minutes of this nonsense, they got the message and joined their comrades back at the barn.

Once they were out of sight, I motioned to Rebecca that the coast was clear. We hustled to her car.

"Should I come in tomorrow morning as usual?" she said.

"I'll call and let you know. Let's stay as far away from the FBI, the cops, and the press as we can. Focus on Nai'ya and Angelina. I don't give a shit about any of these dead bodies."

"Me neither. So I'll wait to hear from you?"

"Right. But don't try to call me. It wouldn't surprise me if the Feds are tapping my phones."

I closed the door to her Accord and waved her down the driveway. Darrell Jackson, the young blonde cop who'd been first on the scene when the initial body was uncovered, intercepted me on my way back to the house.

"Is Rebecca okay?"

"She's stronger than she looks. How's the investigation going?"

Jackson set his hands on his hips and looked toward the FBI trailer. "The Feds pushed us out of the way. You probably know as much as we do on this one."

"Cup of coffee?"

The young cop shook his head. "Better not with Crawford still around. He's super pissed at being squeezed out. Don't want to add to his aggravation."

As if on cue, Crawford emerged, unsmiling, from the barn. He stomped down the hill toward us, all the while talking on his cellphone. "So, McKenna, you're back at last." The phone disappeared into his coat pocket.

"Home, sweet home."

Crawford turned to Jackson. "You're off duty 'til tomorrow morning. Eight-thirty. Don't talk to any reporters."

"Yessir." The young cop gave me a quick glance and walked down the driveway to his patrol car.

I moved closer to Crawford. "Seems like a fine young officer."

"He's got a ways to go. I'm outta here, too. Enjoy the Feds." He buttoned his coat and stepped toward his car.

"I know how you feel. *Buonanotte fiorelino.*"

He turned around and glared. "What the hell does that mean?"

"Good night." I hurried into my house without a backward glance.

A seven-thirty phone call woke me the next morning. Archuleta. "You free? We need to talk."

"Have you found Nai'ya? Or Angelina?"

"Not yet."

"Is this important? I haven't showered or had my coffee." I tried to scratch myself awake.

"All my calls are important. Meet me for breakfast."

"Okay. El Camino on Fourth? Thirty minutes?"

"Don't keep me waiting."

I beat Sam to my favorite breakfast spot and snagged a booth by the front window, where the clang of silverware and order calls to the kitchen weren't quite so loud. A middle-aged woman in white shirt and fluffy red skirt floated over. Maria was one of the owners, but doubled as a waitress when things got busy. "No Irish coffee today, *señor*?"

I shook my head. "Not this time." She filled my mug, set a basket of *sopapillas* on the table, and disappeared into the kitchen. I drank the hot, rich, brew and wondered why Sam had called this meeting. Before I could ask for a top-off, he slid into the seat across the table. He pointed to the plastic menu under my elbow. I slid it over.

"Morning." I squeezed a drizzle of honey onto the corner of a *sopapilla*.

"What were you doing at the Pueblo-66 yesterday?"

I savored the last few drops of my coffee and sighed. "You saw me."

Sam gave me his I-wasn't-born-yesterday look. Maria appeared behind Sam's shoulder and silently mouthed the word "cop."

"It's okay." I waved off her warning with my right hand.

She tapped her pencil. I ordered *huevos rancheros* for both of us. Archuleta wanted his coffee black.

Sam and I played our staring game. I savored another mouthful of *sopapilla*.

"So?" he said.

"Let me finish my breakfast."

"Come on, Gabe. I haven't got all day."

"Look, I told you I couldn't keep out of this. So I visited Klein, met his muscle boys, too. It was worth it."

"You shoulda called." Sam took an electronic cigarette out of his breast pocket and took a deep drag.

"Oh *my*."

"I'm working on my vices, okay?" He winced. "Tell me about Klein."

"He's from back east. Has a New York accent, South Brooklyn. He might also be connected to Klein Associates, the real estate firm that sold the house to Aunt Nellie."

"We know all that. You're right about the real estate angle. It's his company. Has been for more than thirty years. His father ran it 'til he died, now junior's in charge. Got anything else?"

"Klein *says* he was in Santa Fe at the time of the shooting. At an art gallery opening."

"He was."

Maria arrived with our orders. We dug in. I paused to speak first. "I drove to Santa Fe yesterday afternoon and scoped out the place. Sun Mountain Art Gallery. It's a front."

"How do you figure?"

"The owner's a guy named Reginald Addison. Doesn't know shit from shoe polish. Didn't know the artists I mentioned. Way overdressed for Santa Fe. Guys don't wear pinstripes on Canyon Road."

"That proves nothing. But I'll send Crawford up there to check him out." Sam rubbed his forehead. "Now that the FBI's taken over the investigation at your place, it'll give him some red meat to chew on."

"Just keep him as far away from me as possible." I sliced up an egg and stabbed the largest piece with my fork.

"You haven't experienced Crawford's softer side."

I gagged on the egg.

Sam drummed his fingers on the table and studied my face. "Have *you* heard from Nai'ya yet?"

I stared blankly and moved some beans around on my plate.

He pocketed his fake cigarette, took out a real one and rested it between his lips. "I suppose you wouldn't tell me even if you had?"

"No, I haven't, and no, I wouldn't. Sorry."

"Look, Gabe. I'm telling you as a friend. Angelina's gotta come in. I know you're worried about her. So am I. I'll see she gets treated right." He motioned to Maria for a refill.

I passed on more coffee. "I'll take that under advisement. Now I've got a question or two for you."

He looked at his watch. "Go ahead."

"The murder victim at the casino. Who was he?"

"We don't know yet. White male, fifty, fiftyish. No identification, no wallet. We rolled his prints and sent them to the FBI. Still waiting to hear. Until then, he's John Doe."

"How'd he die?"

"Nine millimeter to the front of his head from close range. There's an entry wound on his right palm and an exit wound on the back of the hand. Like he raised it to protect himself." Sam demonstrated the motion.

"Tough way to go."

"We have no idea why the victim was there. Klein swears he'd never seen him. I'm wondering if Angelina or Nai'ya might have known him."

I gazed into my empty coffee cup and felt a burning inside. "What the hell do you mean?" I set down my fork so I wouldn't stab his hand.

He tried nonchalance. "Or maybe you know him. Maybe you want to come down to the morgue and tell me if you've ever seen this guy before. Hanging around Nai'ya's, wherever."

I picked up my fork and fumbled it back onto the table. "You want me to view the body?"

"You said you wanted to help."

I shook him off. "I'm busy."

He leaned forward like he was in pain. "It might help."

I crumpled my napkin, tossed it on the table, and motioned Maria for our check.

"Listen, Gabe. I want to find this killer as much as you do." He waited for a response, but I gave him nothing. "You're already in the middle of this, pal."

He was right. "How long do you figure this will take?"

"One hour. Tops."

Viewing dead bodies isn't my thing. But if I agreed, Sam would owe me. "Well..."

"Maybe we find out who this stiff is, it puts Angelina in the clear."

He cocked his head to the side and gave me a slight nod.

"That's something. Okay. I'll do it." I looked across the table. "You're okay. Some of the time."

"Don't spread that around."

I paid our tab and accepted a hug from Maria at the door. Sam led the way into blazing morning sunshine.

CHAPTER ELEVEN

I kept a respectful distance behind Sam down Fourth Street to the Albuquerque Medical Investigator's Office. We pulled into a circular driveway before he motioned me into the administrative parking lot. A minute later he marched over and slapped a sticker on my windshield. We walked across a semi-circular red brick entrance and into a four story white building.

Large fluorescent lights hummed overhead. A shrouded dead body on a gurney was escorted at a funereal pace down a corridor. The living bustled around in uniforms and lab coats. The cold sterility of the place gave me the creeps.

Sam and I followed the gurney to a desk barely visible beneath a precarious stack of manila folders. A rotund gentleman rocked in a desk chair and muttered under his breath. He popped an Altoid, pushed his glasses back to the bridge of his nose and looked at us.

"Lieutenant Archuleta. Welcome." A fleeting smile turned to a frown. "Oh dear, I'm afraid you'll have to put out that cigarette, sir. Regulations."

Sam dropped his smoke and crushed it underfoot. "We're here to see the shooting victim from Pueblo-66."

The attendant handed Sam a clipboard. "You'll both have to sign in, of course." He checked me up and down. "Have you come to identify the body?"

"Something like that," Sam said. "If you don't mind, Oliver, we're in kind of a hurry."

"Of course. Follow me." He hauled about three hundred pounds out of his chair and led us through a pair of silver swinging doors. We moved through a large rectangular room with the sides of Oliver's unbuttoned lab coat flapping as he stepped.

Inside the morgue, we followed him past two metal tables that held a pair of bodies, one male and one female. Three bloodstained young women in medical garb held a hushed conference over the body of the dead man.

"Here we are." Oliver unlocked a three-foot square door in a wall and slid an aluminum shelf out until it stopped about a foot away from me. The body was covered except for the feet. Oliver's eyes seemed to sparkle as he looked my way. "Come closer."

While Sam remained at the corpse's foot, I inched around the tagged toe and up the other side of the slab. I paused for a muffled breath behind my hand. "Ready. Let's take a look."

Oliver grabbed the sheet with stubby yet delicate fingers and inched it down, until the dead man's head lay fully exposed on the slab.

I leaned forward and stared into his lifelessness. *What the fuck?* I caught my breath and checked the corpse's left ear. I grabbed the side of the slab to steady myself. It couldn't be…I rolled back the years, trying to picture this guy first as a kid and then as a teenager. My stomach and legs cast their votes, but I needed to be sure. "May I borrow your glasses, Oliver? I left mine at home."

He pursed his lips. "Well…they're probably not right for your eyes, but if you think they might help…" He pried the spectacles from his nose and passed them across the body.

"Thank you." I held his glasses open and bent down. In a flash, I slid them over the ears of the corpse until they rested firmly on the dead man's nose.

Oliver recoiled. "Here now! Don't do that!"

"Gabe, what the hell?" Sam reached across the corpse and grabbed my arm.

"Sorry." I lifted the glasses from the dead man's head and handed them back to their flustered owner. "Guess I shouldn't have done that."

"We need to go. Now." Sam tugged me toward the door.

"Nice meeting you, Oliver. Thanks for your time."

"Move it," Sam dragged me with such force I nearly stumbled.

I regained my balance but not my composure at what I'd seen.

"Jeezus, man." Sam lit up as soon as we walked outside the building. "I ask you for a favor and you go pull a stunt like that."

"I had to. It was the earlobe...I needed to be sure."

"What are you talking about?"

"Your dead man is Tommy O'Donnell. Fifty-five years old. From New York City. Queens, to be precise."

Sam's mouth fell open. "How the hell do you know all that?"

"He was one of my best friends. We grew up together."

Archuleta wasn't buying it. "Really? You're talking half a century ago."

I ignored him and continued, "Tommy got a puppy for his eighth birthday. I remember walking over to his place to see it after Mass. The little rascal bit Tommy's left ear and tore part of his lobe off. Made like it was a chew toy or something. I never forgot it. Of course, we all called Tommy 'Ears' from then on."

By now Sam was interested. "No shit? Still, the business with Oliver's glasses, what was that all about?"

I grabbed the arm of Sam's coat before he could turn away. "Last time I saw Tommy was high school graduation. He wore glasses by then. I wanted to see the corpse's face that way. It's him."

Sam scratched the side of his head. "If you say so, I'll believe you—for now. At least it gets us off Square One."

I barely heard him. "That was so long ago...Tommy entered the military the week after graduation...I heard he got married."

"You don't say."

The closer we got to the parking lot, the farther away my thoughts drifted. "Siobhan."

"What?"

"That was her name—Siobhan. Red hair, freckles, long legs. My first girlfriend." I half-smiled. "Only reason I showed up for homeroom each morning."

Archuleta sniffed the air and buttoned his coat. "Fascinating."

"I never went back to the old neighborhood, Sam. Not once in more than thirty-five years. Hell of a way to be reminded." I shook my head. "Tommy…"

"Skip down Memory Lane if you want, I've got work to do. And I'll need you to put your identification in writing."

"When?"

"Stop by my office by the end of the day tomorrow." He tossed his cigarette butt on the ground near my feet.

"Okay." I heard him walk back to his car and drive away.

Tommy's youthful face wouldn't leave my mind. I slid behind the wheel of my Cruiser, swung over to a Central Avenue drive-in and had a couple of burgers in his honor.

CHAPTER TWELVE

Sale signs plastered the windows of a shabby electronics store on Central. I couldn't see into the place, so I opened the door and maneuvered my way through a jumble of display racks to the nearest sales clerk.

A pockmarked teen behind the counter was all angles, his face inked and pierced, his eyes full of arrogant, youthful sass.

I dropped three one-hundred dollar bills onto the countertop. That bought me a moment of his attention. "Whaddya want, pops?"

"I want three new cellphones. Put fifty dollars of pre-paid credit on each. How soon can they be ready?"

"Kids going away to school?" He turned and grabbed three plastic packages from the shelf and laid them on the counter.

"How soon can you activate them?"

"The codes and instructions are included. You can do it online. It's easy." He totaled the cash register.

I considered the Feds might have my computer key-logged and my e-mail intercepted. "I got another fifty for you if you do it right now."

Twenty minutes later I sat in the Land Cruiser with three new cellphones, updating each speed-dial with the numbers of the other phones.

The local news came on the car radio. Some guy in the South Valley had gone postal and blown his girlfriend into the Hereafter.

He'd had enough class to save the last bullet for himself. A puff piece followed on the culinary delights featured at the State Fair. Then the weather. No word on the Pueblo-66 killing.

I took my old cellphone out and turned off its GPS applet. *Shoulda done that before.* The first call on my new phone went to Rebecca at her apartment.

"Good news," she said. "Got a ton of info on Klein."

"Stop—don't say another word."

"Okay…"

"Meet me at our favorite rib joint. How fast can you get there?"

"Twenty-five minutes?"

"Great."

I made a pit stop at my house. No phone messages, no word from Nai'ya. Otis got a can of "Shredded Salmon Fare in a Delicate Sauce." A small group of reporters trailed me back to my car, undeterred by my litany of "no comments." I waved good-bye and drove down Fourth Street.

C.J. worked on a late lunch behind his desk. He looked up when I entered. "If it isn't the ringmaster!"

"Don't get up," I said.

"I wasn't about to."

I sat across the desk and rested the bag of phones in my lap. "Ringmaster?"

"That's some circus you have going at that *casa* of yours. Busier there than here, for sure."

"You heard."

"Be serious, man. I saw your house on the news ten minutes ago. CNN update. Congratulations, you're famous. Again."

"Shit."

"*Jimmy Hoffa?*" C.J. put down his pulled-pork sandwich. This allowed him to waggle a finger at me.

I rubbed my temples. "Gimme a beer."

"Aren't you on the wagon?"

I waved off his concern. "Beer's not real booze. Anyway, drinking's just something I do from time to time now."

"Like five o'clock, nine, and eleven? Stop and think, man."

"Give me a beer now, or I'll buy a six-pack later."

"Just one." He reached into his small refrigerator and pulled out a brew.

I grabbed it and popped the tab. "Thank you, Mother."

"Heard from Nai'ya?"

"Nothing." My first chug slid down easy. "Just as well. With the Feds crawling all over, my phones are probably tapped. They'd track her if she called me." I put the beer down and reached into the plastic bag. "That's why I brought you this." My hand slid one of the new cellphones across his desk.

C.J. picked it up and turned it over in his huge, brown hand. "What's this for?"

The office door opened and Charmaine appeared. "Any room in here for this lovely young lady?" She backed away and a red-cheeked Rebecca entered.

"Just in time. Here." I pulled a straight-backed chair over to the desk and set it next to mine.

Rebecca held a yellow file folder out to me before she sat down. "You want this now?"

"In a minute. I have something for you first." I handed her one of the two remaining phones.

"I already have a phone."

I held up a palm. "Let's assume the Feds are bugging my phones. Yours too, maybe. So from now on we use these to call each other."

C.J. rolled his eyes and forked a dollop of potato salad into his mouth.

"Okay, so maybe it's a bit paranoid. But from now until Nai'ya, my daughter and grandson are safe, use these any time we need to contact each other. Understood?"

"What about my regular cellphone?" Rebecca said.

"Call my old cell and home phones with it once in a while so the law won't figure out we have these new ones. If Nai'ya calls either of you on your other phones, let me know on these new ones."

"Game of Phones, eh?" C.J. dabbed at his lips with a napkin. "Got to hand it to you, pal. When you turn psycho, you go all the way."

My old cellphone rang. Archuleta again. I placed a finger against my lips. "What can I do for you Sam?"

"Did you know Tommy O'Donnell was an investigative reporter?"

"Really?"

"*New York Daily News.*"

"Did not know that."

"I thought, you being from the Big Apple, you might still read the local papers. Maybe tell me what kind of stories he did. If one of them could have brought him out here."

"I need to speak with you in person. Can you come to C.J.'s?"

My friend shook his head from behind the desk and mouthed a silent *NO WAY.*

I held up my hand to assure him. "How about we meet in the parking lot out front?"

C.J. nodded.

"Why all this secrecy?"

"I'll explain when you get here."

Sam exhaled so deeply into his phone I could almost smell the tobacco. "Okay. I'm five minutes away. Be right over."

I shut off my old cell and turned to C.J. "Don't worry. I know how you feel about cops. I'll keep you out of this." I cleared my throat and tried to clear my head. What to do next?

"You okay?" C.J. bit his lower lip.

"No." I told them about my trip to the morgue and about Tommy and his job as an investigative reporter.

"This is getting weird," Rebecca said.

"The answer lies in New York. I can feel it. I gotta go back." I glanced at her. "Would you mind staying at my place to keep an eye on things there? And see to the cat?"

"Of course not. Otis and I will take care of everything."

We stood. I took Rebecca's hand. "Sorry about our dinner." I pulled a couple of fifties from my wallet and folded them into her palm. "For food and expenses. If that isn't enough, I'll send more. Don't know what I'd do without you." I kissed her forehead and her cheeks flushed once again.

C.J. laughed in Rebecca's direction. "Don't you worry, I'll make good on the old guy's dinner promise. Eat here tonight. On the house."

"Thanks. There's a red-eye from Albuquerque to New York just

67

before midnight. If I'm lucky, I can still book a seat." I looked at Rebecca. "My travel info will be on the library desk. I'll keep in touch and let you know when I'm coming back."

C.J. struggled up from his chair. "Be careful, Gabe. Call if there's anything I can do."

"Just be around in case my girl here needs backup."

"You forgot the info on Klein." She handed the folder to me.

"Right. I'll read it on the plane." I hugged her, gave C.J. a thumbs-up and left.

Waves of heat from the afternoon sun shimmered above the pavement. The restaurant's front awning sheltered me until Sam pulled into the lot. I hustled over to his car.

He was on the police radio. I rapped on the window. He rolled it down. "Right," he said into the phone. "I'll get on that once I'm finished here."

"Stay there." I motioned him to remain seated and walked around to the passenger's side. I sat inside.

He hung up, then lit up and shared his irritation. "What the hell is going on?"

"I think my phones are bugged. Didn't want the Feds to hear us."

"You're losing it, Gabe." He looked at me like my ears were on backward, then gazed out his front window. A flicker of a smile showed when he turned back to me. "Then again, you might be right. Aw, fuck the Feds. What do you want to talk about?"

"Tommy," I said.

"Me too. I want to know why he was at the casino."

"I can't help you on that. Yet. I've been out of touch with him for more than thirty years."

"Can you help me get through to his widow? She won't talk to the New York cops and his editor at the paper has clammed up. Something stinks."

I hesitated. Working too closely with the police risked losing Nai'ya's trust. Then I got an idea. "How about you give me Tommy's address and phone number?"

"I can't go giving out information on an active case. You know that."

"Listen, I'm flying to New York tonight on personal business.

I used to be close to Siobhan. Maybe she'll see me. Maybe I could drop by and pay my respects?"

"After your antics at the morgue, you're in no position to ask favors."

"You got your I.D. You expect me to sit around and do nothing?"

"Say a rosary. But if you think you can get anything out of the widow, go for it. Just do it on your own."

I wrenched the car door open and slammed it once I was outside.

Sam leaned out his open window "You hear from Nai'ya, I still want to know."

"Forget it." I turned away and took the car keys out of my pocket.

"Wait a minute. Come back here." He waved a small index card at me.

"What's that?"

He handed me the card and stared out the front window. "Your old girlfriend's address. Get the phone number on your own."

CHAPTER THIRTEEN

I thought about Tommy and the old days all the way up Fourth Street. The dashboard clock read half past four—six-thirty back in New York. I got a couple hundred bucks from a drive-through ATM, picked up Otis's food and a bag of coffee for Rebecca.

Back at the house, I called the *New York Daily News* from my new phone. Given the hour, my call went to the night desk. A computerized voice told me how important I was and suggested I hold for the next available operator. After listening to a lifetime's worth of Kenny G, I reached a human being.

"I'm sorry, sir. We don't give out personal information."

"Of course. But Mr. O'Donnell was an old, dear friend of mine. I want to offer my condolences to his family. How about I give you my name and phone number? You can pass it along to Tommy's wife. It would mean a lot."

"Well…"

I had her. "That way—if Siobhan wants—she can call me back. And you haven't broken any rules."

She took my name and new cellphone number. Then she hung up.

I logged in online and reserved a seat on a non-stop midnight flight to JFK. It would get me into the Big Apple just before six in the morning.

My stomach rumbled, but there wasn't enough time to dine out. The freezer coughed up a box of microwavable lasagna. I settled for that.

I packed enough for a couple of days, donning one of my better suits and cramming everything else into a single carry-on. My laptop, electronics, and Rebecca's folder on Klein went in a shoulder case.

The day's mail sat on my desk in the library. No bills. Otis stopped by and nuzzled my hand when I jotted down a few last minute notes for Rebecca. Then I called her.

"I left you some coffee. Once I get settled I'll text you with my hotel info. I'll go through your folder on Klein during the flight."

"Don't worry about anything, Gabe."

"Did you *really* say that?"

The library clock chimed seven times. I set out linens and towels for Rebecca and fresh litter for Otis. Almost ready to go.

I poured three fingers of whiskey and slugged it down. No word from Nai'ya in two days. And now Tommy. I refilled my glass, sat back and spent a half-hour remembering him and the rest of the gang from my old neighborhood. It seemed so long ago, it could have been some other guy's life.

My cellphone rang, a New York number. The female voice sounded frail and beaten down. "Gabe?"

"Siobhan?"

"Hello."

I hunched over my desk and softened my voice. "I'm so sorry about Tommy. I had to reach you to see if there was anything I can do."

"It's been so long."

"Nearly thirty years." An uncomfortable silence followed. "I'm sorry to reconnect like this." I fidgeted with the Mont Blanc pen on my desk.

"How did you find out?"

I paused a moment. *Should I tell her?* "I identified his body in a morgue, here in Albuquerque." No response. I wondered if she was still on the line. "Siobhan?"

"How did he look? Did he suffer?"

"Uh…I don't think so." I kicked myself for not expecting the question.

"We were happy. Tommy was a good man." Another silence. "What am I going to do without him?" Her voice trailed off with each word.

"Do you have any children?"

"They're all grown."

"Of course. They would be by now. Any of them out here in New Mexico? I thought maybe Tommy was—"

"No. Jenny lives in Boston with her husband and Timmy, our grandson. Mark is a journalist, just like his dad. He works for Reuters in their London office. They're all coming home the day after tomorrow."

"I'll be there, too. I'm flying into New York tomorrow morning."

"It'll be good to see you again."

"Siobhan, I have to know why this happened. What was Tommy doing in New Mexico?"

"He didn't tell me. Not exactly."

"Not exactly?"

"He only said it was the biggest story of his career. That's all. Except that it would be too dangerous for me to know any more."

"Did he keep any records or files at home?"

"What? Well…Tommy used the front room as his office. There's a safe in there. He kept our tax records and personal files there. He usually kept his business files at the *Daily News*, but there could be something in there, I don't know…why are you asking me these questions?"

"Don't you want to know why he was killed?"

"What difference does it make now?" Her voice heaved and I heard her cry.

"I'm sorry Siobhan. There's something big going on here. Is there a computer at home?"

"Yes, but…Gabe, I don't understand this at all. It has nothing to do with me."

"There are things I need to tell you. My daughter works at the casino where Tommy was killed. She may have been a witness to Tommy's murder. She's missing. I'm afraid whoever killed Tommy is after her now."

She blew her nose. "I'm sorry. I really don't know what I could do or say that might help you."

A knot grew in my stomach. My tongue was dry as sand. "Please, try to think what happened before Tommy left. Something he said. Anything. Maybe by tomorrow—"

"Please, stop!" Her crying grew loud enough to force the phone away from my ear.

I looked at the clock. Less than an hour to get to the airport. I was ready to hang up when at last she spoke.

"I suppose I could look around for the combination to his safe..."

"That would help. May I stop by the house while I'm in town? We could talk."

"Well...okay, for a little bit anyway. Tommy always did like you."

I checked Sam's index card on the desktop and read off the address. "Is that still—"

"Yes, that's our address."

"I'll stay in town for the funeral."

"It'll be at Saint Sebastian's, of course. They're releasing his body tomorrow. We're waking him all day Friday. The funeral is Saturday morning."

Her words sounded so final. We agreed I'd drop over at ten the next morning.

The mention of St. Seb's stirred a flood of memories. Tommy and I attended grammar school and drank our first wine there as altar boys. We'd starred on the baseball and CYO basketball teams. At last, I'd be going back to my old neighborhood.

A drink for the road, and then a smooth trip to the airport. Once aboard, I sat by a window and had a whole row to myself. Until a beefy guy with a gym bag came aboard at the last minute and parked himself in the aisle seat. His sweat-stained shirt suggested he'd come straight from a workout. He leaned forward to stow his bag under the seat. It became clear he hadn't bothered to shower. At least the flight left on time.

I asked a flight attendant for a pillow, turned on the overhead reading light, and leaned against the window. Once we attained cruising altitude, I slipped Rebecca's folder from my carry-on bag and settled back in my seat. The first few pages of her research contained background information on Klein Associates. Real estate, mostly investment properties, plus a few commercial and residential buildings added to the mix. I noticed they'd incorporated in New York State way back in 1930.

Before I read any further, the combination of stress, exhaustion, and body odor from the guy two seats away took its toll. I couldn't focus. The folder would wait until New York.

We touched down at JFK ten minutes early, but I hit traffic on the Van Wyck Expressway. Seven-thirty in the morning, yet bumper-to-bumper all the way. Welcome home, McKenna. It took me two hours to reach the Woodside neighborhood in Queens.

Siobhan lived on Sixty-first Street, one of the few remaining with a visible, vestigial Irish presence—two bars and Finnegan's Funeral Home. Most of the store signs were in Spanish now. Colombians owned my old neighborhood.

My stomach growled, so I stopped at a diner on Roosevelt Avenue that touted *arepas con chorizo*. Time for a quick breakfast.

My front window seat gave me a clear view of the avenue. Donovan's Pub, where I earned my first dollar as a busboy, still graced the far side of the street.

I sipped my coffee and sighed. It's a bitch to feel so old on a sunny morning.

After breakfast, I drove to Sixty-first Street and grabbed the first available parking space, two blocks from Siobhan's. Her building's entry door was ajar. I walked up the front steps and took the stairs to her second floor co-op, hoping to work off my breakfast sausages.

The door buzzer made no sound. I looked around. The hallway was quiet, clean, and brightly lit. Another buzz and then a knock. The apartment door swung open, wide enough for me to peer inside.

"Siobhan?" I took a cautious step forward. "Anybody home?"

Once through the door, I edged to my left, toward the front of the residence and the room Siobhan had described as Tommy's office. The drawers of the desk against the window had been pulled out. Three of them lay scattered on the floor. The fourth sat upside down on the desktop.

A small office safe stood open against the far wall. No signs of forced entry, so whoever opened it knew the combination. I knelt in front and peered inside. Empty.

I stood and retraced my steps to the entry hallway, then crept into the living room. An overturned table rested on its side. Papers and books were scattered about the room. A stand-up lamp had smashed on the floor. I stepped over it.

My shoe stubbed against a silk pillow on the carpet in front of a couch. A few inches away, a dark red pool the size of my fist stained the rug. A spotted, rust-colored trail wound across the room and disappeared down the main hall.

I held my breath and stepped back over the lamp, listening for any sound coming from the rest of the apartment. Nothing. I wiped sweat from my forehead and leaned back against the door. It slammed shut. I rested my weight against the knob and listened again. A bus pulled into the stop in front of the building. Its doors opened, then closed. It drove on. Faint sounds from a television or radio filtered down through the ceiling.

One careful step at a time, I tracked the path of blood to the kitchen. A bowl of Cheerios sat on a small dinette table. A spoon had fallen to the floor. Next to it, two feet stuck out from behind the counter, heels up. A light blue slipper half clung to the left foot.

Siobhan lay facedown. I touched her neck for a pulse. Her body felt warm, but there was no doubt about it. She and Tommy were together again.

The red hair of her youth was mostly gray. I didn't turn her over. I wanted to remember her the way she looked in a long-ago, happier time. I rose and walked back to the living room.

Footsteps clattered from the hallway and a man's voice shouted. I looked for another way out of the apartment. The front door exploded with cops. The one in front swiveled a gun straight at my face.

"Freeze."

CHAPTER FOURTEEN

They hustled me to 114th Precinct headquarters on Astoria Boulevard before I could catch my breath. My words of protest went unheard.

I stood in front of a sergeant's desk, wrists shackled behind my back. He took down my name, address, and social security number. A muscular guard patted me down. They removed the cuffs so I could empty my pockets and sign a receipt. Luckily, I'd left my new cellphone under that morning's *Daily News* on the front seat of my rental car.

"Mr. McKenna, you're being held for interrogation." The sergeant wrote on a form in front of him on the desk. He never looked up.

"When will that be?"

"Soon as we see if there are any outstanding warrants against you."

"There aren't. Will I be free to go after that?"

"Now that ain't up to me." He motioned toward a couple of nearby cops. "Take his prints." They did, and then escorted me to a holding cell without a word between them.

I expected a lockup filled with a colorful palette of street-wise characters, like in the movies. But except for a teenaged kid and one grizzled old man unconscious on a cot, I had the place to myself.

The large holding cell had a brown and tan checked linoleum floor, bars on three sides, cinder block on the fourth, and a toilet I smelled all the way across the cage.

The kid and I made eye contact. He gave me a "thumbs up" that I dutifully returned. The old guy snored like a rhino. Nothing else happened for an hour. I spent each of those sixty minutes trying to ignore the stench.

Detective Lieutenant John Cuozzo—so read his I.D. tag—appeared, one of the cops who'd ridden to the precinct with me from Siobhan's apartment.

"Let's go McKenna." He unlocked the cell. A hungry-looking cop joined us for a walk down a long, empty corridor to an interrogation room. I'd been through this routine once before. It wasn't any lovelier the second time around.

A rectangular table filled most of the ten-by-ten room. The lieutenant waved me to a wooden chair on its far side. A large wastebasket in the corner overflowed with styrofoam coffee cups. Another officer stood in front of the door, arms folded. A single window several feet above my right shoulder was barred. I wasn't going anywhere.

Cuozzo unfolded a large white handkerchief from his breast pocket and blew his nose with such force that a pencil on the table rolled several inches in my direction. I followed it until it stopped. Once the handkerchief disappeared it was throat-clearing time. First him, then me. I looked up at the cop by the door. He wasn't playing.

The lieutenant switched on a video cam behind him. Its red light blinked several times. He adjusted a small microphone on the desktop, introduced me by name as a person of interest, and pronounced the time to be fourteen-thirty hours. My stomach growled. I wondered if it would become part of the official transcript. He recited my Miranda Rights for the benefit of the recorder.

Showtime.

"Your name?" He grabbed the pencil in his left hand.

"Gabriel James McKenna."

He scribbled away. I braced myself for his flurry of questions. "Occupation?"

"Archeologist and Professor of Pre-Columbian North American History."

"Place of residence?" Either he was bored already or he'd done this a thousand times before. His voice was dull and lacked any emotion.

"Albuquerque, New Mexico, U.S.A."

He dropped the pencil and stared at me. "With *that* accent?"

"Yeah, with that accent. Born and raised in Woodside, Queens. Lived in Elmhurst after that. Moved to New Mexico six months ago."

"Any family here who can vouch for you?"

"My wife died eighteen months ago. I do have a brother-in-law. Dan Mooney." I coughed up his address and phone number.

"What were you doing at the O'Donnell residence?"

"Siobhan was married to Tommy O'Donnell. Tommy was a long-time friend of mine. He was murdered three days ago. I stopped by to pay my respects to his widow."

Cuozzo's eyebrows shot up in surprise. *Was it possible he didn't know?* "Where did this murder take place?"

I swallowed hard. "Albuquerque."

His eyes flicked a bit of fire. Nostrils widened. There was blood in the water.

"I'm the one who identified Tommy's body after the killing. You can check with Detective Lieutenant Sam Archuleta of the APD. He'll vouch for me."

"Why you?"

I looked up. *Had that vein always been there on his forehead?* "What do you mean?"

"How come they had you identify O'Donnell's body?"

"Tommy and I were classmates back in the neighborhood. Saint Sebastian's, over on Fifty-First Street. Served Mass together. Check with Monsignor John Egan. If he's still around."

For the first time, a glimmer of warmth appeared on his face. Then it vanished and he was all business again. "The old monsignor passed away last year. You came all the way back to New York just to see the wife?"

Careful, Gabe. "I had to come back to New York on personal business. I took the opportunity to pay my respects to the family at the same time."

"Yeah?"

"Six months ago I moved to Albuquerque rather abruptly. Left things undone. A bank account, a safe-deposit box at Queens County

Savings on Thirty-ninth Avenue. I'm technically on leave from Dumbarton College and needed to sign my termination papers. Had to take care of these things eventually, so I figured, why not now, when I could pay my respects to Siobhan? We were friends."

I wanted those words back as soon as they'd left my mouth.

"Friends?" Cuozzo leaned across the table a couple more inches. "Good friends?"

"*Just* friends. From more than thirty years ago. Nothing more than that."

"The story you're telling makes a bit of sense, but *only* a bit. For all I know, this could be a romantic triangle gone bad. You kill your rival in Albuquerque, and then come to New York to confront the woman."

I knew he was baiting me, but my fist landed on the table just the same. "You're crazy." I stood up half way.

Cuozzo didn't move. "Sit down, McKenna. Cool off." His voice was low key. Matter-of-fact.

"Sorry." I settled back in my chair. "I can account for every minute I've been in New York. I took the red-eye from Albuquerque last night. Sat in seat 16C by the window. The boarding pass stub is in the envelope with my other belongings. The car rental receipt is in there as well. Ask the sergeant at the front desk."

Cuozzo sounded unimpressed. "I will. That still doesn't account for your whereabouts at the time of Mrs. O'Donnell's death."

I felt my cheeks flush. "I haven't finished. I rented an Impala at 6:30 this morning, at the airport. Hertz. Got stuck on the Van Wyck for nearly two hours. Check the traffic reports. Breakfast at a Colombian diner on Roosevelt at 8:30. The waitress's name was Caleña. Little slip of a gal with glasses. I left a big tip, maybe she remembers. That receipt is in the envelope, too. Maybe it's time-stamped."

"Too much detail, McKenna. You choreograph everything you do?"

"I'm an archeologist. Details matter. Look, I was in the O'Donnell co-op for less than two minutes before you arrived. I'll even give you a DNA sample."

"Yes, you will." Cuozzo took a breath and let it out the way a tired man will at the end of the day. The clock behind him said it was not yet noon.

"You have my prints. Other than the front doorknob, I only touched Siobhan's neck."

Cuozzo flashed a killer smile. "That might not help you too much."

"Why not?"

"Mrs. O'Donnell was strangled to death."

"But all that blood—"

"The way we see it, maybe she left the breakfast table to answer the door. Maybe she was expecting someone. A confrontation ensued. She was struck several times and tried to escape through the kitchen. Her assailant finished her there."

Someone pounded on the door to my left. The standing cop opened it and stepped out into the hall. I tried to slow down my breathing.

"Assistant D.A. Milner is here, Lieutenant." A gray-haired gentleman with half-glasses and an impeccable blue pinstripe suit entered the room. Cuozzo rose. The two conferred in whispers. The other cop came and stood between them and me. I couldn't see much of Milner until he stretched out his arm and checked his watch.

Shit, another one? On the fourth finger of his left hand—a black onyx ring with the raised golden figure of Chief Tammany in the middle.

I rubbed my eyes and looked again. Milner turned and left the room. The cop resumed his post in front of the door. Cuozzo sat down. His eyes toyed with me, like a cat toying with a wounded bird.

"I know my rights, Lieutenant. I'm not saying another word until my attorney is present."

Cuozzo reached into his pocket for his handkerchief and detonated his nose again. "Sure." He looked at the cop by the door. "Clancy, take him back to the tank."

I stood up and shook off Clancy's sudden grasp. "I know the way." With his hovering presence by my shoulder, I trudged back up the corridor and into the holding cell.

The door clanked behind me. The kid was gone. Just the old man, still snoring.

CHAPTER FIFTEEN

Cuozzo returned an hour later. "D.A. Milner will take your formal statement at four-thirty."

I pressed my forehead against the bars. "I'm not saying anything without an attorney. I want to make a phone call."

The lieutenant sighed and unlocked the cell. "Follow me." We walked down the corridor past the interrogation room to a wall-mounted public phone. No privacy.

"I need a local directory."

He pointed to a large book hanging from a wall by a chain. I used both hands to page through the New York City yellow pages. On page sixty-five, under "Attorneys at Law," I found my man—Gerald O'Toole, Esquire.

I hoped my best friend from high school and college would come through for me one more time. "Sloppy" was the only guy I knew who'd worn a sport coat, dress shirt, and bow tie to school each day. Brown shoes, even on weekends. With his wardrobe, and my reputation as an amateur boxer, you could say I functioned as Sloppy's bodyguard.

"Gerald O'Toole, Attorney-at-Law. How may we assist you?" She was young, bright, and full of Brooklyn.

"Hello. I'd like to speak with Sl—with Mr. O'Toole. Tell him it's Gabe McKenna calling." I stared Cuozzo down. He took a step back and pretended to read the posters on the wall.

"Mr. O'Toole will be with you momentarily, Mr. McKenna." Sweet voice.

After a brief silence, my call patched through with a click.

"Sister's ass! This is a surprise."

"How ya doing, Sloppy?"

"Rich and free, Brain. Where the hell you been hiding?" He sounded the same as always.

I explained my situation. He told his secretary to cancel all his appointments and promised to make my four-thirty date with Milner.

"Just one thing," he said.

"What's that?"

"Don't call me Sloppy in front of Milner. I have a reputation to uphold."

Cuozzo walked me back to the holding cell. I wondered if the still-motionless old man on the cot might have lapsed into a coma.

At precisely four-twenty, Cuozzo came back and let me out. "Time for your singing lesson, McKenna."

"Can I leave when it's over?"

"Not my call. Come along."

My stomach tightened. I had a problem in Milner. I had to figure he knew everything. I had to find that sweet spot between cooperation and self-protection.

We walked through the open door. Milner pointed to the chair opposite his. "Professor McKenna."

"Mr. Milner." I squeezed out a smile and sat.

Half-glasses wobbled a bit on the end of his nose. He peered over them with the look of a hungry man at a smorgasbord. Where to begin? He sipped from a Starbucks cup. No jailhouse coffee for the Assistant District Attorney of Queens County.

"You understand why I'm here?" he said.

"To get to the truth, I presume."

"Have you ever given a deposition before?"

"No. Where's my lawyer?"

My answer came with a knock on the door. Gerald stuck his head in, saw me, and gave me a wink. Milner winced like he'd just swallowed a bitter pill.

My old friend pulled a chair up next to mine. We shook hands for the first time in three decades.

Milner turned on a recorder and gave the date and time of day. "Assistant District Attorney Milner questioning Gabriel McKenna. Counsel Gerald O'Toole present at the request of Mr. McKenna."

"Has my client been Miranda'd?" *Atta boy, Sloppy.*

"Of course."

I nodded my head to confirm Milner's assurance.

"Mr. McKenna," he began, "you were discovered at the scene of a homicide on Sixty-first Street in the Woodside neighborhood shortly after nine-thirty this morning. Is that correct?"

"Yes."

"Were you acquainted with the victim?"

I nodded.

"Speak your answer, please. Were you acquainted with Siobhan Carnahan O'Donnell?"

"Yes." I felt Sloppy's hand on my right shoulder.

"Are you also aware that her husband was found murdered in Albuquerque, New Mexico, three days ago?"

"Yes."

"And were you present in that city at that time?"

"Yes."

Sloppy looked at me, puzzled.

"Tommy," I half-whispered to him.

His face turned pale. "May I have a moment to confer with my client?" Gerald now gripped my arm.

"It's okay," I assured him and turned back to the D.A. "I intend to cooperate with your investigation in every way possible, Mr. Milner." *Except telling you anything that would hurt my family or me.* I looked him in the eye, conscious all the while of the ring on his right hand.

For the next half hour, I responded to all of the D.A.'s questions, tossing in exonerating details wherever I could. I'd heard of Tommy's murder from a friend on the Albuquerque police force; I'd flown to New York to clear up personal business, pay my respects to Siobhan, and attend Tommy's funeral; I could account for every minute of my time since arriving in town that morning—the chits and receipts I'd turned over to the police would back me up.

I told my story with growing confidence, sure that Sloppy would interrupt me if I said anything that could be damaging.

Milner lowered his nose to peer at me over his glasses. "Mr. McKenna, who is Joseph Klein?"

I stared at the table. My mind raced and my heart pounded in my chest. I chose my words with great care. "The only Joseph Klein I know runs a real estate brokerage firm in Albuquerque. His company once held the title to my home. They sold it to my great-aunt Nellie more than twenty years ago."

"I see." He ruffled through a few pages on the desk in front of him.

I leaned forward, meeting his gaze when he looked up. "And Mr. Milner, as I'm sure you know, Tommy O'Donnell was shot dead in Klein's office three nights ago. Are you going to be interrogating Mr. Klein?"

Sloppy kicked me hard under the table.

Milner ignored my question. "Did you recently visit the Sun Mountain Art Gallery in Santa Fe, New Mexico?"

"Don't answer that." Sloppy leaned over the table and eased me out of his way. "My client has told you what he knows about the murder of Siobhan O'Donnell. He has been forthright and cooperative. He is also cooperating with the Albuquerque police investigation into the death of her husband."

I nodded solemnly.

"Unless you're prepared to connect Mr. Klein or the art gallery to the murder of Siobhan O'Donnell, I'm advising my client not to answer any more questions."

"Very well." Milner flashed a millisecond smile. He glanced at his watch.

Sloppy was now on a roll. "Furthermore, if you are not prepared to charge my client with a crime at this time, I demand his immediate release. If you intend to hold him as a material witness, I demand his release on bail."

Milner raised his hand. "You needn't worry about that."

"My client has cooperated with the Albuquerque police from the time Tommy O'Donnell's body was discovered. Holding him here in New York may well hinder their investigation. I will assure you that, should Mr. McKenna's presence be required at a future point in your proceedings, my client will present himself voluntarily. Given reasonable advance notice, of course."

"Have you finished, Mr. O'Toole?" Milner's smile smacked of condescension.

"Have you?" Sloppy fired back. I was impressed at what a pit bull my friend had become. I stifled the urge to fist-bump him.

"I'll have a transcript of Mr. McKenna's deposition drawn up. As soon as we have his signature, he'll be free to return to New Mexico." Milner put his papers into a manila folder and sat back.

"How soon will that be?" I said, not wanting to be left out of the decision.

"Will tomorrow noon be satisfactory? I can have the papers sent to Mr. O'Toole's office. He can return them with your notarized signature."

"Fair enough."

"Then our business is finished. For now," Milner said.

We rose together. I reached out and shook hands with the D.A. His hand felt clammy. The ring felt cold.

Sloppy and I walked out the front door of the precinct house. He bundled his overcoat against the evening chill. "Where to, Gabe?"

"Donovan's still any good?"

"Their food's slipped a notch, but beer's still beer."

"That'll do."

"I have to stop by the office first." He checked his watch. "Nearly five-thirty now. Seven-thirty? That too late for you?"

"It might be too early. I have a couple of calls to make. Gotta find a hotel, shower, and change out of these clothes."

"Try the Quality Inn on the Boulevard. Let's make it eight."

"Eight o'clock. Listen, you still in touch with Deke Gagnon?"

"Onion?" Sloppy used the nickname we'd hung on Deke as kids. "I should say so."

"How's he doing these days?"

Sloppy shook his head. "The same."

"Still able to pick a fight in an empty room? He became a cop, right?"

"Until they kicked him off the force. Now he runs his own investigation firm. A regular shamus—trench coat, the whole bit. I toss him some work every now and then. He and wife number three live someplace in Astoria. Married a Greek gal. At least I think this one's Greek."

"Give him a call, see if he can join us, okay? Maybe we can hoist one to Tommy's memory."

"Will do. Eight o'clock. Donovan's."

Gerald O'Toole, Esq. ducked into a shiny, red BMW 6 Series convertible and bad-assed his way down the street. I walked the half-mile to where I'd left my rental car.

Somehow, Milner had known about my meeting with Klein and my visit to the Sun Mountain gallery in Santa Fe. How? Did somebody from inside the APD tell him? Did that ring mean he, Klein, and the guy at the gallery were somehow connected? I didn't like any of it.

I needed to get together with old friends and drink to remember, and to forget. First, there was business that couldn't wait.

CHAPTER SIXTEEN

I sat in my car and opened the driver's window, fanning myself with the two parking tickets some traffic cop left under the wiper blades. I rolled the window up and fished around under the newspaper on the seat for my new phone. Six calls, all from Rebecca.

"Hey kid, what's up?"

"Gabe, where have you been? I've been trying to reach you all day. You're not going to believe it but—"

"Is this good news or bad news?"

"Both."

"Give me the good news first, I could use it."

"C.J. heard from Nai'ya."

I gripped the wheel tight in my left hand. "Are they okay?"

"They're fine. She tried to call you on your old phone, but her calls wouldn't go through."

"I turned it off and left it in my desk back home. Did she say where they are?"

"They've gone up north. Those were her exact words. Nai'ya's family is hiding them until everything blows over."

"Her family?" I waved off a grizzled panhandler who slapped a greasy hand against my passenger side window.

"That's what she said. I thought her family was from Laguna Pueblo? That's west of here, not north."

"She must be with her younger brother Estefan. He married a

woman from Santa Clara Pueblo. That's north of Santa Fe. I only met him a couple of times. They're not close."

"She's going to try and call you tonight after everybody goes to bed."

I looked at my watch. Six-fifteen. She'd be two hours behind Eastern Time. "Does she have my new number now?"

"Yep. C.J. gave it to her. When will you be back?"

"Tomorrow night."

"Want me to stay here at the house tomorrow until you get in?"

"No. I'm taking the last flight out. You go home. How's Otis?"

"He's fine. The little guy misses you."

"Sure he does. Tell him his regular staff will resume its duties tomorrow night."

"Gabe, aren't you forgetting? There's bad news here, too. You better sit down."

My stomach tightened. "I'm sitting in my car. How bad is it?"

"They dug up six more bodies."

"What?" I jerked back hard and accidentally hit the horn.

"First one early this morning. The others at regular intervals throughout the day. Six so far. Looks like your barn was also somebody's private cemetery."

"Is Sam still there?"

"You mean Crawford?"

"Oh, jeez. I forgot."

"He was, but he left for the day. Want to know the funny part?"

"There's a *funny* part?"

"Remember the body they first identified as that guy Hoffa?"

"Kind of hard to forget."

"Turns out it wasn't him after all. It's the body of a trucking company official from New York City. A teamster's union pin was on the dead guy's coat. According to Darryl, Sergeant Crawford thought the remains looked like that guy Hoffa. But DNA tests showed he was wrong. Guy's name was Blazek, or Blassic, or something like that."

I didn't care if the corpse was Tiny Tim. My main concern was that the dead man came from New York. "Is Officer Jackson still there?"

"Yes, he is." Her girlish voice paused. "He's taking me out for a bite to eat when he gets off duty."

"Really?" I pictured two blondes at a taco stand.

"Yep. When *some* men promise to take you to dinner, they actually do it."

"*Touché*. Listen, after you two enjoy your little rendezvous, I need you to do something for me."

"Sure. What?"

"Find out if any of the other bodies have been identified. See if any more are from New York. Get any names you can. Leave the info on my desk before you go home tomorrow night."

"Okay."

"Maybe Officer Jackson can find out for you."

"I'll do what I can."

"The law may not know much for a few days, but check tomorrow anyway. I'll touch base with Archuleta when I get back and fill you in on what's happened here. Thanks for everything. Enjoy your dinner."

"Right."

"One last thing. Nai'ya—did she *really* sound okay?"

"C.J. said she sounded fine but kind of serious. Not scared or anything. Just serious. Determined. And one other thing—"

"What?"

"She said to tell you she's sorry for leaving the way she did."

"Thanks. A lot."

I hung up and reached for the folder on Klein Associates I'd left under the driver's seat before walking up to Siobhan's place. It wasn't there. I looked on the rear floor, under the seat, on the back seat. I climbed out and circled the car. No sign of forced entry on any of the doors or windows.

This didn't figure. It looked like a professional job, but how could they have missed my new cellphone? I called Rebecca back.

"Sorry to bother you again. I either misplaced the folder you made up for me or I've been robbed."

"Gabe, be careful. Don't worry about the folder. I have copies of everything back at my apartment."

"You're a lifesaver, kid. Talk to you tomorrow." I pulled out of the parking spot. My uneasy feelings tagged along for the ride.

The Quality Inn was three blocks away. I stopped at the bar after checking in. A double whiskey accompanied me to my room. The air conditioning was already on and the king-sized bed was firm. I punched in a soft music channel on the TV, stripped off my clothes and nursed my drink through a long, hot bath.

CHAPTER SEVENTEEN

Donovan's hadn't changed. Thirty feet of mahogany bar, a jukebox filled with oldies, high-backed booths along exposed brick walls. The waitresses were still old, but somehow no older. The menu above the bar looked familiar, except for the higher prices.

Different faces, same crowd. Only the old, thick haze of second-hand smoke was missing.

I lucked into our old booth, second one on the right, straight across from the bar. My view of the front door and the street beyond brought back a surge of memory.

A waitress came over. I ordered a Smithwick's Irish Red and reflexively took out my photo ID. The gray-haired lady smirked. "Don't flatter yourself, grandpa."

New York. I slipped the ID into my wallet and looked around. Maybe my friends and I left something of ourselves behind when we stopped coming here, but damned if I knew what it was.

The beer arrived. I took a couple of generous slugs of the reddish-amber liquid before Sloppy and Onion ambled through the front door. They immediately honed in on our old booth.

I stood and waved and stepped out onto the floor. We met in an awkward group-hug followed by some cobwebbed shoulder punches. The same tired wisecracks flew back and forth.

Onion took a half step back and motioned toward my upper lip, a friendly "foam alert." I brushed it aside with my sleeve.

"Sonofabitch. I better stick to whiskey. How you doing, Onion?"

His physique resembled an onion even more now; rounder and heavier than when we'd last met. "Brain, I thought you'd be punch drunk by now."

"I'm working on it. Let's sit down." We sat where we always sat, except for Tommy's empty space to my right. I looked across at Sloppy. "Thanks big time for helping me out today. I owe you."

O'Toole shook his head. "You owe me nothing, Brain. My turn to play bodyguard, that's all."

The waitress returned. I could have predicted my old friends' Guinness draughts.

"Fucking shame about Tommy," Onion said. "Sloppy told me on the way over. Why would anybody want to bump him off?"

"No reason I can think of." I took a slug of beer. Then I told them how Tommy had been shot to death at the Pueblo-66 Casino. I told them the cops had me identify his body. I told them everything, except the part about my daughter. "And so I flew back to the Big Apple to pay my respects to Siobhan."

"Siobhan too." Onion sniffled. "That sucks so bad. That dame was class all the way."

Once their beers arrived, I proposed a toast. "To Tommy. To Siobhan." We raised our glasses and drank in silence.

"I can't believe he's gone." Onion took out a tissue and collected some tears. "And Siobhan… You had a thing for her, didn't you Brain?"

"Yeah. In Junior high. My first girlfriend."

"Beautiful girl." Sloppy shook his head.

"What would you know? You were never interested in girls." Onion stared at O'Toole. "That's why I get married so many times. To make up for your inaction."

"I just never met the right girl."

"Careful, Slop," I warned. "That's what Liberace used to say."

He stiffened in his seat. "What's that supposed to mean?"

"That you're a lousy piano player." I glanced across at Onion and we busted up.

"If I was so lousy, then why did you guys make me leader of Collateral Damage?" Sloppy referred to our 80's punk band that withered and died without ever getting any traction.

"You were the leader because you were the only one with a garage." Satisfied, Onion returned to purposeful drinking.

"Look, you two," Sloppy's Irish was now officially up, "the only reason Collateral Damage didn't make it big time was we lacked proper management."

"Yeah, that and talent," I said. "What was the name of that God-awful song of yours we auditioned at CBGB's?"

"You mean, 'Love is a Death March'? Best thing I ever wrote."

Onion drained his glass. "Then Tommy had to go and spoil it by singing on key."

"Guess we weren't rotten or vicious enough." I looked across at Sloppy. "But we *were* the only punk rock act in history whose keyboardist wore a bow tie."

O'Toole grinned over his Guinness. "What's wrong with a bit of style?"

We shared some good laughs and recalled more of the old times before the waitress came our way again. Onion pointed to each of our glasses in turn.

By now, I was struggling to organize my thoughts and words. I hadn't eaten anything since breakfast. "How 'bout some food? It's all on me tonight."

We started with a double order of baked clams. Onion and Sloppy tried the fish and chips. I ordered a shepherd's pie.

"So, Gabe," Onion said, "we kinda lost track of you. Whatcha do with your life?"

What to leave out? They knew I'd ditched my amateur boxing career to finish college.

"After Fordham, I didn't know what I wanted. My dad was pushing the army. So I enlisted and served for two years—Rifleman, 1st Battalion, 75th Rangers."

Sloppy leaned forward. "See any action?"

"They sent me to Grenada in '83. I was part of the drop at Port Salines airport. Small-scale really, but it was enough. Two of my buddies came back in pieces." I looked past the bar. A pair of tired-looking gals danced with each other in front of some besotted neighborhood gents.

"Know what you mean, man." Onion's voice brought me back to our booth. "Eight years after I joined N.Y.P.D., my partner bought it. Some punk shot him. I emptied a full clip into that motherfucker. Turned out he was fourteen years old. Asshole Sharpton started marching and I got suspended."

I looked up in surprise. "When was that?"

"Summer of '87."

"I was in New Mexico that summer. No wonder I didn't hear."

"That was it for me. Quit the force and my first marriage that same week. If it weren't for O'Toole here, I might've taken the bridge."

"I always figured you'd make it in professional baseball," I said. "You were a damn good high school pitcher. What happened with that?"

"Another almost. Pitched for a year at a junior college down in Texas. Can't even remember the name of the place now." Onion shook his head.

"No shit? I had a cousin who pitched in the minors for a year."

Onion shrugged. "I could always throw hard, but never knew where the damn ball was going. My lack of control turned off the scouts, I guess. Got a nibble. Never got drafted, never got an offer."

Sloppy turned to Onion. "Lack of control has always been your problem."

"It's not my fault I've never been appreciated." Onion's gaze dropped below the rim of his glass.

"Everybody has tough times." Now I was looking into *my* beer. "My marriage ended a year ago this February. Twenty-two years."

"Damn, Gabe, I'm sorry," Sloppy said. "Your wife cheat on you?"

"No. She died on me. Cancer. It ate her up, bit by bit…fuck, where's our food?" I squinted the moisture from my eyes.

Our three plates arrived, balancing on the waitress's forearms. An acrobat, yet. But she did follow it up with another round.

As we ate in silence, I tried not to think of Holly.

There we sat, pals from simpler times. I gazed across the table at a slick New York lawyer and a rumpled, washed-out private investigator. What did they see when they looked at me?

My cellphone interrupted my thoughts. I didn't recognize the

Caller ID. "McKenna."

"Gabe?" Nai'ya sounded far away.

I bolted upright. "Are you okay? Where are you?"

She said something, but her words were lost in the din.

I shouted in response. "I'm in a restaurant. Too much noise in here. Hang on, I'm moving outside."

It sounded like she said "okay."

"Sorry guys, this call's important. I'll be right back." It took me a minute to work my way through the front door of Donovan's and out to the boulevard. A fire engine roared by, sirens at full-blast, an ambulance wailing behind it.

"Damn. Hang on another minute." I walked past a laundromat and a small deli and turned down a driveway into a secluded rear parking lot. Not much moon tonight, just a dim light falling from a second floor window above the deli. Two dumpsters, a beat-up white paneled van, and me. I moved to the center of the lot to improve my cell signal.

"That's better. Honey, how are you? I thought you were going to call me later tonight."

"I'm okay. This is the only time I have alone." She coughed softly. "Sorry."

"I've been going out of my mind."

"Don't worry, Gabe. We're safe. I'm calling you on my brother's landline. It's secure. We're staying with him in his trailer."

"Why did you leave like that?"

"I had no choice. I heard you talking with the lieutenant and worried he'd try to use me to get to Angelina. I did what I thought best."

"You still have that gun?"

"Yes. I saw you put it in the drawer. I took it for protection."

"I could have protected you. Leaving that way makes everything more difficult. What—"

"I did what I thought was best."

"Right." I tried a different approach. "So you're all together at Santa Clara Pueblo?"

"We're safe."

I looked around and took a deep breath. I had to calm down.

"Nai'ya, I can't help you if you don't let me."

Nothing but silence.

"Please, listen. That new cell number C.J. gave you—"

"What about it?"

"We'll use *only* that number from now on. Okay?"

"Okay."

"I'll be back in New Mexico tomorrow night."

"Where are you now?"

"C.J. didn't tell you? I'm in New York."

"New York? What's going on?"

"Much more than you realize. You need to trust me. Will you do that?"

She paused. "Yes."

"I'll come up to the Pueblo day after tomorrow. I want to be with you."

"Gabe—"

"Lay low until I get there. Don't go anywhere. Don't talk to anyone you don't know. All of us are in danger. Wait for me right where you are."

"Okay."

"Is Angelina there? I'd like to tell her I'm coming to see her soon. Tell her not to be afraid."

"Estefan took them into the village. I wanted privacy so we could talk."

"Will you have Angelina call me when they get back?"

The light from the window vanished.

"I don't think that would be wise. She's too frightened. This isn't the time."

My voice rose. "I'd say it's about twenty-five years past time. Why won't you let me speak to her?"

"Gabe, have you been drinking?"

"What's that supposed to mean?"

More silence.

"Nai'ya, I'm Angelina's father."

"She doesn't know that yet."

Her words hit me as hard as any punch I'd ever taken in the ring. I stood there like a fool, all silence, waiting for her next word. After five seconds I hung up, afraid I might say something I'd regret forever.

A mournful procession of dull gray clouds passed overhead. I walked back up the driveway to the boulevard. Cold night wind bit my cheeks and swirled the stale exhaust of cars and buses.

I needed both hands to open Donovan's front door. I dreaded my friends' questions. I didn't want to face them, but I needed their help and another drink.

Sloppy couldn't believe I'd hung up on her. Neither could I. I spilled the rest of my story—about Nai'ya, about a daughter and grandson I never knew, about Klein and the dead bodies in my barn. The whole thing exhausted me. I begged off early and left Donovan's around ten-thirty.

CHAPTER EIGHTEEN

I've never been a good morning-after drunk. I crawled out of bed, full of impotent rage at my lack of self-control, and wondered how far my love for Nai'ya would take me.

The hotel's breakfast didn't improve my mood. The coffee and Danish were cold. When I checked out, the "tourist tax" on my bill was $15.75 for one night's stay. It soured me for what lay ahead.

First on my dance card was the managing editor at the *New York Daily News*. My head was pounding. My stomach ached. I didn't phone ahead.

The lobby floor of Four New York Plaza looked and felt so shiny I could have skated into the building. By contrast, the twenty-third floor lobby was whisper-quiet and all carpet. I eased out of the elevator, straightened my shirt collar, and got my bearings.

A left turn and a dozen steps brought me face-to-face with Ms. Leticia Brill. A rectangular gold-plated sign on the front edge of the desk hailed her as *Personal Assistant to Mr. Charles Vacco, Managing Editor*. She seemed to count to ten before she looked up at me.

"May I help you?" Young, Manhattan-slim and poured into a tight-fitting gray shirt. No wedding ring. Scarlet nails flashed as she tapped on her desktop. Wavy brown hair spilled over one shoulder.

"I'm here to see Mr. Vacco."

Her right eyebrow rose. "Do you have an appointment?"

"I want to speak to him about Tommy O'Donnell."

"In what capacity?" No warmth, no welcome, just cool superiority.

"I identified Tommy's body in New Mexico. Gabe McKenna." I offered my card.

She held it between her thumb and forefinger like it had just washed up on the Jersey Shore. She read it and then read me. I studied the soft flow of her hair.

"Stay here, Mr. McKenna. I'll see if Mr. Vacco is free." She rose and disappeared through a mahogany paneled door.

Her desktop looked too neat, like that of an employee without enough to do. But the autographed photo of Derek Jeter on the wall behind her chair scored her some points. She returned before I completed a mental review of the Yankee captain's career highlights.

"This way." She motioned me through the door and led me down a short corridor. The length of her stride flashed a hint of silk slip beneath her black skirt.

Vacco's office was a sterile festival of chrome and glass. Aggressive air conditioning made the room colder still. But a panoramic view of New York harbor made it all worthwhile.

Charles Vacco sat like a wax dummy, dwarfed behind a desk that could have doubled as a helipad. A half-dozen large screen TVs broadcasting the major 24/7 news channels covered the wall to my left. No sound, just a barrage of video cutting and popping like silent firecrackers.

Vacco didn't move when I approached his desk, and his blue-gray gaze never wavered. He looked pleasant enough. Warm eyes, square jaw, solid shoulders. The kind of guy who gets elected fraternity president. "You're here about Tommy O'Donnell?"

"That's right."

"Sit down." He motioned me to a chair across from his. "May I offer you something to drink? Coffee? Mineral water?"

My pounding head screamed for coffee. "No, thank you. I'm fine."

"Miss Brill says you're from New Mexico. That you identified Tommy's body."

"I did."

"You sound pretty New York to me."

"Tommy and I grew up together. Queens, Elmhurst."

"He was a good man. Best investigative reporter I've ever known."

"Whatever you had him working on got him killed."

"You know this for a fact, do you?" Vacco's voice had a sudden edge. He leaned forward.

"It's clear enough. Probably got his wife killed, too," I said.

"What's your source?" His warm, dark eyes went cold. The rest of his face gave nothing away.

"I stopped by their home yesterday. Thought maybe you could help me out."

Vacco shifted in his seat. "If you're here to make me feel bad about what's happened, save it. I feel that way already." His right hand opened the center desk drawer and took a couple of pills from a small silver case. He swallowed them dry. "Bad stomach."

"Help me out here, Mr. Vacco. What kind of story was Tommy working on?"

"I wish I *could* help you. The fact is, I don't know."

"You were his boss."

"Tommy O'Donnell was a respected veteran of his craft. A goddamned icon around here. Your quintessential New York reporter. He knew what buttons to press. And he knew where all the skeletons were buried."

My mind flashed to the recent discoveries in my barn. "Go on."

"Look, I didn't nursemaid every story Tommy did. That's my point. He worked on his own, pursued his own leads. He'd earned that much over the years. Later, he'd check things out with me before we ran with the story. That was our routine."

"So what did he share with you about this one?"

"Not a thing. That's what made it so unusual. He was downright secretive. Said it was too soon. But he did call it *the hottest thing I ever handled.*"

"That's how he described it?"

"His exact words. Tommy said I shouldn't know. I needed to have plausible deniability in case anything turned sour."

"He was looking out for you."

Vacco nodded. "That's the kind of guy he was." He made a fist of his left hand and rubbed it furiously with his right. "I should have stopped him right there and demanded to know more. I feel responsible for what happened."

"I don't think Tommy would want you to carry that around."

Vacco dragged himself from behind his desk and paced to the window. He stood with his back to me, looking out across the harbor. "He was my friend, too, Mr. McKenna."

His cellphone chimed the first four notes of Beethoven's Fifth. I swallowed my other questions for the time being.

"Vacco." He looked over his shoulder at me, his face stricken. He lowered his voice, but not so much that I couldn't hear. "I see... right away."

Who gives this guy his marching orders?

"Of course. No. Nothing." He stole a second, more furtive glance at me. "Nothing, I swear."

I cleared my throat and checked the clock behind his desk. Eleven-fifteen already. I was due at my old bank in half an hour.

Vacco slid the phone back into his pocket without another word to his caller. "I forgot I have a previous appointment. I'm afraid I can't help you any more, Mr. McKenna." He sat back down. His hand trembled a bit on the desktop.

"That's a shame. If you change your mind or think of anything, would you give me a call?"

Vacco nodded. "Why don't you leave your contact information with Miss Brill? Hotel, phone, your e-mail address, if you have one. If I think of anything more, I'll have her get in touch."

I stood. Vacco rummaged through his desk and avoided my gaze. Our discussion was over. I'd have given my eyeteeth to know who'd just called.

"Thanks." I whisked out of his office past Leticia Brill without giving her any of my personal data Vacco had asked for. I could clam up too.

Frank Darby, a geriatric guard outside the Queens County Savings on 103rd Street and 39th Avenue, greeted me like a long-lost brother. "Mr. McKenna, where ya been?"

"New Mexico."

"You in the foreign service now?" He ran a bony finger along a bulbous nose and held the door for me with his free hand.

"That's in the U.S., Frank." I patted his arm and brushed past him into the bank.

My meeting was with a Mr. Charles Bishop, Senior Vice-President. A portly five and a half feet of milquetoast, he helped me close out my accounts and stood guard as I emptied my safe deposit box.

The sight of Holly's jewelry staggered me. None of her items were all that expensive, but my heart ached more with each piece I removed from the box. I thanked Bishop for his time, crossed the street to a FedEx store and mailed them to my home in Albuquerque.

Angelo's Pizza was right across 39th Avenue from the bank. Onion sat waiting for me at the popular lunch spot, hogging one of the few small tables by the front window.

"Feeling any better today, Brain?"

I told my first lie of the day. "I'm okay."

"Hope you're hungry." He unfolded his napkin and tucked it into the front of his pants.

"I won't embarrass you."

"Listen Gabe, I know it wasn't easy for you unloading on us last night. Just remember you've got two guys in your corner. Slop and I want to find whoever killed Tommy and Siobhan as much as you do."

"I appreciate that. Listen, about last night…"

Onion cocked his head. "What about it?"

"I've got a mess back in New Mexico that can't wait. You think Tommy and Siobhan would mind if I flew back before their funerals? You and Sloppy—"

"Course not, Gabe. Tommy would tell you, do what you gotta do. Besides, once we put O'Toole's legal ability, my detective skills, and your brains together, we'll find whoever killed them soon enough. Right?"

"Thanks." The waitress stopped by with two menus. "You know this could get messy," I said.

Onion glanced at the menu for about five seconds before he put it back on the table and looked at me.

"Life is messy. Sloppy and I talked last night after you left. This case needs somebody on each end anyway, in New York and New Mexico. He's going to dig into the Chief Tammany angle and find out what he can. I have a few N.Y.P.D. guys who still talk to me. They can keep me updated on the investigation into Siobhan's murder. Sloppy and I will keep in touch with you every day. You go take care of your business in Albuquerque."

"Sounds like a plan." The waitress returned. I ordered a cold antipasto salad. Onion opted for something called the *Deal 3*, a large cheese pizza, a dozen wings, and six garlic knots with cheese.

He must have noticed my jaw drop. "It's my dinner, too, okay?"

We dug in and he gave me a slice, the best I'd had in a long, long time. *Why can't somebody make New York pizza in Albuquerque?*

Onion wiped a long string of cheese off his chin and pointed a finger at me. "You be careful when you get back there. My gut says we're dealing with something big."

"Tommy called it 'the hottest story he'd ever had.' "

Onion stopped chewing and thought about it. "I'm between cases right now, so I can—"

"Between cases?"

"You could say that. Anyway, I can be flexible, come out to New Mexico if and when you need me."

"You're a pal, Onion. And I may take you up on that. If I do, I'll cover all your expenses. In any case, we keep in touch every day, right?"

"You got it." He looked toward the heavens. "Hear that, Tommy?"

My spirits rose. Ten minutes of good food and small talk later, my phone rang.

"Mr. McKenna?"

"Speaking."

"This is Mr. O'Toole's secretary. He wanted me to tell you he's tied up in court this afternoon. He said for you to stop by and sign your statement transcript from the Queens D.A.'s office."

"Is it there now?"

"Yes. Dropped off about an hour ago."

"Great. I'll stop by after lunch. If Mr. O'Toole calls in, tell him I'll stay in touch when I get back to New Mexico. Thanks." I hung up and turned to Onion. "I better get going. Got a couple more stops to make before my flight."

"Okay, Brain. Don't forget what we talked about. And watch

your back."

I put money on the table. "I won't forget. Call you in a day or two. Here. Take this." I wrote my new cell number on the back of my card and slid it across to him. We shook hands and walked away in opposite directions.

CHAPTER NINETEEN

I flipped a mock salute at the statue of Elijah Dumbarton and strode across the concrete quad of his college. The old nineteenth century codger turned his fortune, built on the labor of his textile workers, into a school for their descendants.

Nowadays he stands proud and serene, a roosting and feeding spot for New York pigeons. Larger-than-life, Elijah still carries out the motto of his institution, *Sustinere et Servare*, to support and serve.

My old office had been reassigned as soon as I'd taken my leave of absence. I proceeded straight to Personnel.

"Good afternoon, Marge." I winked at portly Mrs. Lonergan. Rumor had it Dumbarton College had been constructed around her desk. No one had ever seen her anywhere else.

"Professor McKenna! Welcome back, you're certainly looking well."

"An illusion I've cultivated for years."

"Ms. Blanch is waiting for you in her office."

"Ah. The Divine Ms. Blanch. How is she?"

Marge checked right and left and lowered her voice. "The same, I'm afraid."

"Nuts." I walked past a row of eight-foot cubicles and waved at all the worker bees. At the end of the corridor, I knocked on the large oak door of their Queen.

"Enter."

I poked my head inside. "Good afternoon." I continued into a Gothic chamber darkened by purple velvet drapes. Two rococo sofas flanked an enormous desk. A plain wooden chair at the foot of it was Iris Blanch's only concession to her visitors.

"Sit down." She gave me the flinty-eyed stare that earned her the title of "Dr. Warmth" among my former colleagues.

My footsteps echoed off the hardwood floor and walnut-paneled walls. I gripped the back of the wooden chair to steady it as I sat down.

"You're late." She looked at a small wooden desk clock and tapped its top, like we were playing timed chess.

I stared at the woman, a sour artifact weathered by thirty years of administrative overreach. I offered no apology.

"So, you've decided to leave?" Something about my leather jacket seemed to catch her eye, perhaps the tan lamb's wool on its collar.

"I've decided not to return."

Ms. Blanch paged, machine-like through a manila folder in front of her. She slid two stapled sets of papers across the desktop. "Initial the bottom of each first page. Sign in the middle of each second page. Keep the second copy."

"Mind if I read it first?" I studied the document. It terminated my employment and held the school blameless for any future mayhem I might inflict upon the world.

"The college will henceforth make no further contributions to your retirement account. You are, of course, free to keep contributing on your own."

"How kind of you." I signed where I was supposed to sign.

"Professor McKenna, I don't think I like your attitude." She punctuated the remark with an acidic glare.

"I don't think you ever did, Ms. Blanch." I sighed audibly for effect, folded my copy of the papers and slipped them into the breast pocket of my coat. I reached into my wallet and took out one of my cards. "In case you ever need to reach me."

She stabbed out for it and brought the card up to eye level. "New Mexico?" She made it sound like I'd taken a rental in a trailer park.

"Happy trails, Iris." I gave her a wink and slid out of her lair.

The drive to Sloppy's office took less time than the search for a parking space. My friend was still in court when I arrived. I read my witness statement on Siobhan's death twice. After I signed it, his attractive secretary notarized it.

I asked her to tell her boss I'd call him from Albuquerque. We bantered for a bit before I walked out to my rental car. Enough time remained on the parking meter for a snort or two at a bar across the street. I needed some liquid courage before visiting my wife's grave on the way to the airport.

My daily visits to Holly's burial plot in the year after her death did little to process my grief. But the last time I'd knelt and touched her gravestone, I did experience a small sense of closure. During the past six months I felt I'd managed, with Nai'ya's help, to make some progress toward a healthier emotional life.

Three quick doubles and I was in no shape to drive. I couldn't dare let Holly see me like this. By the time I'd filled my stomach with salted snacks and two cups of coffee, it was quarter to four.

CHAPTER TWENTY

Outbound traffic on the Van Wyck proved lighter than the morning before. Still, it was pushing five when I turned in my rental. I snaked my way through the line at airport security and placed a call to Rebecca.

"What's up, boss?" Her voice was a cool evening breeze against the side of my face.

"Lots. My plane's leaving on time. I should be home by ten."

"I'll wait for you."

"That's okay, I've leaned on you enough these past few days. Go home and get a good night's rest. Tomorrow morning will be soon enough to get together. Any word from Nai'ya?"

"Nothing today. And I think the cops found all the bodies yesterday. No new developments there either."

"I guess that's good. Did you leave that extra copy of the Klein file on my desk?"

"I didn't have a chance. It's back at my place. Okay if I bring it with me tomorrow?"

"That'll work. I'm too tired to look at it before then anyway. How's Otis?"

"Still Otis."

My smile took some effort. "Guess that's good, too. Thanks for all your help. So...how did your dinner with Officer Jackson go? Decent first date?"

I thought I heard a quiet giggle. "Much, much better than that."

"Oh?"

"I'll tell you what I want you to know tomorrow."

"Can't wait."

The boarding call sent me hurrying for a cellophane-wrapped sandwich as my makeshift dinner. A man can't live just on pretzels and booze. When I returned to the gate, the passenger line was moving.

Part of me still wanted to stay in New York to attend Tommy's and Siobhan's funerals. The larger part of me wanted to find their killers.

Most of the people I passed down the aisle of the 737 looked as tired as I felt. At Row 11, a pink-cheeked, grandmotherly woman in a print lilac dress sat in the aisle seat. She was knitting a scarf.

"Pardon me." I pointed across to 11A. "My seat's against the window."

"Of course." She put her needles and yarn on the middle seat, stood and moved into the aisle.

"Thank you." I heaved my carry-on into the overhead storage bin and swung past her; my shoulder bag in one hand, my sandwich in the other.

I buckled up and settled in against the headrest as we left the gate. The middle seat remained empty. *Excellent. Room to stretch.*

They dimmed the cabin lights shortly after takeoff. I leaned my forehead against the window and closed my eyes.

The stress of recent days must have caught up with me. I woke up four hours later during our final descent to the Albuquerque Sunport.

"I thought I might have to wake you." Grandma stopped knitting a black and gold scarf, neatly folded it, and stuffed it inside a woolen tote bag on the floor between our seats.

"I was exhausted." My sandwich was still on the seat next to me. The glow of the cabin lights on the cellophane made it look green.

The old lady's incessant smile coaxed me fully awake. "Do you like New Mexico?"

"It's interesting." I turned on my phone for a quick, forbidden check. No messages.

After a smooth-as-silk landing, the plane taxied toward the

terminal. Grandma looked away and busied herself with the tote bag. Once we came to a stop, she checked her phone too. The sweet smile changed to a frown. "Oh my."

"Something wrong?"

"My son-in-law was supposed to pick me up. His car won't start."

"Nuts. Is there anyone in town you can call?"

Her eyes were now misty and her hand trembled a bit as she brought it to her lips. "My daughter and her husband are the only people I know here. This is my first visit. Oh dear."

"Ma'am, my vehicle is in the long term lot. May I drop you off somewhere? I'm a careful driver," I lied.

She looked at me like I was ice cream and balloons. "Would you? I would never ask such a thing, but it's so late. You seem like a decent young man."

So the 'Decent Young Man' would be getting home a few minutes late. With four hours of sleep under my belt, I'd be up for a while anyway.

"Gabe McKenna." I held out my hand.

"Elaine Houseman. Mrs.—Mr. Houseman passed twelve years ago next week." She gathered her things when it was our turn and stepped into the aisle.

"I know how that is." I leaned my head under the edge of the overhead bin, slid my carry-on down to the seat and lifted my shoulder bag.

We shuffled behind a line of weary passengers toward the front of the plane. I nearly tripped over a bag left on the floor. Its handle strap stuck out into the aisle at Row 7. A man sat slumped against the window, lights out to the world. I picked up the bag and nudged him with it. "Buddy, you better take this. Somebody might get killed."

His eyes opened a slit. He blinked. It was the same gym rat that sat near me on the flight to New York two nights before. He grabbed the bag without a word, put it on the floor between his legs and turned back to the window. I felt a jolt in my stomach. Then I realized he was probably flying on to San Francisco.

"Mr. McKenna, it's so kind of you to give me a lift." Mrs. Houseman opened her purse. "Let me at least pay for the gas."

"Forget it." The carry-on was digging into my left arm. I shifted it to the other side. "Did you check any luggage?"

"Just one suitcase. With wheels."

"Right. Meet you at baggage claim." I slipped the old sandwich into my jacket pocket and made a pit stop at the first men's room in the terminal. I looked around for something different to eat, but at this hour everything was closed. Damn. I rode down the escalator to meet Mrs. Houseman and her luggage.

Her suitcase was the size of a small circus car, but it did have wheels, like she said. After some struggle, it fit into the back cargo area of the Land Cruiser.

I settled in behind the wheel. Mrs. Houseman scribbled on an index card and handed it to me. "My daughter's address. She said her house is in the Northeast Heights. Wherever that is."

The address was twenty-minutes away. She unfolded an Albuquerque street map. While I drove, she tried to locate her daughter's street with the aid of a penlight from her bag. We barely spoke the entire way. I had problems of my own to think about.

I stayed on I-25 north to the Paseo del Norte exit, and then drove eastbound toward the Sandia Mountains. A mile or two along, Mrs. Houseman patted my forearm. "This should be the turn-off coming up." She pointed to the left side of the approaching interchange. "Yes it is. Turn left."

Less than half a mile north of the intersection, her daughter's spacious two-story modern adobe palace stood alone, dominating the largely undeveloped area. House lights were on as I motored up a winding driveway. Rows of ground-level solar lights edged both sides of the blacktop.

I swung around a small traffic circle, stopped the Cruiser in front of a wrap-around porch, and climbed out. Mrs. Houseman waited for me as I wrestled her luggage out of the car. The suitcase and I banged our way up the steps beside her.

A thirtyish blonde woman opened the door with her right hand. In her left, she cradled a little blue-eyed boy who was rubbing sleep from his eyes. There were lots of tears and hugs all around.

A man's voice called from the dark interior, "That you, Mom?"

"Charles, since when don't you come to the door and greet your mother-in-law?" Mrs. Houseman snapped.

"Mixing you a drink. Be right there."

Mrs. Houseman brushed a hand on my arm and gave me a final, disarming smile. "Thank you for your help. I'm sorry to have inconvenienced you, especially at such a late hour."

Her daughter chimed in, "Thank you for driving my mother home. May I offer you a drink?"

"No thanks, got to be going. Lovely boy there."

"Isn't he? You can leave the suitcase inside the door. My husband will take care of it."

Mrs. Houseman waved good-bye. I moved across the porch and heard the door shut behind me. I paused a moment at the bottom of the porch steps. A million stars dotted a clear, dark New Mexican sky. My problems seemed far away.

When I turned the ignition key, my stomach growled along with the engine. I slid my right hand into my jacket pocket and pulled out my sandwich. The cellophane looked more edible than what was inside. "No sir." I left it on the seat and decided to stop at a 24/7 Lotaburger on my way home.

I circled back down the driveway toward Eubank. The dark outline of two cars I hadn't noticed on my way in bracketed both sides of the driveway entrance.

When the Cruiser drew within twenty feet, their headlights came on in tandem. Brights. For a moment, I couldn't see the driveway at all.

A shot exploded from the car on my right and pierced the passenger side windshield. I ducked as low as possible, pressed the accelerator to the floor and split the two cars.

At the entrance to the driveway, I swerved hard left and sped back the way I had come. A glance in the rearview mirror confirmed my fears. Both cars were after me.

The Land Cruiser holds 380 horses under its hood, but its off-road capability was my best chance. I ran a red light at the Paseo Del Norte intersection and raced east toward the Sandia Mountains.

I maneuvered around a pair of slower moving vehicles and left them in my dust. Up to seventy-five now. A small chunk of windshield glass broke off, hit the dashboard and fell to the floor.

Eighty-five. Let the cops come. Only one car in my rearview

mirror. Outside and to my right, a second vehicle pulled up alongside. The driver's window slid open.

Riding the center lane gave me options. I sped up enough to edge ahead of my pursuer and swerved into his left front fender. The Cruiser bucked from the impact, but I kept control. I drifted further into his lane and forced him onto the shoulder.

He slowed, trying to clear himself. I matched that move and kept pushing him to the right, into the darkness of a roadside culvert. I cut my wheel to the left and grabbed the highway again.

Then I floored it. Another gunshot sounded above the scream of my engine. The light at the upcoming intersection glowed solid red. A panel truck, its turn signal flashing, approached from the right. I held the horn down and flicked my brights.

The headlights of my second pursuer flashed in my left side mirror. He was less than twenty feet behind me.

The panel truck rumbled into the intersection. I let up on the horn, clasped the wheel with both hands and floored it again.

The next seconds clicked by like individual frames of a motion picture. I flew through the red light. The panel truck didn't stop. My headlights lit up its driver. He stared at me, wide-eyed. His mouth opened. I swung the wheel left and hit my brakes. Too late.

The front end of the panel truck clipped my rear bumper and sent the Cruiser sideways through the red light. The impact jarred my hands from the wheel. My body thrown forward, I struggled to regain my grip and swerved to the left. As the rear of my vehicle continued to turn, I counter-steered and held my foot steady on the brake.

An ungodly squeal of tires and the shattering sound of compacting metal rang out behind me. I twisted my head to see.

The panel truck spun a full circle in the middle of the road and came to rest facing the wrong way. The second car chasing me hung suspended in the air for an eternal second. It nosed into the concrete, flipped once, twice, and then again. The car landed upside-down in the left-hand lane, parallel to the road. It burst into flames.

I crawled from my Cruiser, dazed, yet drawn to the burning car. The two vehicles I had passed a lifetime ago pulled up and stopped. Their headlights flooded the scene with an unreal brightness.

"Stop!" The driver of the panel truck stood by his vehicle,

somehow unharmed. "Don't go any closer. You've done enough damage. Stay back!"

"We have to reach that guy." I tried to walk but stumbled to my knees.

"There's an extinguisher in the back of my truck. Hold on."

I held my head and waited for the world to stop spinning. Nothing but silence, except for the footsteps of the truck driver and the lapping of flames inside the overturned car. Then a piercing, agonized scream from deep inside it. I held my stomach to keep from retching.

The man from the panel truck emptied an extinguisher into the burning vehicle. The fire gave way with an angry hiss. Low smoke covered the area. An acrid odor surrounded me.

At last the cops arrived and took control. A minute later a pair of emergency vehicles pulled up, red lights flashing. One team of EMTs clustered near the overturned car, the other hurried over to where I knelt.

I've been hurt enough to know I didn't need medical assistance, but I couldn't sell the EMTs on the idea. They checked me for head injury and major trauma. When they slow-walked me over to the ambulance, we passed by the smoldering wreck that had pursued me. A half-burnt gym bag lay in the road beside the car.

CHAPTER TWENTY-ONE

The usual tests at UNM Trauma Center showed only a soft-tissue bruise to my left shoulder. The doctor recommended an overnight stay for observation. No way. I signed myself out at 2:35 a.m.

My concern over finding a cab at that hour proved unfounded. Sam Archuleta stood just outside the hospital entrance, waiting for me. "So. The Angel of Death returns." He flicked a cigarette butt to the ground and gave me a *what-the-fuck?* look.

"Don't you ever sleep?"

"Detective Lieutenant Cuozzo of N.Y.P.D. called. Told me you were coming in tonight. That was some entrance you made."

"How the hell did Cuozzo know what I was doing?"

Sam gave me a dismissive look. "So what's the big deal? He heard it from the Queens' D.A.'s office. We're coordinating on the homicide investigations of your friend and his wife."

"Someone followed me from Albuquerque to New York. And back. That's the big deal. And the guy who died trying to kill me tonight was on both of my flights."

"That so?" Sam took out another cigarette and flicked his lighter.

"The only people who knew I was flying to New York were Rebecca, C.J.—and you."

Sam blew a lungful of smoke. "I didn't tell a soul. You have my word on that. You sure nobody else knew about your trip?"

"Not on this end. Of course, Siobhan O'Donnell knew. I talked with her before. And I called the *Daily News* office before my trip. But I didn't mention anything about my travel plans to them."

"Interesting." He pointed to his left. "My car's in the lot."

"You still charge by the quarter mile?"

"Pay for my coffee. We need to talk."

"Damn right we do."

We sat in the Frontier Restaurant on Central under a large mural of John Wayne. Sam stirred his coffee as he layered in the sugar. The first bite of my green chile cheeseburger burned like a first swallow of whiskey on an empty stomach.

Sam scalded his mouth and then set down his cup. "Was your trip worth it?"

"I know a lot more now, if that's what you mean."

"Like the fact we're dealing with an extensive criminal enterprise?"

I nodded. "How'd you figure that out?"

"Has to be," Sam said. "Too many New York connections. New York money behind the casino. The Albuquerque murder of a New York reporter in Klein's office. And we dug up more bodies in your barn while you were away."

I put down my cheeseburger. "Did any of them turn out to be long-missing persons from New York?"

"You didn't hear that from me, smart guy." Sam took a more careful sip of his coffee, holding the cup with both hands.

I winked. "Rebecca told me."

"Wait 'til I get my hands on Officer Jackson."

"Go easy on him. My secretary can be quite persuasive." I sipped as much Coke as I could before the straw collapsed. I pulled it out of my drink and tossed it on my tray. "Find out everything you can about the Sons of Tammany."

"That business with the rings?"

I nodded.

"But Tammany Hall fell apart in the early 1960s."

I nodded again. "I'm impressed with your historical knowledge. Actually, their political power declined during the two preceding decades, when the Luciano and Genovese crime families gained influence over the organization."

"So why should I suspect them now, half a century later?"

"Play a little 'what-if.' What if, after Tammany officially disbanded, some of its members diversified, moved on to other avenues of power and wealth?"

"That's a stretch. But I'll look into the rings, if you really think it might lead somewhere."

"Sam, the first body in my barn had one. Klein flashes one." I paused. "And the Assistant D.A. of Queens just happens to wear one, too."

"Oh?" His eyes widened.

"You heard me. His name's Milner. There's a connection somewhere."

"If there is, I'll find it. Better let Cuozzo know."

I raised my palm. "Don't. You don't know anything about him."

"He's well respected. Heard him speak a few years back at a Violence Against Women conference in Chicago."

"Not enough. You don't *know* him. That's the point."

Sam waved away my comment. "I cooperate with law enforcement guys I don't know every day of the week."

"Don't trust those guys back in New York. I'm telling you."

His cellphone interrupted what I expected would be at least a mini-lecture. "You don't say." He looked at me and raised a finger. "Okay. I've got one stop to make first. Be there in half an hour." He hung up and slipped the phone back in his coat. "Well, well."

"What?"

"No registration in either of the vehicles that pursued you tonight. We ran the plates. Both belong to Pueblo-66 Enterprises, Incorporated."

"Did you arrest the driver of the car I ran off the road?"

Sam frowned. "He got away."

"Nuts."

"The Commissioner expressed his disappointment in somewhat stronger terms."

"What's your next step?"

"The casino. I'm going to be there when Klein shows up for work." He checked his watch. "Finish your cheeseburger."

"Take me home, okay?"

Darkness enveloped my house. I turned on the light in the foyer and the ceiling light in the library before collapsing into the desk chair. The corner clock chimed four times. Otis appeared out of nowhere and jumped on top of my desk. He rubbed his head against my hand until I switched on the lamp. His Lordship then curled up under its warmth.

I lifted my Bohemian crystal paperweight and examined a single sheet of paper beneath it. Four names, all male, written in Rebecca's hand. She'd listed an address under each of the names. Three were from the New York area, one from a high priced New Jersey suburb. Under all that, a solitary sentence: *Two sets of remains are still unidentified.*

The answering machine held no messages. The clock said four-fifteen. Rebecca would be arriving in less than five hours and we had a lot of ground to cover. I filled Otis's food bowl and glanced out the kitchen window at the barn. Seven bodies.

Turning off the lights on my way to the bedroom, I set my alarm for 8:15 a.m. and crumpled on top of the covers fully clothed.

The alarm wasn't necessary. Sam called from the casino around 7:30.

Propping myself up on an elbow qualified as morning calisthenics. "What?"

"Sorry to wake you. I just thought you ought to know." A hint of defeat tinged Sam's voice.

"Know what?"

"Klein's disappeared."

"When?"

"Overnight. I drove here right after I dropped you off. We interviewed all the night workers. Apparently, Klein and two of his assistants left about three-thirty with a couple guys nobody's ever seen before. Two cars. At least one had Colorado plates."

"That it?"

"In light of what happened last night, you should be warned. Want me to send over a patrol car?"

"No thanks." I sat up and scratched my head with my free hand. "Rebecca's coming in around nine. We have tons of stuff to do. Then I need to arrange for car repairs and file an insurance claim. You just find Klein and let me know when you nab him."

"You're starting to sound like my boss."

"You are a public servant, right?"

"About your car...plan on driving that older rig of yours for a while. We need to keep the Cruiser until we conclude our investigation."

We hung up and I called Rebecca. With Klein on the lam, her research into his connections was more important than ever.

No answer. Probably on her way over. I dragged myself into the shower, dressed, and started a pot of coffee.

I sat at the library desk and read Rebecca's list of names. After pouring my first cup, I went over the list one more time and phoned Sloppy back in New York.

"Offices of Gerald O'Toole, Attorney-at-Law." How do secretaries sound so damn perky so early in the morning?

"It's Gabe McKenna. Is your boss in?"

"One moment please." At least there wasn't any sugary elevator music.

"What's up, Brain? How was your trip back?" Sloppy's staccato voice was music enough.

"Aside from the two guys who tried to kill me, it was smooth as silk."

"What? Where?"

"Here in Albuquerque. On my way home from the airport."

"Somebody knew you were on that flight."

"Obviously. And somebody followed me to New York, too. Look, forget that for now. I need your help."

"Name it."

"I'm going to give you a list of names. Four of them. Find out everything you can about these guys—background, jobs, and families. Any information about the circumstances of their disappearances."

"What's the connection? They got anything in common?"

"Yeah. They were all buried in my barn."

"Jeezus. These names, can you e-mail them to me?" Sloppy said.

"Afraid not. My fax, e-mail, and phone lines are probably tapped."

"You think so?"

"Yeah. And do us both a favor."

"What?"

"Hang up and call me back at this number on your secretary's cellphone."

"You're kidding me."

"Not at all, Slop. You might be bugged too."

He let out a deep breath. "If you say so."

"Thanks."

We hung up. A couple of minutes later O'Toole called me back. "I agreed to reimburse her for the minutes and gave her the afternoon off. Fire away."

I spread Rebecca's sheet in front of me. "First guy is Angelo Zappeli." I spelled the surname. "Last known address 6607 19th Avenue in Brooklyn. Out on bail and awaiting trial for embezzlement from the New York Transit Authority. Last seen July 12th, 1971."

"Next."

"Sergei Dmitrov."

"A Russian?"

"Indeed. Member of the Soviet Union delegation to the U.N., believed to have defected to the U.S. in November of 1962."

"Right after the Cuban Missile Crisis?"

"Yep. But I doubt you'll find his disappearance is connected to that."

"If the C.I.A. *was* involved, that would be classified," Sloppy said.

"So how the hell does his body end up in my barn?"

"Beats me. Who's next?"

"Brian Livingstone. Upper Saddle River, New Jersey."

"Expensive real estate."

"Ran his own financial management company. Disappeared in October of 1979, along with more than fifty-three million in his clients' assets. Left behind a wife and a couple of kids."

"I remember that one," Sloppy said. "One of my Profs used it as a case study in estate law."

"All that dough bought him was a ticket to my barn."

"And the fourth?"

"I saved the most interesting for last. January of 1958. Guy named Richard Van Heyer."

"Never heard of him."

"Get this: he was an investigative reporter for the *New York Daily News*."

"No shit. I'll get Onion on this right away."

"Tell him to text me his bank account info, I'll do an E.F.T. for fifteen hundred. That should cover his initial expenses."

"Listen, Gabe. You watch your back."

I smiled into the phone. "Same thing Onion told me."

We hung up. Nine-thirty. Rebecca was late. I called her again, but there was still no answer.

My phone rang. "Welcome back, Gabe." C.J. sounded downright perky.

"Flew in last night. How'd you know I'd be back today?"

"Rebecca buzzed me right after we closed yesterday. Said things were popping. So what's the current body count?"

"Then you heard about the cemetery in my barn."

"Yeah. But I kept that little nugget from Charmaine. Then she saw it on the TV news. You better not show your face around here, man. She might try to rearrange it."

"Don't joke about that. Two guys tried to kill me on my way home from the airport last night."

"You shitting me?"

"I wish. Cops traced both cars to the Pueblo-66 outfit. And now Klein's disappeared."

"So what happened?"

"They took a couple of shots at me and then tried to run me down on Paseo del Norte. I used my driving skills to full advantage."

"Cops get 'em?"

"One's dead, the other escaped."

"Damn." C.J.'s voice picked up a bit. "You hear from Nai'ya yet?"

"We talked night before last."

"She okay?"

I paused. "Yeah."

"What's wrong, Gabe?"

"Nothing I can go into now. I may go see her tonight."

"Give her my love."

"I sure will. Listen, did Rebecca give you any hint that something might be wrong when she called you last night?"

"No. She sounded happy you were coming home. Thanked me again for dinner the night you left. That was it. Why? Is something wrong?"

"Probably nothing. She's late for work."

"Man, you worry too much."

"Bullshit. How about Rebecca and I stop by for lunch later?"

"Not until one-thirty. Charmaine has her weekly beauty parlor appointment then."

"I could use a mess of ribs. Bye."

I called Rebecca a third time. Her voice recording asked me to leave another message. I felt a jolt in my stomach. After hanging up, I grabbed the keys to the Hudson and headed out to my carport.

It was a quarter to ten when I pulled out onto Rio Grande Boulevard. The Hudson warmed up as the sun hit it, so I opened the driver's side window. Fifteen minutes later, I parked in front of Rebecca's apartment in the Huning Heights neighborhood south of Central.

She lived in a second floor apartment of an old Victorian home that had been converted to multiple units. Her car sat in the small parking area at the end of the driveway.

Thirteen steps up to her door. I knocked and checked the street down below. A blue early '70s Mustang sped down the block. I knocked again and tried the knob.

Her door was unlocked.

"Rebecca?" I pushed it in far enough to edge my head inside. "Rebecca?" No answer. I had a sudden flashback of Siobhan's co-op back in Queens.

I took a step into the apartment and stopped, a sickness rising in my stomach. Papers and pillows were scattered around the living room. Her coffee table and large lounge chair lay on their sides. Her television set had fallen backward onto the rug, its screen now facing the ceiling. A standing lamp leaned against the far wall, its pole bent, splinters of glass around its base. Only her large green sofa appeared untouched.

I yelled her name a third time and rushed through the living room into the kitchen. Her espresso machine was on. A red light indicated its brew cycle was complete. An English muffin peeked out from her toaster. A full glass of orange juice sat on the small dinette table in the corner. It looked like an ad for breakfast.

My growing fear propelled me to her bedroom. My hopes rose when I found the room empty. Then I noticed some ominous details. Overturned vials of creams and perfumes decorated the top of her lace-covered vanity. A small pair of scissors lay on the floor. I knelt down and examined it, careful not to touch.

Thin streaks of red covered the blades and part of the handle. Dark red stained the bed sheet where it drooped down to the floor. Specks, like breadcrumbs, drew my eyes along her carpet, down the hall and into the living room. In my haste, I'd missed them on my way in. I slumped against a wall.

"Dear God, please…" I called 911, gave them my location and sank onto the couch. My gaze caught the corner of a manila envelope that stuck out from beneath her overturned coffee table. I took a tissue from my pocket and lifted the table enough to kick the folder out with the toe of my shoe.

Rebecca had written one word on the front: *Klein.*

Using the tissue, I opened the folder. Empty, except for a yellow post-it note stuck to the inside cover. I unstuck the note and turned it over. There were only two words on it: *Find Mahatma.*

I jammed the paper into my pocket and took another quick tour of the apartment. The bathroom was empty and apparently undisturbed. A neatly folded bath towel hung on the rack. Rebecca's bedroom and hall closets told me nothing more. I returned to the living room a third time and looked out the front window. *Where the hell are the cops?*

Down on the street, two squad cars pulled up to the curb. I let go of the drapes and walked out to meet the patrolmen at the top of the stairs.

Officer Darrell Jackson arrived first, breathless, his face stricken. Sergeant Crawford and two other cops I'd never seen before huffed up the steps behind him.

Jackson grabbed my arm. "Where's Rebecca? What happened?"

"Jackson," Crawford barked, "you look the place over. I'll deal with McKenna."

The rookie officer paused and then glided past me without

another word. The other two cops followed him inside the apartment. It was a *Crawford vs. McKenna* rematch.

"You've been a busy boy these past twelve hours."

"Sergeant—"

"You're a shit magnet, McKenna. The more time I spend with you, the more crap I have to deal with."

I'd had enough of his act. I moved closer and stood toe-to-toe with him. I spat out my words. "This isn't about you, Crawford. I'm sorry about your daughter and whatever problems you have in your miserable life, but an innocent young woman is missing here. Open your goddamn eyes. There are signs of a struggle all around here. Blood in the bedroom and on the floor. Try to wrap your head around that if you can."

He responded with a fat fist that buried itself into my stomach. It was a solid punch that landed where it would leave no mark and could easily be denied. I doubled over, groaned and slid away from him. I blocked his next blow with my forearm. He reached for his gun.

"Hold it right there, Sergeant." Jackson stood in the archway between the kitchen and living room. He aimed his handgun squarely at Crawford's hulking body. "Drop the gun and sit on the couch."

"You're career is over, Jackson." Crawford turned and flashed his distilled hatred at me. But he placed his gun on the floor and sat on the edge of the couch. I picked up the weapon and handed it to Jackson.

The two other cops entered the room and stopped short. The taller one looked at Jackson. "What the fuck?"

"Thomas," Jackson ordered, "go down to the street and secure the area. Don't let anyone up the stairs." He turned his head slightly toward the smaller, swarthy cop, but his gun and gaze never left Crawford. "Garcia, call Lieutenant Archuleta. I don't care what he's doing. Tell him to get over here right now. Then keep the sergeant quiet."

Crawford leaned against the back of the couch and glowered at his young subordinate. "You're dead, Jackson."

The young officer called for a forensic unit while he stalked the premises, a frantic perpetual motion machine. At last it was time to question me.

"What were you doing here this morning, Professor?" Jackson

kept eyeing Crawford as he spoke.

"I flew into town last night after a couple of days in New York. Rebecca didn't show up for work this morning or answer any of my calls. I came over to check on her. I was worried."

Deep lines formed across his brow. He looked at the overturned coffee table, then bent down and examined the empty manila folder. He noticed the single word Rebecca had written there. "Klein? What's this all about?"

"Rebecca was doing research for me on Joseph Klein."

His voice cracked like a rifle. "Why?"

"Klein's real estate company used to own my home. And he knew my daughter was a witness to the killing of Tommy O'Donnell in Klein's office."

Jackson scowled. "You realize you put Rebecca in danger?" He turned away and stomped out of the room.

I looked at Crawford and his Cheshire cat grin. "What's so funny?" I said.

Crawford let out a muffled yet defiant laugh. "Haven't you ever watched a young man drown before?"

Garcia prodded the back of the sergeant's thick neck with his gun. "Knock it off, Sergeant."

Forensics arrived first. Jackson met them at the front door. He looked back at Crawford as he spoke. "We've found blood stains that need to be tested and typed. Check the entire apartment for prints. Lieutenant Archuleta should be here soon. Report back to him."

As if on cue, Sam appeared at the front door. He took one look at me and threw his hands up.

"Lieutenant," Jackson stuck out an arm to halt Sam's entrance into the room. "I need to speak with you in private." He motioned toward the hallway.

"That's right, Sam," Crawford bellowed from the couch. "Go ahead and listen to what the young fool has to say. Just don't believe a word of it."

"Can't you just shut up, for once?" I glared at him from across the room.

"We're not done, you and me," he said. "Not even close."

Garcia again poked Crawford from behind.

Crawford turned his head. "Watch it, Beans. I'm not forgetting you either."

A minute later, Sam marched into the living room, staring at me. "Did Sergeant Crawford physically assault you?"

I nodded. "Twice. His first punch hit me in the stomach—"

"Liar!" Crawford shouted.

"I blocked his second punch with my forearm." I rolled my sleeve up. A red welt on the bone had begun to swell. I showed it to Sam.

"Did you instigate the use of force or retaliate against Sergeant Crawford with anything other than words?"

"No, sir. He started to draw a gun on me, but Officer Jackson intervened."

"Lies!" Crawford stood and shook a fist at the world.

"Sit down and shut up." Sam's hands slipped into his trench coat but came away empty. He turned to Garcia. "Remain with Sergeant Crawford. Make sure he doesn't leave the couch. Lieutenant McAuley from IA is on her way. When she arrives, I want you to accompany her and the sergeant back to headquarters."

Crawford's smile disappeared faster than the whiskey at my father's wake.

"You'll need to make a statement, Gabe." Sam hands continued to fidget.

I nodded. Another statement.

"Jackson," Sam turned to the officer. "You'll have to go downtown, too. Tell them what you told me, all of it. For now, I want you to wait downstairs."

Jackson nodded in a daze and turned for the door just as Sam's phone rang.

"Archuleta." Sam looked around the room. "You found him? Good. Where? Excellent—what's that?" His free hand clutched his forehead. "Aw, fuck!" He waved his hand about, like he was trying to brush away a swarm of gnats. "Shit. Yeah, I'll call you back." He shut off his phone. "Judas Priest!"

"Sam?" I said.

"They found Klein and his two muscle men."

"This could be the break you need. Where were they?"

126

"At a rest stop off I-25 near Raton Pass. Huddled behind the restroom building."

"Are they talking?"

"They can't. Each guy has a bullet hole in the back of his head."

I walked to the front window and peered through the blinds. Three black and whites and Sam's car clogged the street in front of Rebecca's building. Neighborhood onlookers surged against the police barriers when the medical investigator arrived. Things were moving quickly, just not quickly enough.

Sam showed no interest in the view. He sat on the couch and ran his hand over the bald spot on the top of his head. No words, no cigarettes, no emotion registered on his face.

"What now, Sam?" It was something to say.

His weary voice barely rose above a whisper. "I have no idea."

I felt for him. "Can I help?"

"Go down to Internal Affairs and give Lieutenant McAuley your version of what happened between you and Crawford. But take it easy, okay?"

My back stiffened. "What the hell for?"

"Crawford was way out of line, I know that. We've taken his gun. He'll get desk duty, an official reprimand, and only after a full psych evaluation."

"He needs one. He's a danger to himself and others."

"He's a hard ass, but an effective cop. Abrasive, but effective."

"Fuck it, Sam. You're breaking my heart." My gut throbbed from Crawford's punch. "I'm not letting up on anything or anyone until I know Rebecca and my family are safe."

Archuleta looked up at me, wounded. There was no fight left in his face. "I should never have let him go out on duty today."

"What are you talking about?"

"Crawford's wife left him night before last. He told me on the condition that I wouldn't let anyone else know."

I must have appeared insufficiently sympathetic. Sam stood and put his hand inside his coat. I waited for the usual cigarette to emerge, but an empty arm dropped to his side. "She walked out on him with their seven-year-old daughter in the hospital. The kid's dying of leukemia." He gazed in my direction, but I don't think he saw me.

"What the hell was I thinking?"

I thought about my own family. "Maybe I can cut him some slack one time, if it will help. But dammit, see that Crawford gets whatever help he needs."

"He will now."

"And keep me posted, okay? Anything. Everything." I started for the door, but turned and looked at Sam. "I don't know what to do either."

He waved a feeble good-bye. I walked down the front steps to my car and dialed Nai'ya's number. No answer.

My deposition at Internal Affairs took half an hour. I didn't sugar coat anything, but did sound a note of conciliation, reminding McAuley about Crawford's family issues. I decided for Sam's sake not to press any charges and left the matter for APD to resolve.

CHAPTER TWENTY-TWO

C.J. and Charmaine chatted with a young couple whose infant son sat propped up on their table like a drooling centerpiece. I stood inside the front door and motioned C.J. to meet me in his office. Charmaine caught my action and stared me down. I couldn't blame her.

I waited at the office door while he limped over, cane in hand. Just before he reached me, I snuck a glance back at Charmaine to see if she was still glaring. She sure was.

"What's up, man?" C.J. turned the door handle.

I whispered. "Inside."

"Uh-oh." He said nothing more, just hobbled across twenty feet of threadbare carpet to his desk. It hurt to watch him. He set his cane on the desktop and landed hard in his swivel chair. "What's happened now?"

"Rebecca." I sat across from him.

C.J. rested his forearms on the desktop and leaned toward me. "What?"

I told him about her disappearance, about the blood in her apartment. About my confrontation with Crawford.

"Shit."

"That's not all. The State Police found Klein and his two muscle men up near Raton."

"Good."

"Not good. They'd been shot in the head, execution style."

"Fuck." He leaned back and let out a deep breath. "Fuck."

I pounded the desk with both fists.

"Easy man!" C.J. made a gesture toward the small refrigerator beyond his chair. "Need a beer? This time, I'll understand."

My phone rang.

"Gabe, it's Sam."

I grabbed the edge of the desk. "What is it?"

"I *think* it's good news. We got the results back on those blood samples from Rebecca's apartment."

"And?"

"It's not her blood. We checked the records from her hospitalization last April. She's O negative. The stains in her apartment were AB positive. Very interesting."

"Why?"

"AB positive—it's uncommon in the Western Hemisphere, except for people of Oriental extraction. A couple of American Indian tribes too."

"Meaning what?" I hoped Sam wasn't suggesting Nai'ya or Angelina was somehow involved in Rebecca's disappearance.

"I don't know, Gabe. But it's interesting."

"Any idea where Rebecca is?"

"Not yet. We'll let you know as soon as we have anything."

"Thanks." I hung up and shared Sam's message.

C.J. held out his hands. "What can I do?"

I thought for a moment. "If you don't mind, I'd like to give your name and number to a couple of friends from New York. Sloppy and Onion are working with me. I'll tell them, if they ever can't reach me, they can leave a message here. You okay with that?"

"Either one of them a cop?" C.J. suffered from allergies and the badge was one of them.

"No. One's a lawyer and the other's a private dick. Old friends of mine. From Queens."

"A couple of micks, probably." He slid a notepad and pencil across the desk. "Give me their names and numbers."

I wrote down their contact information.

C.J. tapped his cane. "Might not be able to keep pace with you in my present condition, but I can still watch your back."

The office door flew open and Charmaine stood there, hands on hips.

"I was just leaving." I gave her a lame wave of my hand. "Nice to see you again."

"A bag of ribs is waiting for you at the register." She held the door for me. "On your way out."

Onion called from New York just after I started the car. I turned off the engine to give him my full attention. "Got anything for me?"

"Too much coincidence on those bodies, that's what we got. Brian Livingstone—the financial guy from Jersey—and the other guy, the one who embezzled from the Transit Authority."

"Angelo Zappeli?"

"Yeah, that guy. They both cashed out sizeable assets days before their disappearances."

"So their exits were *arranged*?"

"It looks that way. And get this. Each of them drew a certified bank check for a quarter of a million dollars on the day before he vanished."

"They paid someone to get them lost."

"Sloppy found out both these guys were under indictment when they disappeared—Livingstone in Jersey, Zappeli in Manhattan."

"Anything on the other two guys—Dmitrov and the *Daily News* reporter?"

"Nothing yet on Van Heyer. The Russian guy we may never know. What about you? Any IDs on the other two bodies?"

"Maybe later today." I paused and took a deep breath. "I may need you to come out here and help me."

"What's going on?"

"My secretary just disappeared. I had her doing research on Joseph Klein, the guy who managed the casino. Looks like she's been abducted."

"Shit. I'm sorry, Gabe. Was Klein involved?"

"Not this time. He's dead. A professional whack job."

"I can be there tomorrow."

"Stand by. I'll let you know in the morning. Thanks for all the info. Good work."

"I always do good work."

"Call you tomorrow."

I phoned Sam before driving home. "Any update on Rebecca?"

"Nothing. Sorry."

"Listen, I need your help. What time are you free tonight?"

Sam grunted. "I wish. I won't be free until these cases are solved."

"This is about the cases. I need to knock heads with you and the Feds. Tonight at my place?"

"The Feds?"

"It'll be worth your while. Trust me." I noticed the bag of ribs was leaking grease onto the seat. I reached over and put it on the floor.

"Why the Feds?"

"We need to coordinate."

"You want the FBI to coordinate with the APD? Are you a dreamer or a magician? Not a chance." A whiff of his smoke hit the phone.

"What's the guy's name? The top Fed in town."

"The FBI Field Director is not about to come over to your house."

"How about somebody underneath him then? Somebody you've worked with before?"

Sam was silent for a moment. "There's Carlson."

"Who?"

"Carlson. Walter. Good agent. Crew-cut, attitude, knows everything, tells you nothing."

"Got his number?"

"He'll never take a call from you. *Might* take a call from me. Maybe."

"Call him. See if he can meet us at my place at 6:30."

"Gabe, you're asking a federal employee to work nights."

"Tell him I have information he'd be willing to spy for."

"Then he probably already has it."

"I'll take that chance." On the way home, I worried about Rebecca and how widespread this mess had grown.

The ribs needed reheating and I needed to cool down. The doorbell rang before either could happen. Outside the front window, a FedEx truck blocked the foot of my driveway. I opened the door to a muscular, tanned woman in Navy blue cap, shirt, and shorts.

"I need a signature." She handed me a shoebox-sized package and pointed to a line on her silver clipboard. "Right there."

I did my best with the attached electronic pen, but couldn't read my signature.

"Have a good day, sir."

I locked the door and carried the box to the library. *Same Day Delivery.* I wasn't the only one in a hurry.

The box weighed next to nothing. I shook it. Something shifted inside. I listened closely. Nothing. My neck muscles tightened.

The return address on the local shipping label read *P.O. Box 57092 Albuquerque, N.M.* I grabbed my letter opener from the desktop, looked around and noticed the bay window to my left. I walked over and closed the shades.

A brown outer wrapper covered the package. My hands shook a little as I slit it open. A second, smaller box lay inside. It held two envelopes. The top one had the same P.O. Box number. The bottom envelope read: *McKenna.*

I slit it open and unfolded a single sheet of typed paper.

Your secretary is alive. Whether she stays that way is up to you. The price is $500,000. I know you have it. Make out a certified bank check to cash. No tricks or you both die. Mail the top envelope with your check inside to the address listed. I have added a stamp for your convenience.

You have 48 hours to respond. Don't wait. No cops.

Mahatma

I read the message a second time, recalling that Onion said the two guys back east each laid out a quarter of a million when they disappeared. The price had gone up over the years. I dropped the letter opener onto my desk and slid the lower right-hand drawer open. My whiskey bottle was less than half full.

It stayed that way. This called for clear thinking.

Rebecca's cryptic *Find Mahatma* would be my starting point. Her disappearance and Klein's had to be connected. Mahatma's M.O. seemed consistent with what Onion and Sloppy discovered about the disappearance of at least two of the dead men in my barn.

But what tied it all together?

My right hand reached for the Mont Blanc on the desktop, my left pulled a clean piece of paper from a drawer. I jotted down everything I could think of that seemed to matter.

Why all the bodies in my barn? Klein Associates owned the house for years. That was an obvious connection. But a couple of the bodies were men who disappeared *after* Aunt Nellie moved in. Wouldn't she have known?

I went to the kitchen, poured a tall glass of water from the tap and tossed in a handful of ice cubes. The ribs from C.J.'s sat on the countertop. I put them in the refrigerator for later. Otis's food bowl was empty, so I filled it. I walked to the empty bedroom and stared at all the boxes.

Three-thirty. Three hours to rummage through Nellie's things. Three hours before my hoped-for meeting with Sam and Carlson.

Archuleta called the minute I opened the first of Nellie's boxes.

"Your lucky day, Gabe. The FBI wants to talk with you after all."

"Wonderful."

"You may find such enthusiasm premature."

"I'll take that chance. We're on for tonight?"

"Carlson will give you half an hour."

"Do the Feds care about Rebecca's disappearance or is that case all yours?"

"If it ties in with the bodies in your barn and with Klein, I'm sure they're interested."

"Good. Because FedEx just dropped off a ransom note. I need to decide what to do."

"Don't do anything until we get there."

"Six-thirty?"

"Six-thirty."

He hung up. I turned to the first box, not quite sure what I was looking for, not sure I'd know it if I found it. The first time I searched through Nellie's things, I passed over the six boxes labeled "Clothing." Today I'd check them all.

The first two boxes contained hand-tooled boots, women's vintage Western clothing, several hats, a cream-colored formal gown, and a pile of blouses and skirts. Good stuff in its day. The third box weighed more. I'd found her jewelry.

My Aunt Nellie was a wealthy woman. When I first met her in the late 1980s, she wore enough turquoise, silver, and gold to pass as a Santa Fe doyen. But James O'Connor, the crooked lawyer who'd been executor of her estate, skimmed off the best of her pieces. This box held the glass and silver plate leftovers.

A small, battered cardboard box at the bottom of the carton caught my eye. I took it out and lifted its top.

I couldn't control the sick feeling in my stomach. A black onyx ring with the head of Chief Tammany stared up at me. I picked it up and turned it over in my hand. The inscription inside the band was both clear and puzzling: *To N.McK. from J.F.C – 6/8/1948*

I slipped the ring into my pocket and set the rest of the jewelry aside. Who was *J.F.C.*?

Four boxes near the window contained Nellie's financial records. I dragged them into the center of the room and opened them. They were filled with bank statements going back to the mid-1930s. That was even before she'd moved to New Mexico in 1942, one of the stipulations in the inheritance she'd been left by her uncle, James A. McKenna.

I concentrated on the bank records from after her move-in date and examined handful after handful of forms. Her initial balance at New Mexico National Savings Bank stood at just under $20,000 thanks to her inheritance from the man everyone in my family called Uncle Jimmie.

Weekly deposits of $85.00 from the New Mexico State Department of Records must have been her paychecks. She once told me she'd worked at their Albuquerque office. These entries ended in 1946.

On August 16, 1946, Nellie deposited $500.00 cash from a James Frederick Cannon. On August 23rd, another cash deposit, listed as "JFC," same as the inscription on her ring. Cannon, no doubt. I checked the days of the week for that year. Both dates fell on a Friday. Paydays, perhaps?

I paged through more records—every Friday, a $500.00 cash deposit from *J.F.C.* Each successive monthly bank statement showed the same pattern of deposits until November 8, 1962. Her bank balance that day read $206,877.

James Frederick Cannon paid Nellie more than twenty-five grand annually for seventeen straight years.

I called Onion. "Got a job for you."

"Can it wait until after dinner?"

The two-hour time difference had slipped my mind. "Sorry. When you're done, see what you can dig up about a man named James Frederick Cannon." I took the ring out of my pocket and turned it over in my hand. "See if he disappeared like all the others. And if so, when?"

"Got more than a name for me to go on? Business? Approximate age? Date last seen?"

"Hold on a second." I held the ring up to the light and checked the date. Same ring as the skeletal body in the barn that started all of this.

"Gabe? You still there?"

"Check that name against the names of former Tammany Hall officials. High level public servants, police officials, judges, New York Port and Transit Authorities—those kinds of guys. And maybe he dies in the early1960s. Say, 1962 or 1963."

"Criminal records check too?"

"Yeah, guess you'd better. Call me back if you find something."

I read the inscription on the band one more time, then put it back in my pocket. I gathered up Nellie's bank records.

The library had more space for my work. Still, Nellie's papers covered most of my desktop, leaving just enough room for a glass of whiskey.

It was five-thirty. Sam and Mr. FBI were due in an hour. I logged in online and read up on Tammany Hall. Mostly, I checked on one of their famous "bought" judges.

I switched off my monitor half an hour later and downed what remained in my glass. Time for an after-hours phone call to the Bernalillo County Medical Examiner's office.

A recording greeted me: "*After the beep, please enter or say the extension or the name of the party you wish to reach. Please leave a callback number. Thank you.*"

"Dr. Rachel Holtzmann," I intoned after a loud beep.

Her recorded voice asked me to leave a message.

"Dr. Holtzmann, this is Gabe McKenna. I need to check with

you about the first body discovered in my barn. I need to know if—"

"Hello?" It was the medical investigator herself.

"Dr. Holtzmann? I didn't think you'd still be in your office."

"With all the bodies you've been sending us? Get real."

I ignored her complaint. "I have a question about the teeth on the first body they dug up. The guy with the ring."

"What teeth? The skeletal remains had none. He probably had full dentures, but wasn't buried with them."

"How long do you think he's been dead?"

"No telling for sure. If you push me, I'd say fifty years, give or take a decade."

"Thank you so much." It all fit.

"Mr. McKenna, what's this about?" There was more irritation than curiosity in her voice.

I smiled to myself. "Ask Lieutenant Archuleta in the morning."

Onion beeped while I talked with Dr. Holtzmann. I wished her well in her investigation and bid her a quick goodbye.

"Found something interesting for you, Gabe."

"That was fast."

"I checked James Frederick Cannon against a historical database of New York City employees and officials. Nothing. No record of anyone by that name associated with the Tammany machine either."

"Didn't think you'd find—"

"However," Onion interrupted, "I checked instead for the initials 'JFC.' Guess what?"

I felt a jolt of electricity. *We'd both found the same key.* "You found Joseph Force Crater."

"Fuck it, Gabe, how—"

"History professor, remember? I've been checking everything I could find about Crater."

"Find anything?"

"I did."

"So what do you need me for?"

"To confirm my suppositions. And you have. You and the Bernalillo County medical examiner—"

"Whaddya talking about?"

"She reminded me that the skeletal remains didn't have any teeth."

"This is important *how?*"

"Joseph Force Crater was a vain, overly fashion-conscious guy. Something of a dandy. His disappearance from the New York scene created a sensation and led to a nationwide manhunt. *Big news* for months. Turned out there were no dental records on the guy. He bought new dentures every year."

"Something to chew on."

"Lousy joke. Listen, I need you out here."

"Tomorrow soon enough?"

"That'll do. Keep a list of your expenses and airfare. I'll cover it all. Call and let me know when you're arriving. We'll meet at the airport."

"Roger."

"And be ready to travel again as soon as you get here."

"We going somewhere?"

"To help a couple of women in trouble."

"A specialty of mine." I caught a fresh enthusiasm in his voice.

We hung up. I cleared off the library desk, except for the first bank statement from April of 1942, and the one from November of 1962 showing the final $500 deposit from "JFC." I selected a few statements from dates in-between as well, enough for Sam and the FBI guy to see the pattern.

Just after six. I called Nai'ya. She was expecting me at her brother's place on Santa Clara Pueblo. That wasn't going to happen.

No answer. I let it ring until Felipe's recorded voice asked me to leave a message.

"Nai'ya, this is Gabe. Something's come up that I can't explain over the phone. Sit tight. I'll be up there in a day or two. Say hi to Angelina and Matty, and give my thanks to your brother. I love you."

CHAPTER TWENTY-THREE

At 6:30, I opened the door and let Sam Archuleta and Walter Carlson into my home. Sam's shoulders slouched. His jaw seemed to be stapled to his tie. Must have had another tough day.

"Come into the library." I'd set a couple of chairs on either side of my desk. Divide and conquer. "Can I offer you a drink?"

Sam waved my offer away. "No thanks. I'm working."

Carlson checked his watch. "I don't drink."

His gray hair matched the suit. I wondered if the bulges in its sleeves were muscle or just padding. His head was large, his jaw wide and his crew cut flat as an airport runway. Nice scowl, too.

I looked at the ring on his right hand. A college ring. "Fordham, eh? What year?"

Carlson's brows rose as his eyes narrowed. "Class of '72." Each word emerged slowly, like gravy through a strainer. He stared at me all the while.

"I'm Class of '80, myself." Maybe here was a way to break the ice. "So you were there for Digger Phelps's great NCAA team in '71? Twenty-six and three, weren't they?"

Carlson stiffened. "They never should have let that son-of-a-bitch break his contract and leave for Notre Dame."

Whoa. He was talking about something that had happened forty-five years ago. *This guy knows how to hold a grudge.*

Sam spoke up. "You bring us here to talk about college basketball?"

I shook him off. "I know you're both busy. I brought you here to make your lives easier." I pulled out my bottle of whiskey and a clean glass from the desk drawer. "Do you mind?"

Neither man moved.

I poured three fingers worth, took a sip and let it roll around on my tongue for a bit. Carlson checked his watch again.

"Let me share what I discovered about the bodies in my barn, the murder of Tommy O'Donnell, and the executions of Klein and his muscle boys." I took another sip. "I believe it's all tied together, part and parcel of a criminal enterprise that's been going on for more than fifty years."

Carlson leaned forward. "Go on."

"The FBI runs a witness protection program—"

Sam interrupted. "Would you get to the point?"

"That *is* my point, Sam. The point at which this all began. Eighty percent of what I'm going to tell you I can verify. The other twenty percent is up to you to check out."

The FBI agent glared at Sam. "Is this guy always so full of himself?"

"Former college professor."

Carlson winced and shifted his glare to me.

"Mr. Carlson, the witness protection program has been useful in securing the kind of testimony that puts criminals behind bars."

"So?"

"So what if I'm the *ultimate target* of a criminal investigation and I want to avoid prison? What if there was a group willing to provide the same service you do for government witnesses? A group that promises I won't see any jail time? A group that promises me a fresh start without any red tape or hassle?"

"Criminals always think about bolting." Carlson's tone indicated he wasn't impressed so far.

"Yes, but most of them don't know how. We're talking about getting *really lost*. What if an organization with connections, money and influence, used the federal witness protection program as its model? But instead of protecting witnesses, they provide a service—for a large fee, of course—to help *criminal targets* disappear instead of facing prosecution?"

140

Carlson shook his head. "That would take too much manpower, money and ongoing commitment to pay off. The federal witness protection program costs more than we'll ever admit. And that's year after year. Far too expensive for anybody else to afford."

I raised a finger and let each of my words resonate. "*That's because you keep your informants alive.*"

Sam reached into his coat pocket. I pulled an ashtray from the center drawer and slid it over to him. He lit up, took a long drag and looked back at me. "So you're saying this group promises to give their clients safety and anonymity to avoid prosecution for their crimes—"

"And then kills them after their 'clients' have disappeared. And paid a hefty up-front fee, of course." I took a sip of my whiskey. "Afterward, they use varying degrees of 'persuasion' to gain control of their clients' assets, probably with the help of confederates. Lawyers, bankers," I paused. "Maybe even cops and government officials."

Carlson looked at the glass in my hand. "I assume that's not your first drink of the day, Professor." He glanced at his watch a third time, and stood.

"Hang on a minute, Carlson." Sam raised a palm to his FBI counterpart. "Let's hear him out. Gabe can be screwy, but he has helped me in the past."

"Thanks." I put my glass on the desk and looked at the two of them in turn. "What you said about the expense of such an enterprise is true. So I asked myself: who, or what group could possibly pull off something of that magnitude?"

Carlson folded his hands in his lap and gave out with a sigh. "Okay. I'm listening."

I took Nellie's ring from my pocket and flashed it at them. I placed it on the desktop. "A group like the Sons of Tammany, better known as Tammany Hall. A national network. Politically connected. Protected. And with vast financial resources."

Carlson shook his head again. "You're seventy years too late. Tammany Hall lost its power in the decades after World War II. I ought to know. My grandfather was part of the organization."

I swallowed and then caught myself. "Then you know they lost their political clout and connections. But powerful men don't just fade away. They diversify. Explore new avenues of influence and wealth."

It was Sam's turn to sound skeptical. "How do you figure that?"

"Think back a bit," I said. "How did organized crime make most of its money during the '20s and '30s?"

Sam blew out a lungful of smoke. "Illegal booze. Everybody knows that."

"In 1933, Prohibition gets repealed. The end of organized crime?" I looked at Carlson and back at Sam.

He waved his cigarette in the air. "Of course not. The families turned to extortion, heroin, human trafficking, gambling, prostitution, protection—"

"Exactly. They diversified."

"So you're suggesting that Tammany, or at least certain former members, turned to other criminal enterprises." Carlson was with me now.

"It's well documented that Carmine DiSapio, the last Tammany boss with any real power, had ties to mobsters like Frank Costello."

"True. But nothing was ever *actionable*." Carlson pointed to my bottle. "I'll take that drink."

I looked at Sam.

He nodded. "What the hell."

CHAPTER TWENTY-FOUR

We drank, and I shared what Onion, Sloppy and I had discovered, that Angelo Zappeli and Brian Livingstone had faced criminal charges. That they'd both withdrawn significant amounts of money and liquefied assets.

"Sam, remember the rings worn by Klein, Queens D.A. Milner and the first body in my barn?"

"What about them?"

I held up Nellie's ring. "Some of the pieces are falling into place."

Sam shifted in his seat and shrugged his shoulders. "I don't see it."

I spread out Nellie's bank records. "My own great-aunt may have been part of this."

"You don't say." Carlson cracked his first smile of the evening.

"The first body. That's the key. And Nellie is the thread that ties past and present together."

"Hit me again." Sam wiggled his glass until I refilled it.

"The first sign something was wrong was when my P.I. friend found out two of the guys buried in the barn disappeared *after* Nellie moved into this house."

Carlson took out a small spiral notebook and a pen.

I stood by my desk, drink in hand, and told Sam and Carlson about Nellie's bank records and the payments from someone listed as "JFC."

"And who would that be?" Carlson put the notebook down like

this was a waste of his time.

"Joseph Force Crater, *The Missingest Man in New York*."

"Judge Crater?" Carlson laughed out loud. "Not a chance. That guy was murdered in 1930."

"That's what Tammany Hall wanted the world to think," I said. "His orchestrated disappearance became the model for a scheme they launched decades later."

As the clock in the corner rang seven times, I motioned to the bottle on my desk and pointed to my guests in turn. Carlson shook me off.

Sam pointed to his already empty glass. "Who's this Judge Crater?" he said as I poured.

"A playboy New York judge during the Roaring Twenties. A loyal good timer. Owed his seat on the bench to Tammany Hall. One of *their* judges, as they used to say. Called before a grand jury in 1930. His testimony could have exposed the crimes of his Tammany overlords."

"Let me guess," Sam said. "He took out a large sum of money and disappeared."

"While his innocent wife conveniently vacationed in Maine. A nationwide manhunt ensued. But nobody ever found Judge Crater."

"He was killed," Carlson said.

"No," I insisted. "He disappeared from New York, fled to New Mexico and became James Frederick Cannon. He never testified. And Tammany's secrets remained safe."

Carlson eyes narrowed. "That doesn't tie him into anything that's happening now."

I sat down at the desk. "Let me walk you through it. At one point Carter-now-Cannon and Nellie met and fell in love. He confided his past to her. Maybe by then he was legit, had a new life in Albuquerque as Cannon. More likely he went into business with Klein Associates."

"You're saying this is where the other bodies come in?" Sam sloshed some of his drink on the floor.

"My guess is when Tammany lost its political power and connections in the '50s, Crater-now-Cannon and Klein, went to the bosses with an idea: help troubled people of means disappear the way Tammany helped Crater disappear two decades before. Charge them a 'disappearance fee' and spirit them off to New Mexico. Maneuver to gain access to their assets, then have them killed and their bodies buried in the barn behind Nellie's house."

Carlson leaned forward. "You're suggesting a private sector criminal protection program that later kills its clients for their money?"

"Only carefully targeted clients. *That's* the story Tommy O'Donnell was pursuing for the *New York Daily News*. It's why he was out in New Mexico and why he happened to be in Klein's office when he got killed."

Sam put his glass down on the floor next to his chair. "But Klein was in Santa Fe. We checked on that."

"The murder in his office was a screw-up. It wasn't supposed to happen. Klein messed up. He also messed up trying to kill me after I returned from New York."

"What?" Carlson looked up from his notebook. "I wasn't told anything about that."

Sam raised both hands in a peace-making gesture. "I'll fill you in later."

I continued, "Klein became a liability to his bosses. So he stopped a bullet with his head on a road to Colorado."

Carlson put his notebook back in his breast pocket and paced to the bay window. "It's rough, but I'll admit it's not implausible." He turned to leave. "Thanks, McKenna. We'll take it from here. You did some decent leg work."

"Just one thing," I said.

"What's that?" Sam's glassy stare searched for me from across the desk.

"I've just told you all I know. I want a favor in return."

The FBI man stopped just short of the door. "Out with it."

"I want the cops and the Feds to leave me alone for the next forty-eight hours. No tails." I looked at Carlson. "No taps. Stay out of my way. After that, do whatever you want."

He walked back to my desk. "While you do what?"

"That's my business. My *personal* business."

Sam spread his arms, palms up. "Gabe, I'm trying to conduct ongoing investigations into your secretary's disappearance *and* into your daughter's."

Carlson turned to me, his eyes wider than they'd been all evening.

"Your daughter's?"

"Like I said, this is personal. Go ahead with your investigations. Just leave me be, okay?"

Neither of them spoke. I closed the bottle and returned it to the lower desk drawer. "Now if you'll excuse me, I still have things to do tonight. Thank you both for your time and attention."

"Professor," Carlson said as I escorted him to the door, "I'm not making you any promises. None."

"I didn't expect you would. But I've given you enough to keep the Bureau busy, don't you think? I'll pass along any relevant information my friends and I uncover."

He grunted across the threshold into the cool evening air.

"Gabe…" Sam reeled past me without another word.

I grabbed Sam's arm as he passed by and spoke under my breath, "You in any shape to drive?"

He looked away.

"Listen. Get into your car and wave Carlson off. When he's gone, come back to the house. I need to talk to you. Alone."

CHAPTER TWENTY-FIVE

I walked back inside and left the door open for Sam. I ran water from the kitchen faucet and set some coffee brewing.

Sam shambled in and mopped his brow on his sleeve. "Guess maybe I've had too much. Sorry."

"Don't apologize, I've been there a thousand times. Black?" I pointed to the coffee.

"Tonight, yeah."

"Have a seat. It'll be a couple of minutes. I need to talk to you about Rebecca."

"I noticed you hardly mentioned her in front of Carlson."

"I'd prefer the FBI concentrate on the bodies in my barn and any New York-Tammany connections. And leave Rebecca to us."

Sam took out a cigarette, lit up and tossed his match into the ashtray on the desk. "I'm afraid we've got nothing new on her whereabouts."

I opened the desk drawer and took out Rebecca's ransom note. I gave it to Sam. "Read that while I get your coffee."

He was still looking it over when I returned with his cup. He pointed to the name at the bottom of the page. "Mahatma? Like in Gandhi?"

"Not quite." I waited until he took his first sip. "Anything strike you as strange about the note?"

"Mahatma—whoever that is—wants you to send half a million

bucks to a P.O. Box number? That's crazy. We'll watch the box and nab whoever makes the pickup, easy. Unless they really think threatening Rebecca will keep the APD at bay."

"They're going to kill her anyway, Sam. They killed all the others."

"Because of the guys buried in your barn?"

"Because that's how they operate," I said. "Get the payoff, get rid of the payee. Or in this case, the hostage."

"What do you want to do?"

"Pay it. Let them collect from the post office box. Watch from a distance. Let whoever makes the pick-up lead us to Rebecca. I don't see any other way."

Sam's phone rang.

I stood up and pointed to his coffee cup. "Top off?"

"Please," he whispered and then turned his back to me. "Archuleta. What's up? Yeah. Good. Give it to me…excellent."

By the time I brought the pot back, Sam was scribbling on a small notepad. I glanced over his shoulder on the way to my chair but couldn't read his writing.

"Okay," he said to his caller. "Have the photo digitized and sent to law enforcement statewide." He put the notepad and pencil in the hip pocket of his coat. "I'll call you back in a little while. There's a set-up we have to do for tomorrow. Bye."

I leaned forward. "News?"

"The prints came back from Rebecca's place. We have ourselves a suspect."

"Who?"

"Jacob Wallace."

"Who's he?"

"Jacob Gray Wolf Wallace. Muscle for hire. In and out of the New Mexico penal system since his teens. He grew up on a Blackfoot rez in Montana, but he's spent his adult life in New Mexico. Mostly in maximum security facilities."

"How come you know so much about him?"

Sam blew another lungful in my direction. "Wallace was one of my first arrests as a rookie. He's one of those guys who's more comfortable in jail than on the outside." He snubbed his cigarette out in the ashtray. "Maybe Rebecca caught a break."

"How's that?"

"He's a bad one. Aggravated assault, robbery, even grand larceny once, as I recall. But he's not a killer. At least not so far."

"Why would he kidnap Rebecca?"

"It's a game to him. Jacob hires out to do anyone's dirty work. He doesn't care. It's the challenge that gets him off." He drained his cup and thought for a moment. "Strange dude. Not the brightest bulb, but he's fearless and knows how to follow orders."

"You mentioned a picture."

He pointed to my computer. "This thing work?"

I leaned forward and switched the monitor on.

Sam took another cigarette from his coat, but left it unlit between his lips. "You logged in?"

"Yeah." I stood and let Sam sit at the keyboard. I couldn't see what site he opened. APD records, probably.

A few mouse clicks and he leaned back so I could see the picture on the screen. "Jacob Gray Wolf Wallace. Good likeness."

"Recent?"

Sam hunched forward and squinted at the fine print. "December of last year."

I leaned over his shoulder. "Bring that up to full screen size."

Wallace looked about fifty years old. Heavy set, his mostly dark hair pulled back. I imagined a ponytail. Prominent nose. The scowling attitude you see in police department photos. One long, deep scar running down his right cheek.

"Let me have the mouse." I right-clicked on the image, saved it to the computer desktop, and sent it to my cellphone. "Good work, Sam."

"My men will be waiting for him at the post office."

"Don't move in or interfere in any way. Wallace may not be a killer. Mahatma is."

"I'm aware of that." He finally lit the cigarette.

"And don't assign some schmoe to this job. We're talking about Rebecca's life."

Sam let the cigarette hanging from his lips. He rested his hands on the edge of my desk, leaned forward, and frowned. "When have I ever given you less than my best?"

"Sorry. I'm just worried."

He ignored my concern and walked over to the window, just like Carlson had ten minutes before. A cloud of smoke left his lungs and floated through the half-open blinds. He waved it away and looked outside. "When will you mail the certified check? I have to know what time to begin our surveillance."

"I'll be at my bank when it opens at nine. Once I get the check I'll take it directly to the post office on Veranda Road off 4th Street. They open early too. I'll take the fastest delivery they have. Figure it should reach the P.O. box number early the following morning."

"I'll keep in touch by cellphone," Sam said.

"You won't be able to. I have a new phone."

"I know." Sam smiled like a fox. "Carlson gave me its number on our way over here."

"Sonofabitch."

"Relax. The Feds aren't after you. After Klein's execution, Angelina may still be a material witness in the O'Donnell killing, but she's no longer a suspect. You have my word."

With Sam's assurance, I checked to make sure he had the number right. "I'll be coming back here from the post office, but staying only until I pick up a friend of mine at the Sunport tomorrow afternoon. We're going to see Nai'ya."

"So you *do* know where she is."

I paused to stare at him. "I'm not sure what I know at this point, but I'll do everything I can to bring Angelina in to you."

Sam rubbed his stomach.

"You okay?" I said. Before he answered, I reached into my pocket and tossed him a roll of antacids.

He caught them and put the roll in his pocket. "Good luck tomorrow, Gabe." Steadier on his feet, he walked out to his car.

Almost eight o'clock. Nai'ya should be at her brother's place by now, so I called.

"Estefan here."

"It's Gabe McKenna. Can I speak with Nai'ya?"

There was a momentary silence. "Hold on. Let me see if she'll come to the phone."

The frantic barking of a dog drowned out their muffled

conversation.

"Hello." Nai'ya sounded weary.

"Are you all right? How are Angelina and Matty?"

"We're safe. How about you?"

"Not so good. Rebecca's disappeared."

"Oh, no."

"Sometime early this morning. Abducted from her apartment. I had her checking into Klein. She may have gotten too close."

"Klein again?"

"Klein's dead. Listen. Things have spun out of control here. It's one huge mess. Even the FBI is involved."

"Are they looking for Rebecca?"

"APD is. Sam says they have a suspect. Guy named Jacob Gray Wolf Wallace. Ever heard of him?"

"No. He sounds native."

"Blackfoot. From Montana, but he lives in New Mexico. A career criminal. Sam thinks he hired himself out to the people behind all of this. I'm sending his mugshot to your cellphone. You still have it with you?"

"Yes. But wireless coverage here is spotty."

"Does Estefan have Internet?"

"Sure. A laptop with satellite access."

"Then I'll send the photo to your e-mail. Print it out and have your brother post it around the Pueblo. Just in case this guy shows up. I'm hoping—"

"Gabe?"

"What?"

"I appreciate all you're trying to do. I want you to know that."

I let her words soothe me. "This will be over soon. We'll be together. A real family."

She cried softly but didn't say anything.

"Nai'ya?"

Her tears swelled into a sobbing that seemed to shake the phone. Or maybe it was my hand. She moaned and then quieted down, still gasping for breath.

"What's wrong?" I said.

She took an audible deep breath. "I told Angelina about you."

My pulse quickened. "Thank you, honey. Thank you so much! Tell her I'll be coming up."

"She's not speaking to me. She's furious. This morning she took Matty and left. They're staying with Estefan's aunt."

"Where is that?"

"On the western edge of the Pueblo. I've made such a mess of things." She broke down again.

I struggled to reassure her. "Hang in there, it'll be okay. I'll be up tomorrow night. Just hold on until I arrive. An old buddy of mine from New York will be with me. Maybe if I can talk with Angelina— now that Klein is dead—maybe she won't be so afraid."

"Her heart is full of hurt and confusion. You have no idea how upset she is. But go ahead and try. Maybe you can get through to her and—"

"A few minutes ago, Sam assured me Angelina's no longer a suspect in the casino killing. They only want to question her as a possible witness. They'll protect her."

She hesitated. "Okay…"

"Stay with Estefan. Be sure to show him the photo of Jacob Wallace."

"I will."

"My buddy and I will handle things when we get there."

"I love you, Gabe."

"I love you, too. Right now, I gotta go. Bye, Princess."

"Bye-bye." We hung up.

I poured a nightcap, walked out to the backyard and sat in Nellie's battered wicker chair. I looked into a clear, star-filled sky.

Angelina knew about me. I'd talk with her and allay her fears. Her troubles would soon be over. I finished my whiskey and enjoyed the mellow glow.

I glided back inside and stopped in the library long enough to send the Wallace photo to Nai'ya's e-mail.

Onion called. He'd booked his flight and would arrive tomorrow afternoon around two. We'd meet at the airport.

I fed Otis, took a shower and settled into bed. Tomorrow we'd set the trap. Sam would follow anyone who picked up Rebecca's ransom pay-off. Carlson and the FBI would pursue the Tammany angle, both here and in New York. Onion and I would drive up to Santa Clara Pueblo and unite with Nai'ya, Angelina, and Matty.

I closed my eyes and lay in the darkness. This was going to work out after all.

CHAPTER TWENTY-SIX

Otis jumped on the bed and head-butted me. It was eight-fifteen. The sun streamed through my bedroom window. I got dressed and took my cup of coffee out the front door.

I spotted it right away: a Ford F-150 parked back up the road where I couldn't see his license plates. I pulled out and headed downtown. The pickup followed at a distance. Very professional.

Five minutes later, I found a parking spot in front of the bank and watched the F-150 pass by. I thought he made the first right turn, but couldn't be sure.

Ten minutes past nine on the clock in the lobby. I sat in an under-stuffed chair and waited for one of the bank officers.

A dark haired man approached, thirtyish, wearing a starched blue button-down shirt—the kind of guy who probably had a young, attractive wife and two beautiful children. Here I was, about to spoil his day.

He cleared his throat and stretched out a hand. "Welcome. John Garcia. How may I help you?"

"Gabriel McKenna." We shook. "I need a bank check."

"Have a seat in my office." He pointed toward his cubicle. I led the way. He offered me one of the two chairs and sat behind a desk with a workstation computer. Shelves of reference books surrounded a five-foot high glass barrier with enough chrome trim to bounce the morning sun into my eyes.

I settled in, resting my elbow on the edge of his desk while I looked around. Nice photo on his desktop of an attractive young woman hugging two beautiful children.

Mr. Garcia began. "You need a bank check. In what amount?"

"Half a million dollars. Made out to cash, if you don't mind."

"I see." Garcia wasn't seeing much of anything with his eyes squinted nearly shut. He took a slow, deep breath. His hand started for his phone and stopped. "Will you excuse me for a minute?" Before I could reply, he left the cubicle and disappeared through a nearby metal door labeled: Mr. Woolsey, Branch Manager, in large, raised letters.

I drummed my fingers on the edge of Mr. Garcia's desk. Two or three people stood in line at each of the teller windows. A television screen high up on the wall flashed brightly colored summaries of the bank's services, alternately in English and Spanish.

A stocky, round-headed man in a lavender shirt, thin black tie, and dark high-water slacks emerged from the Branch Manager's office followed, puppy-like, by a worried John Garcia.

I stood. "Mr. Woolsey." We'd met in his office six months earlier when I opened my sizeable account.

"Professor McKenna. Nice to see you again."

"I assume Mr. Garcia has informed you of my request."

"Yes." Wolsey dragged the word out to several syllables. "You understand, with an amount of this size—you're not thinking of closing your account, are you?"

"Not at all. I intend to restore these funds to my account within the week. You could say the check is escrow on a deal I'm looking to close." I flashed my most heartening smile.

Woolsey beamed. "Well, that's reassuring. Of course, I'll have to check with the main office downtown..."

"Of course."

"This should only take a short while. Perhaps you'd care for coffee while you wait?" He pointed to a small glass-enclosed waiting room.

"Perhaps I would."

The branch manager disappeared into his office. Garcia gave me a sheepish grin and retreated to his cubicle. I walked into the waiting room and sat between Mr. Coffee and a small square table piled with magazines. I sifted through a handful of them to pass the time. *Running* magazine. *Self* magazine. *Style*. *Fitness*. The one on the bottom was *People* magazine. Sure, it was slumming, but I clutched it like an old, dear friend and put the others back on the pile.

I didn't recognize any of the people on its cover. After flipping my way through its pages, I hadn't recognized any of the people on the inside, either.

"Okay…" On to the coffee machine. I half-filled a white Styrofoam cup and eyed a jar on the counter labeled "InstaCrème." I passed.

For ten minutes, I sipped my bitter brew and tried to ignore a heavily tatted Goth-child who sat across the room working on her nails.

I looked at my cellphone a couple of times. No calls, no texts. When Mr. Woolsey returned with my check in his hand, it was time to leave.

The F-150 sat at the far end of the parking lot, exhaust from its tail pipe visible in the frigid air. I raised my hand and waved. *Doing just what you want, buddy.*

I sat in the Hudson and opened the envelope that came with Mahatma's note. I took the bank check from my pocket, slipped it inside the envelope and held the flap open to seal. My cellphone rang. Archuleta.

"Everything okay?"

"So far," I said. "I've got the bank check with me now. And I picked up a tail. He's—"

"What?"

"Gone. Dammit, he just pulled out of the lot. A dark blue F-150."

"Must be a million of those on the road. Listen, make the drop, then clear out fast," Sam sounded anxious. "We'll back off until the letter gets picked up tomorrow. The Postal Service will buzz us. We'll do loose two-vehicle surveillance and see where he leads us."

"Okay. I'll mail the check and *vamose.*" I slipped the envelope back into my jacket pocket and pulled out of the bank lot. No sign of the F-150.

The post office was a three-block drive. I eased into a diagonal spot right outside the front door. Only one person ahead of me at the single window. As soon as I got in line, a young Hispanic mother with a frisky toddler queued up behind me.

We all waited. I had no idea sending a pair of shoes to Alaska could be such a problem. The woman in front of me finally grabbed her box and huffed off muttering something about FedEx.

"May I help you?" A world-weary postal clerk adjusted his glasses and grasped the counter with both hands.

The little kid behind me grabbed at my pants leg. I gave him a light shake-off and edged up to the window. "I need to send this letter Priority Mail Express. How soon will it get there?"

"Depends on where it's going."

"Local."

"In that case, it'll be there by ten-thirty tomorrow morning. Maybe by the end of the day today."

"That'll do."

The clerk looked at the letter in my hand. "Anything hazardous in there?"

"Not if I can help it."

"What?" He stiffened.

"Nothing. It's just a check."

"That'll be nineteen dollars and ninety-nine cents."

I put a twenty on the counter. "Keep the change."

"Wise guy." The clerk slammed his hand down on a boxy postal machine. A long red strip of paper tape spat out from its side.

I rechecked the address on my envelope: P.O. 57092.

"Better seal that." The clerk pointed at the envelope. "Wouldn't want the contents to fall out."

I raised the envelope to my lips and touched my tongue to the flap. The young boy behind me knocked into the back of my leg again. The envelope slipped from my grasp and fell to the floor.

"Apologize to the man, Cesar," the young mother said.

I turned and shook off her concern. "That's all right. He didn't... dnnn—"

A powerful tingling sensation grabbed hold of my tongue and spread to my shoulder. A jolt of pain stabbed between my shoulder blades, searing deep into my chest and lungs. I gasped for breath. It wouldn't come. I clasped my throat with my right hand and the countertop with my left. My chest tightened even more. I couldn't move. My heart fluttered at first. Then it thudded over and over and over again. I opened my mouth to shout at the clerk, or to the woman, to anyone. "Help me." I formed the words, but couldn't hear them.

Spots appeared in front of me, then a low, buzzing sound rattled inside my head. *Breathe, Gabe!* I sucked air into my mouth as fast as I could, hoping it would reach my lungs.

My whole body prickled. Then all feeling ebbed away, even the pain. I let go of the countertop one finger at a time. The lights in the post office seemed to go out at once. A woman screamed from a hundred miles away. A man's voice answered.

Or maybe it was a bird.

CHAPTER TWENTY-SEVEN

The world was quiet, except for an intermittent whooshing and clicking at my side. Above me, an ethereal murmur. Barely audible. Ominous.

The back of my head throbbed. Acid flames rippled through my stomach and chest. My mouth, on the other hand, felt nothing. I moved my tongue around, but couldn't feel any teeth. I gave up and let myself float into darkness.

When I opened my eyes, everything was blurry and remained that way while I blinked and tried to focus on something in the bright light.

I lay strapped to a hospital bed. Tubes up both nostrils. Needles in my left hand and forearm. A figure in white stood by my bed. I tried to sit up, but something held me down. The room spun around. I leaned back on my pillow, struggled for a deep breath and closed my eyes. When the dizziness stopped, I opened them again.

A nurse was leaning over me. C.J. stood next to her.

"Take it easy, Mr. McKenna." Her words ran together in my head.

"What?" I tried to remember...anything. My head hurt too much to think. I mumbled. "C.J.?"

"Take it slow man," he said.

"What happened?"

"Don't know. Your cop friend called. He told me you were here. Asked would I come by and keep an eye, you know? Charmaine drove me over."

"How long ago? What time—what day is it?" Each painful word required effort and concentration.

"They brought you in before noon, I think. The lieutenant called about one."

"Archuleta?"

"He said you'd collapsed at some post office."

"Post office?" An image flashed in my mind, then it disappeared. "Water. I'm so thirsty."

The nurse rested a hand on my shoulder. "You're not allowed to drink anything. Not yet. Doctor Aguilera will be in soon. Then we'll see. In the meantime, you can have some shaved ice."

"What flavors you got?" I said in a weak voice.

She was all business. "Frozen."

"I'll take it."

She raised a tiny paper cup from somewhere and let a few bits of crushed ice caress my lips. A bit of the ice slid down my throat. "Oww, dammit!" If I hadn't been strapped to the bed, I would have doubled over with the pain.

"What's wrong?" The nurse checked my eyes and then the monitors above my head.

"My stomach. Feels like it's full of rocks." I laid my head back against the pillow and took a couple of slow breaths. Nothing helped.

"Rocks?" The nurse half-smiled. "That's pretty close, Mr. McKenna. We pumped you full of activated charcoal to clear the toxins out of your gastrointestinal tract. Don't worry. It'll pass." She swabbed my forehead with a damp cloth.

"Toxins? You mean poison?"

"You'll have to speak to Doctor Aguilera." She tossed the cup of ice into the wastebasket next to my bed.

A muffled cellphone sounded. *I Heard It Through the Grapevine*, my ring tone. "That's for me."

C.J. looked around the room.

"I keep it in my pants."

"Always a good policy, Ace," C.J. deadpanned.

The nurse pointed behind my friend. "They're hanging on the rack in the bathroom."

He turned and opened the door.

"Get that, would you?" My voice rasped as I tried for more volume.

"Hello? No, this is a friend of his. Who's calling?" C.J. put his hand over the phone. "Some guy named Onion? Says he's at the airport and where are you?"

"Shit! I forgot. Tell him I'm here—nurse, what hospital is this?"

"UNM."

"Tell him to take a cab. Tell him I'm okay."

After C.J. relayed my message from inside the bathroom, the door to my room opened. A bald, bespectacled wisp of a man in a lab coat entered, a clipboard tucked under his arm. His hair was a perfect white. His eyebrows came together over dark eyes.

The nurse gave me a signal. "Hello, Doctor Aguilera."

The diminutive figure studied me from the foot of the bed. "You're a lucky man, Mr. McKenna."

"Convince me."

He picked up the clipboard and stared. "You're alive. You've ingested a deadly toxin. Specifically, the neurotoxin aconitine."

"What's that?"

"A chemical poison from the plant world. Specifically, the flowering plant *aconitum*. The common term is monkshood. Deadly even in small doses, even if absorbed through the skin."

It didn't make any sense to me. "I don't understand. I don't garden. And I didn't eat anything today. I don't think, so…"

"We need to find out where you came in contact with the toxin. If it's still around, the next person may not be so lucky. Aconitum isn't native to this area. Anything you can remember would help."

I tried to think. *What was I doing at the post office?* My memory was still too cloudy.

Doctor Aguilera stepped around to the side of the bed, felt my pulse, and looked into my eyes with one of those little flashlights. "When they brought you in, your breathing was slow and irregular. You had cardiac arrhythmia and were displaying signs of a coronary event. Acute pulmonary distress as well. We gave you an EKG, then blood monitoring, and an EEG."

"And?"

"And your tongue was swollen. That suggested contact with a

toxin or strong allergen. We tested and found a dangerous level of aconitine." He stared at me. "If you were my size, you might be dead."

A shiver coursed down my spine. "My tongue is still numb. I can't feel with it. Sorry if I sound funny."

"We'll proceed on the assumption that's how you ingested the toxin. Did you eat any greens this morning?"

I shook my head.

"Or brush against a blue-flowered, three-foot shrub with your face? This would have been within a minute or two of when you collapsed."

I thought back. The post office... "The envelope." I tried to rise but the straps held me fast to the bed. "I was mailing a letter. I licked the flap of the envelope. A child bumped into me—yes. A little boy bumped into the back of my leg. I dropped the envelope."

Aguilera's brows rose. "That little boy saved your life. It's imperative we find that envelope. Excuse me." He spun and left the room with the nurse close behind.

C.J. looked at the bells and whistles that surrounded me. "What were you doing at the post office?"

"I don't know...I do remember driving somewhere else first."

"Maybe you bought something and took it to the post office to mail?"

I shook my head. The dizziness returned at once. "Don't think so."

C.J. limped to the window and split the blinds with his hand. "Too nice a day to spend cooped up in the hospital. Listen, I'm going down to get some coffee. I'll try to be back before your friend gets here. Can I bring you a cup?"

"I can't have anything to drink, remember?"

"That was *before* the doc checked you out. You still take it black, right? Maybe a magazine or something to read?"

My mouth dropped open. "The bank—I stopped at my bank on the way to the post office."

"Paying a late bill?"

"No. I took out some money, I think—holy shit, no!"

"What's wrong?" C.J. returned to my bedside.

"There was a check in that envelope. A bank check."

"How much?"

"Half a million dollars."

"Say *what*?"

"Unstrap my arm and hand me my phone."

C.J. held up a hand. "I don't know about that."

"Come on," I pleaded, "I'll make like it came loose. I have to call Archuleta."

He opened the door a crack and peered out into the hall. "Okay." He swung around to my right side. After a short struggle, we managed to loosen the strap. Reaching into his pocket, he gave me my phone.

"When did Onion say he'd be here?"

"A.S.A.P. No cab. He's doing a rental."

I punched in Sam's number and waited. The pain in my gut increased when I sat up. Damn. "Sam. It's Gabe."

C.J. gave me a quick nod and left for the cafeteria.

"You okay?" Archuleta said. "Almost didn't recognize your voice."

"My mouth is numb. My body feels like shit. I've been poisoned."

"That's what Dr. Aguilera told me."

"He says I'm lucky to be alive. The flap of that envelope was laced with aconitine."

"Bad stuff."

"Aguilera's gonna call you. You need to find that envelope in case—"

"Hold it. While you were dancing with the angels, we've been busy. Halfway down the block from the post office, we found a dark blue F-150, like the one you said was following you. Stolen plates. We combed it for prints. Should know within twenty-four hours what we've got."

"That makes no sense. Why leave that truck behind?"

"Because they had another one waiting at the post office. One you wouldn't be able to identify in case you survived. We're dealing with pros here."

"How can you tell?"

"That F-150 was waiting at your house in case you didn't come out."

"Huh?"

"If you already had the check and you sealed the envelope at home. Then they followed you to the bank, in case you sealed the envelope there. They'd have picked up the check before you ever got to the post office. That's what they hoped would happen."

"At least I messed up their plans a little."

"We also have an ID on the man who grabbed your check and fled the post office. Probably a Honda Accord with Colorado plates. We questioned everyone at the scene. Lots of confusion, as you'd expect. But we do know this much—after you dropped that envelope, a man grabbed it and ran to a red car. We have two corroborating IDs, one from a teller, one from a customer who was just entering the bank."

"So who made off with my check?"

"Jacob Gray Wolf Wallace."

CHAPTER TWENTY-EIGHT

I shifted in my hospital bed, feeling uncomfortable about everything. "I guess some of it fits."

"The Colorado license does suggest a connection between Wallace and the deaths of Klein and his bodyguards. The car that whisked them away from the Pueblo-66 Casino had Colorado plates. So maybe I'm wrong about Wallace not being a killer."

"We gotta find Rebecca."

"That check of yours is our best chance."

"Should I stop payment?"

"You can't. It was a chasier's check. So we cross our fingers and hope they cash it immediately."

"What if they don't? What can we do?"

"Call in the Feds. I already notified Carlson. The FBI will monitor transactions in that amount from New York to the Cayman Islands."

I shook my head and glanced at the wall clock.

"Hey, it's something," Sam said.

"But that won't save Rebecca. I have to get out of here."

"You're in no shape, Gabe. Look, I had one of my men drive your car back to your house. I'll stop by the hospital tonight and give you your key ring. We can talk. When you're good to go, call me. I'll drive you home."

"Okay." I hung up. Aguilera and a nurse came in and stood on opposite sides of the bed. She replaced the drip on one of my IVs

165

and disconnected the other.

The doctor checked my pulse and shone his flashlight into my eyes again. "Open wide and stick out your tongue." He looked inside. "Uh-huh."

"Uh-huh, what?"

"Is your mouth still numb?"

"Not as much as before. When can I leave?"

"That depends."

"Give me a little more than that, Doc, okay?"

He pulled up a chair and sat next to my bed. A frown creased his face. "What happened to this strap?" He lifted it and looked at the nurse.

Her face turned crimson. "Doctor, that was secure last time I left this room." She scowled at me. "Mr. McKenna—"

I raised a hand. "Don't blame her, Doc. I had to use my cellphone."

Aguilera glared. "The more you follow the rules, the sooner you'll be out of here. I'll authorize your discharge when it's safe for you to go and not one minute before."

"What's the earliest I can hope for?"

"The half-life of aconitine in the human body varies from six to fifteen hours. We gave you atropine as an antidote and lidocaine to steady your heartbeat. We'll ramp up your fluid intake and hope that clears the toxin by tomorrow morning."

"Can I do anything to make it happen faster?"

"Drink as much as possible."

"Not a problem."

"No solids tonight," he continued. "Soft food only in the morning. We'll monitor the toxins in your urine over the next twelve hours. Your body should pass most, if not all of the poison by tomorrow. Then I'll let you go, but you'll have to take it easy for a few days."

"Got it."

"I'll stop by in the morning. Like I said, drink as much as you can. If you experience any sudden weakness or if the numbness increases, call a nurse immediately. Use the button by your pillow." Aguilera stood, hung my chart on the foot of the bed and left without turning back.

"Here's your water." The nurse handed me a full glass with no ice.

"Look, I'm sorry about the strap. I didn't mean to cause any trouble."

She ignored my apology and put a metal pitcher on the table arm next to my bed. "The more time you spend in the bathroom, the faster you can leave."

"Duly noted." I rubbed my forehead with my free hand. "The glare is giving me a headache."

The nurse walked to the window, reached for the cord and let the blinds down most of the way.

"Thank you." I took another swallow of water.

She rummaged through a pile of old magazines on the window ledge. "Here's something for you to read." *People*. The same issue I'd paged through at the bank. She placed it on the table next to my bed and crossed to the door.

Onion brushed against her on his way in. He made a sour face and watched her walk down the hallway. Then he closed the door behind him. "What the hell happened?"

"I was poisoned."

"Figured it must be bad for you to fly me out here."

"I'm knee-deep in shit." For the next half hour, he listened to the long-form account of all that happened since my return from New York.

"Put me to work." His smile reassured me. "Just one thing, Gabe."

"What's that?"

"I won't carry a gun. Never again."

I imagined how he must have felt when he shot and killed that fourteen-year-old boy. "Understood."

There was a tap on the door. C.J. entered with a magazine under his arm and two cups of coffee.

I grabbed Onion's arm. "I want you to meet a friend of mine. Curtis Jester, this is Deke Gagnon, my old buddy from New York. His friends call him Onion."

C.J. put the coffee down and the two men shook hands.

"Curtis Jester?" Onion said. "Used to be a pretty tough prize fighter by that name back in the day."

"You're looking at him," C.J. said.

Onion's face lit up. "In that case, you owe me two hundred bucks.

That's how much I dropped on you in the Harold Johnson fight."

C.J. rubbed his jaw. "I paid for that night in a lot of ways."

"Six rounds, right?" Onion said.

"Coulda been eight. I don't remember any of them."

I cut in. "C.J. runs the best barbecue joint in town. Maybe you can stop there on your way to Santa Fe."

"What's in Santa Fe?" Onion asked.

"The Sun Mountain Art Gallery. I need you to look the place over. A guy named Reginald Addison is the supposed owner. Knows less about art than I do. Find out everything you can about him. See if anything out of the ordinary happened at the place last week."

Onion wrote it all down on a small spiral notepad. "Will do. Anything else?"

"Get yourself a room in a good Santa Fe hotel. Stay in touch. I'll meet you there as soon as I can."

"When's that gonna be?"

"Tomorrow afternoon, if we're lucky." I looked at C.J. "Make sure this guy is well fed before he leaves. As you can see, he's had lots of practice."

C.J. checked Onion's waist for a split-second. "What kind of ribs you like?"

"Baby backs."

"I'm your man." C.J. turned toward me. "You be okay here, Gabe?"

I shrugged and picked up the coffee he'd brought. By now, the brew had cooled. "Maybe I'll see what's on TV."

"Okay Brain," Onion said. "I'll call from Santa Fe in the morning."

C.J. laughed. "Brain?"

I ignored that. "Check in with Sloppy too, okay? Keep him up-to-date."

"Done. Rest up." Onion led the way to the door.

C.J. stopped and turned. He grabbed the magazine from under his arm and tossed it onto my bed. "In case there's nothing good on the tube. See ya." He eased the door closed behind him.

The current issue of *Maxim*, much more like it. I set it on the nearby table, right on top of *People*, lay back against the pillow and closed my eyes.

The cellphone woke me at nine-thirty. It was Nai'ya.

"Gabe, where are you?"

"Nai'ya—"

"You told me you'd be here tonight. You and your friend."

"I'm sorry. Something came up. I didn't have my phone until just a few minutes ago."

"Where are you?"

I looked around. What could I say? "I'm in bed."

"In bed?" There was a sharpness in her tone now. "Would it hurt to have called? I've been waiting all day for you."

"I apologize." Time for the truth. "Actually, I'm in a bed at UNM hospital."

"Gabe!"

"I didn't want to worry you. Everything's fine now. Onion's here and we'll be up to get all of you tomorrow, I promise. He's already gone to Santa Fe. I'm meeting him there in the morning and—"

"Are you alright?"

I tried to sit up. Everything still hurt. "Really, everything is okay."

"No, everything is not okay. Don't shut me out."

"I don't want my family hurt."

"I've seen to it that Angelina and Matty are safe."

"Not safe enough." *How could I convince her of the danger?* "A chance came up here to free Rebecca, or so I thought. It didn't play out that way. Jacob Wallace got away. Rebecca's still gone and I ended up here. But I'll get up to the Pueblo tomorrow night, one way or the other."

"Do you want me to come down to Albuquerque? Angelina and Matty can stay with my sister-in-law."

"No, don't do that. I'll be fine, but Wallace is loose. We don't know who hired him. You're safer where you are."

"Promise you'll call me this time if there are any changes?"

"I promise. Will you try again to convince Angelina that the cops want to protect her, not arrest her?"

"She's still not speaking to me."

"Then at least make sure she doesn't leave. All of you just stay where you are. Did you get the photo of Wallace I sent?"

"It's posted all over the Pueblo."

"Good…that's good. And pray for Rebecca. She may be in more

danger than any of us right now."

"I will. Be careful, Gabe."

"We're going to make it."

"I hope you're right."

"Listen, can you have dinner waiting tomorrow? My friend Onion loves to eat."

Nai'ya forced out a weak laugh. "I'll see what I can do. I love you."

"I love you, too. And love conquers all, right? Get some sleep."

"Okay," she said.

We hung up. I struggled off the bed, stretched and grabbed hold of my IV rack. I wobbled into the bathroom.

CHAPTER TWENTY-NINE

I rode the bed-to-bathroom shuttle most of the night. During those ten hours, I drank more than I ever had before. What a shame it was all water.

But I felt more like myself with each hour that passed. By sunrise my mind was set on getting up to Santa Fe and hooking up with Onion.

For breakfast, the staff rewarded me with a small plastic bowl of diluted Cream of Wheat. I washed it down with water, like they asked. The mac and cheese on the lunch menu called to me like a three-inch thick tenderloin.

Sam stopped by around eight-thirty. He carried a cup of coffee in his hand and a large plastic bag over his shoulder.

"How're you doing?" He slugged down a mouthful of the coffee. "Can I get you a cup? The bag is fresh clothes for later, if they let you out today."

"They will. Could you put them in the bathroom? Under where they hung my pants."

He disappeared for a moment and then returned to my bedside, shutting the bathroom door behind him. "Somebody die in there last night?"

"You might say that." I propped up on my elbow. "Anything new on Rebecca or Wallace?"

Sam pulled up a chair and sat down. His unbuttoned tan jacket covered a white shirt that appeared to be stained with coffee. What remained of his hair stuck out on either side of his head. His usual tie was missing. Maybe he was auditioning for a revival of *Colombo*. More likely, he hadn't slept last night either.

"I'm afraid the trail is still cold on Rebecca. As to Wallace, six-thirty this morning we found an Accord. Red, with Colorado plates. Same color and model as the one he got into at the post office."

"Where?" I sat up the best I could.

"Long-term lot at the Sunport."

"Damn. He could be anywhere by now."

"Not so fast. He's on the security video. His car entered the lot at one-fifteen this morning. That's more than an hour after the last flight departed. One man driving."

"Wallace?"

"Looks like him. Same size, same build, same kind of jacket Wallace had on earlier in the day. That car was dumped. We got video of a second vehicle that came in behind it. The guy I assume is Wallace got into it and they drove off at one-seventeen."

"That's something. Did you get a make on the second vehicle?"

"It was a large SUV. That's all we could make out. Too far from the camera and not enough light. We're trying to enhance the video, but it's grainy. Might be all we can get."

"So they left the Accord at the airport—"

"To throw us off their trail. My guess is Wallace and his friend are still in New Mexico—maybe still in Albuquerque."

"You have the major roads covered at the state line?"

"Of course. Bus terminals, Amtrak, car rentals, all the state airports have been notified to be on the lookout for them."

"How do you know the Accord at the airport the same one that picked up Wallace after I collapsed?"

"We found an empty envelope addressed to P.O. Box 57092 on the floor of the front seat."

"Any poison and prints?"

Sam nodded. "Yes to the poison. Enough aconitine residue on the envelope flap to be fatal. No on the prints." He stood, walked to the window and raised the blinds. Morning sunlight flooded the room. "You're one lucky S.O.B."

"I know." I pushed the covers off. "Now if they'll just let me out of here."

"The weather's changed the past twenty-four hours. Car barely started this morning. The clothes in that bag should be warmer than the ones you had on yesterday. Make sure you bundle up."

"Yes, Mother."

He reached into his coat pocket. "Your keys. Call me when you're good to go. I'll swing by or have one of my men take you home."

I rested the keys next to my water glass.

Sam slugged more coffee. I struggled out of bed, grabbed the IV rack and headed for the john.

"Gotta get going." Sam headed for the door, then turned around and smiled. "On my way to Pueblo-66 Casino. We got a court order to shut the place down until the murders are cleared up." He tossed his coffee cup into the wastebasket.

"Way to go." I turned the knob on the bathroom door.

"Hey, Champ," Sam called after me. "Isn't that thing supposed to tie up in the back?"

"You must be looking in the mirror."

"Fuck you."

I closed the bathroom door behind me. The door to my room slammed shut.

A nurse came by twenty minutes later and drew my blood. Dr. Aguilera stopped in around ten-fifteen. He checked my chest, eyes, tongue, pulse, blood pressure, and hopeful smile.

"You bounce back pretty well for a man of your age," he said.

"Thanks, I guess."

"There's no reason to keep you here any longer."

"Great." I stood, stretched and grabbed my bag of clothes.

"We need this bed." Aguilera wagged a finger at me. "Be careful the next couple of days. No excitement. Watch what you eat. Go easy on the spices."

"No problem, Doc." I grabbed a fresh pair of jeans from the bag and stepped into them.

"No alcohol, either."

I paused with the jeans around my knees. My legs shook visibly.

"I'll do my best."

Aguilera's brow furrowed. "Mr. McKenna, there's a slight chance of weakness in your extremities and blurred vision. If either of these occur over the next forty-eight hours, go to the nearest urgent care facility immediately. Have them call me. Here." He handed me his card.

"I promise." I snaked a belt through my jeans and cinched it up.

"Lieutenant Archuleta asked me to call when you were ready to be discharged. I just talked with him. He'll have a car waiting for you downstairs at eleven o'clock. Good luck."

We shook hands. He smiled for the first time in our brief acquaintance, turned, and left me to finish dressing.

I added a flannel shirt and socks to the jeans, slipped into my shoes, put on my leather jacket, and packed all of my other clothes into the plastic bag. I made my way downstairs and checked out. Patient Services gave me back my secured items. The clock on the wall said I had fifteen minutes before Sam's arrival. I passed on a cup of coffee. Too much beautiful sunshine to spend another minute indoors.

The cold hit me before the back of the door did. Sam was right about the change in the weather. A biting north wind swirled around me. I turned up the collar of my jacket, slipped my free hand into my pocket and took out my cellphone.

Onion sounded like he'd slept in. "Gabe?"

"They just discharged me. Gotta stop home for a bit and then I'll haul ass up to Santa Fe. Look for me sometime between one and two."

"Take your time, Brain. You've been through a lot. I'm doing fine."

"Uh-huh." I paused. "What's her name?"

He whispered, "Juanita."

"Be ready by one. We've got a lot to do. No time for distractions." I hung up and turned my back to the wind.

An APD squad car swung into the front circle and skidded to a stop in front of me. Dust and leaves scattered in the air. The passenger side door popped open a few inches. A second push from inside opened it all the way.

Officer Darrell Jackson leaned out the open door. "Climb in,

Professor."

"Hello." I eased into the front seat and tossed the clothing bag on the floor. "What happened to Sam?"

"The lieutenant's stuck out at Pueblo-66 Casino. We're shutting it down."

"Yeah, he mentioned that. Hope there's no more trouble out there."

"Drive you home?" he asked.

"Thanks. No siren, please."

Jackson coaxed a smile and eased onto Lomas. The smile didn't last. "Still no word about Rebecca. Professor, I'm worried she's—"

"Stop it," I snapped. "Rebecca's been in tough spots before. She's always survived."

Jackson blinked rapidly. His hands gripped the wheel so tightly I could see the veins.

"You care about her, don't you?"

"Yessir." He looked straight ahead and cleared his throat.

I stared out the side window. We turned onto Fourth Street and headed north. Nobody spoke until the squad car pulled into my driveway.

"Hang in there." I gave him a thumbs-up. "We'll find Rebecca. Soon, I hope."

The rookie cop kept staring out the front window. He pursed his lips and nodded. I stepped out of the car, grabbed my bag of clothes and closed the squad car door behind me. Jackson sped out of sight before I had my keys out.

The air inside smelled stale and clung to my clothes. I started the swamp cooler fan and opened the bedroom and library windows until the house felt too cold. Once in the kitchen, I filled Otis's food bowl and hiked back to the library.

Rebecca's desk looked lonesome in the corner. A sick feeling settled in my stomach. I sat at my desk and my hand found its way to the lower drawer. Then Dr. Aguilera's admonition about drinking booze echoed in my head.

"Fuck." I took out my phone and carried it with me to the kitchen. After piling ice into the tallest glass in the cupboard, I filled it at the tap and set up the coffee maker before dialing the phone.

"Archuleta."

"It's Gabe. Thanks for sending Jackson round to get me."

"He tell you I'm tied up here at the casino? Damn lawyers."

"Yeah. Listen. I'm heading up to Santa Fe and then further north to get my people. I'll keep in touch. Just wanted you to know."

"Do that. You'll be out of my jurisdiction, but I have friends if you need anything. Where exactly are you going?"

I hesitated.

"Oh come on, Gabe," Sam's voice sputtered. "I gave you my word. Doesn't that mean something to you? We want to protect Angelina, not arrest her, remember?"

"I'm not the one you have to convince. My daughter doesn't even trust me, how the hell do you think I can get her to trust the cops?"

"She's safer here under our protection than she is hiding out on Santa Clara Pueblo."

"Sonofabitch. How did you—?"

"I was notified last night that Nai'ya's brother—what's his name?"

"Estefan."

"Yeah, that he lives on the Pueblo. Figured. Listen, if you need any help, the Tribal Coordinating Officer up there is a friend of mine. Sheriff Pedro Naranjo. I can call ahead if you'd like, tell him to expect you."

"I guess so." I grabbed a mug from the sink and filled it with hot coffee. The brew burned my stomach. I needed something real to eat.

"Word to the wise, Gabe—Naranjo's a guy you definitely want on your side, not against you. One tough S.O.B."

"I'll keep that in mind. Now what about Rebecca?"

"Not a thing. Absolutely cold trail." A match was struck. Sam was silent for a moment before he coughed into my ear.

"Call me the minute anything breaks," I said.

"Will do. I'm sorry, Gabe. I know how much Rebecca means to you."

"You better keep an eye on Officer Jackson too. He's carrying a Big Hurt." We hung up.

I checked my mail and e-mail, paid an overdue utility bill online and rubbed Otis's chin a few times. After five minutes under a hot shower, I ignored doctor's orders and filled a shot glass with whiskey.

One for the road.

I lifted my revolver from the library desk drawer. It was loaded. I emptied a small matchbox into the drawer and filled it with extra .38 S&W Special rounds before tucking it into my jacket pocket. Back in the kitchen, I filled a thermos with hot coffee. One more call to make before leaving for Santa Fe.

"You out already?" C.J. sounded surprised.

"I'm heading to Santa Fe. Onion and I are driving up to Santa Clara Pueblo to round up my family. I need a favor."

"Anything."

"Stand by in case they find Rebecca while I'm out of town. Be my legs." I cringed as soon as the words left my lips.

"You got one sick sense of humor, you know that?"

"Jeez, I'm sorry. I'm not myself yet."

"Let it go. You need me to be somewhere, this cane won't stop me."

CHAPTER THIRTY

The sun disappeared halfway to Santa Fe. I switched on the Hudson's heater for the first time. A sharp, burning smell filled the car. Smoke poured from the vents on both sides of the dashboard. I pulled off onto the shoulder of I-25 while I could still see and breathe.

I struggled out of the car and opened both doors. My coughing continued. I opened all the windows. *Thank God for the gusty winds.* I zipped up my leather jacket and flipped its collar. When the air inside the car cleared, I closed the windows and crawled in behind the wheel.

Thirty frigid miles to Santa Fe. I drove one-handed all the way, blowing alternately on each of my hands to maintain some feeling in them. As I passed Santo Domingo Pueblo, snowflakes swirled in the air. At least the wipers worked.

Onion had taken a room at the Galisteo Hotel, a recently renovated establishment off the Plaza in the heart of Santa Fe. I pulled into the guest lot. The way I saw it, paying for Onion's room entitled me to a parking spot for a few minutes.

I hurried through a massive wooden portal with hand-carved columns and stepped onto the copper tinted ceramic tiles of the hotel's lobby. A series of burnt-red leather couches bordered the walls to my left and right. Soft flamenco music fluttered from above. A mezzanine level Spanish-style balustrade let enough light reach the lobby that I thought about my sunglasses.

A misty-eyed, stoop-shouldered bellhop struggled past me, his arms full of tan suede luggage. The desk clerk was dressed in black. He rang Onion's room with deft fingers and a poker face. I guess he heard what he needed to hear and nodded me toward the elevators. "Room 223. Up one flight. Down the hall to your right."

Southwestern landscape prints lined the second floor hallway. Somebody spent a fair chunk of change on the recent renovation. Might be a nice getaway with Nai'ya, once our current problems were resolved.

I turned the corner and almost collided with a black haired woman who stood outside the first door on my right. She didn't see me at first, bent over as she was, adjusting the strap on a six-inch stiletto heel.

"Excuse me." I smiled and pointed to the door behind her. Room 223.

She stood upright, fussed with her hair and drew a black lace shawl around her bare shoulders. At first, her face seemed lopsided. Then I noticed one false eyelash had slipped its mooring.

"Nice to meet you, Juanita."

"Huh?" She fluttered her eyes with a start and the lash fell, kissing her ankle on its way to the carpet. I stooped to retrieve it. She spun on her heel and wobbled around the corner and out of sight.

I slipped the eyelash into my breast pocket and knocked on Onion's door. "It's me."

"Come on in, the door's unlocked."

Onion stood across the room by a bed, a crystal coffee cup raised to his lips. At least his pants were on. The spare tire around his waist obscured any belt.

"Hungry?" Often a rhetorical question where Onion is concerned, but I said it anyway.

Onion lowered the cup and pointed to the empty silver tray that rested on the seat of a small bedside chair. "Nah, we ordered room service." He returned the cup to the tray. "Can you believe I had a BLT, fries, a salad, *and* a slice of chocolate cake for less than twenty bucks? It costs more than that for a beer and brat at a Mets game. Fuckin' nine-fifty for a hot dog last time I was there. And that's without fries or anything."

"Onion—"

"Eleven-fifty for a brewski, plus tax."

"Shut up, please. We have work to do."

He struggled to tuck the shirt into his pants. "Okay, Brain. You won't see Juanita again, I promise."

"Just don't let me see her on your expense account. Did you at least find time to check out the Sun Mountain Art Gallery like I asked?"

"I did." He crossed the room, took his small notebook from the top of the dresser, and thumbed through it. "Interesting stuff. The joint's been closed for the past four days. I talked with the shop owners on either side of the gallery. No sign of Reginald Addison. So I checked the New Mexico taxation and revenue records."

"And?"

"Addison's listed as sole proprietor. I found out his home address and checked there too. Beautiful old adobe in what I'm guessing to be a gay neighborhood. Nobody home. Mail in the mailbox, lots of it. I left it there."

"I wonder."

"Wonder what?" Onion closed his notepad.

"Is Addison running from the cops or from whoever killed Klein?"

I paid Onion's bill on our way out. When he promised not to complain about being hungry for the rest of the day, I even covered his room service.

"Thanks, Gabe." He pulled a tan trench coat over his shoulders and loosely cinched the belt.

I tucked the receipt into my shirt pocket. My fingers brushed against Juanita's fake eyelash. "Here you go, champ," I whispered as I handed it to my friend. "A keepsake from the Land of Enchantment."

Onion's face turned light crimson. That didn't keep him from running the item under his nose and slowly inhaling. His face glowed. "Patchouli."

"Come on." I led the way outside to the guest parking lot. By chance, I'd parked right next to Onion's rental. We'd be driving to Santa Clara Pueblo in two cars. He already had my cellphone number. I entered his on my speed-dial, so we could stay in touch no matter what.

I pulled out first and headed north past the Santa Fe city limits. Onion followed in a dark blue Dodge Avenger. Santa Clara Pueblo was a half hour drive away in good weather, but the snow flurries I battled earlier found me again. So did the howling winds.

In downtown Española, I turned off the highway and into the drive-thru lane of a Lotaburger. My stomach growled in anticipation of my first real food of the past two days. I asked them to hold the green chile on my cheeseburger, skipped the fries and soft drink. My Hudson predated the arrival of built-in cup holders, but a thermos of still-hot coffee held more appeal than cold soda anyway.

Burger in hand, I pulled ahead into a parking slot and took my first bite. Onion had parked alongside. When he got out and came over to my window, I opened it a couple of drafty inches.

"What's that?" He pointed to the paper-encased burger as I lifted it to my mouth a second time. I gave him a wicked grin and rolled the window back up.

He knocked against it. His ring making a grating sound.

"What?" I yelled through the window.

"You gonna eat all your fries?"

"I didn't order any." I took Onion's middle finger in stride. He gave up and returned to his car. All these years and so little about him had changed.

When my burger was reduced to its paper wrapper, I had a final swallow of coffee and phoned Nai'ya. The call routed straight to voicemail. I left a message to tell her we'd be there in fifteen minutes. With a blast of my horn to signal Onion, we resumed our journey to Santa Clara.

The snow flurries held steady. The winds intensified. Ten minutes later, I led our two-car convoy off the highway at a convenience store/gas station/mini-mall outside the Pueblo entrance. I climbed out, filled my tank, and refilled my thermos when I walked inside to pay for my gas. Onion waited in his car. Maybe he was still pissed about the lack of fries.

We turned to leave the mall. A hook and ladder from the Española Fire Department roared by and nearly sideswiped me. It passed through the Pueblo's entrance arch and spit a shower of gravel in its wake. A small red and gold vehicle with a screaming, rotating emergency light, and a larger rescue ambulance, swept past and chased the fire truck like a couple of angry dogs.

I rang Onion. "Let's follow them until we're sure they have nothing to do with Nai'ya."

"Check."

By now the three vehicles were several hundred yards ahead on the single-lane Pueblo entrance road. They passed over a rise and disappeared from view.

I braked at the top of the hill and squinted through my snowflake-streaked windshield. A burning doublewide off to my left lit up the entire valley floor. I turned my dual-speed wipers on high, but that only made things worse. I opened the window, raised my body and stuck my head outside for a clearer view.

Flames from the trailer shot twenty feet into the air. A second later, my car rocked from an explosion. A propane tank must have ignited.

I called out to Onion, who by now was standing outside. "Let's go in closer. We'll park on the periphery in case we need to make a quick exit."

We climbed inside our cars and sped within fifty yards of the blaze. A crowd of people parted momentarily as the emergency vehicles and their crews deployed. The back door of the rescue ambulance flew open. Two figures jumped out and moved toward the burning trailer.

My pulse raced. My breath came fast and shallow. I tightened my grip on the steering wheel. Less than three months before, I sat in that very trailer on a warm summer night, sharing good times with Nai'ya, her brother Estefan, and his wife.

CHAPTER THIRTY-ONE

I sat frozen in the Hudson, unable to move. The wheels inside my head spun and went nowhere. My ringing cellphone snapped me out of it.

"Gabe? What do you want me to do?"

A glance in the rearview mirror showed Onion climbing out of his car. I hung up without responding and slid outside to meet him.

We stood together atop the ridge and looked down at the fire. I leaned a hand on Onion's shoulder.

"What's wrong, Gabe?"

I stared into the flames. A second fire truck roared past and joined the other vehicles at the bottom of the hill. I got that sick, after-the-fact, helpless feeling. "Nai'ya's brother lives in that trailer. It's where they were hiding."

"Then for God's sake let's get down there!" Onion pushed me the first couple of steps. I took a deep breath to clear my head and ran as fast as I could, leaving Onion in my wake.

A ring of people blocked my path fifty feet from the trailer, a human wall as solid as the flames. I picked two flannel shirts at random and wedged my way between them.

"Excuse me," I was panting now. "Let me through."

The burly guy to my left recoiled at my intrusion and pushed back. "Watch it." He turned to face me, a fist raised and ready.

"My family is in there!" I kept pushing forward and struggled free of the crowd. Then I ran toward the fire.

"Stop!" A loud voice bellowed from the shadows. "Where the hell are you going?" An older man in uniform stood facing me, a massive silhouette against the flaming backdrop. His burly, rounded shoulders hunched forward, a Grizzly ready to pounce. He ran forward, crashed into me and caught me before I fell. Nose to nose with me, his voice cut through the jumble of sound surrounding us. "Get back to the crowd. You're in the way."

"Officer, my family's in that trailer!" I struggled against his grasp but couldn't break free.

"Take it easy, fella. We found only one man inside. He's laying over there." He let up on me and pointed to my right. A paramedic with a long braid down his back and a female EMT aide worked over a body prostrate on the ground. The man's jeans and boots caught most of the light from the fire, his head and chest remaining obscured. The EMT worker held either a transfusion of blood or IV bottle over the body. Shadows made it impossible to tell.

I turned back to the burly officer. "Is that Estefan?"

His eyes narrowed. "How do you know him?" He gave me the once-over and studied my non-tribal face. "Who are you?"

"I'm Gabe McKenna. I've come from Albuquerque to—"

"McKenna, eh?" His features softened only a little, like it hurt him to drop the scowl. "Sam Archuleta phoned that you'd be headed this way. Told me all about you."

"Sheriff Naranjo?"

"That's me." The fire crew drew closer as they moved to get a different angle on the blaze. "Let's you and me get out of their way." He stepped me back fifteen feet toward the gawking crowd.

Onion broke through the line and stumbled forward. He doubled over to catch his breath. I put an arm on his shoulder. "You okay?"

Naranjo motioned with his head. "Who's this guy?"

Onion remained breathless, so I spoke up. "He's Deke Gagnon. A detective friend of mine from New York."

"N.Y.P.D.?"

Onion shook his head. "Private," he gasped.

Naranjo made a dismissive sound and turned toward me. "You two stay out of the way. We'll talk later." He took a step to leave.

I caught his arm. "One question first, Sheriff. Was this an accident?"

He shook his head. "Not a chance. Somebody worked Estefan over real bad. The way he is now didn't come from the fire." Before I could say anything else, he moved away to confer with the fire crew.

"Come on." I pointed over to Estefan and the emergency crew.

Onion winced. "Gabe, the sheriff told us to steer clear."

"I have to see if Estefan can talk. Maybe he can tell us what happened. And why my family isn't here."

"I'll stay behind and keep an eye out for the sheriff. If he heads back this way, I'll let you know."

I moved through the shadows to where Estefan lay. A Coleman lantern lit his face. He wasn't saying anything. He was hardly breathing, his only movement coming from the erratic heaving and sinking of his chest. Blood dripped from his purple, swollen chin. A large patch of hair and skin was missing from the front of his scalp. Beneath that, an angry hole was all that remained of his left eye.

Onion snuck up next to me. "Sheriff's coming," he whispered.

His movements alerted the paramedic to our presence. He turned, looked up at us, and motioned with his head. "Get out of here. Now!"

I pulled Onion away. "Come on, let's go back to our cars."

"Right." He turned up the collar of his trench coat. We staggered back to the top of the ridge.

The farther we got from the fire, the colder the air became. The wind gusted with such ferocity I struggled to remain standing.

"What now?" Onion inhaled a couple of deep breaths.

I didn't have an answer.

CHAPTER THIRTY-TWO

The cold wind blew through to my bones. I scanned the valley from the top of the ridge. The last light of the vanishing sun withdrew over the dark outlines of distant western hills. How much time did I have to find my family?

On my one previous visit to Estefan's doublewide, an old woman stopped by for a visit. Her dog had gone missing. Estefan and I put off dinner to aid in the search. We found the mutt in less than an hour, leashed him and returned the animal to the woman's small home on the east side of the village.

The old woman seemed well acquainted with Estefan, his wife Belana, and Nai'ya as well. Aunt Pablita was the only other Pueblo resident I knew by name. I'd start with her.

"Well?" Onion flapped his arms around his torso to ward off the cold and stood with his back to the wind.

"Stay here and learn what you can," I said. "Nose around discreetly. Tell anybody who asks that you're a detective. I'll get the print of Jacob Wallace's mugshot from my car. Find out if anybody has seen Gray Wolf around here recently or knows what happened at Estefan's."

Onion nodded. "Where are you going to be?"

"There's an old woman who lives about a quarter mile from here. An elder in Estefan's family. I'm gonna see if she knows anything. Meet you back here within the hour."

He glanced at his watch. "By six-thirty then. Let's get that photo."

On my way to Pablita's, I told myself the absence of my family was a good thing. Nai'ya must have had time to flee with Angelina and Matty. Estefan must have been tortured in an effort to make him talk. It had to have played out that way.

The trek to Pablita's felt longer than it actually was. I warded off several dogs, walked into Northwest headwinds and felt my way over uneven terrain. It was nearly fifteen minutes before I arrived at a tiny adobe home, nestled between a pair of lofty blue spruce trees.

I knocked on its thick wooden door. Nothing. I knocked again, waited, and peered through the single front window. The curtain was drawn, with only a dim, flickering light visible inside. I pressed my ear against the window and caught a low growl and then a deep, throaty bark of a dog. A woman's voice gave a command, in Spanish I thought, and the barking stopped. I took three quick steps back to the front door.

Another knock. "Pablita? This is Gabe McKenna. I'm looking for Nai'ya Alonso-Riley."

Nothing.

"Please open up. My daughter and grandson have disappeared. I've come to take them home. Please help me."

The front lock turned. The door opened a crack, still secured by a heavy chain that clacked against the wooden frame. The features of an old woman's face emerged from the darkness inside as she moved closer to the narrow opening.

"*Señor* McKenna?"

"Yes." The door opened enough for us to make eye contact. "Good to see you again, Pablita."

"Come in." She unlocked the door. The old woman held a large-eyed, dappled hound by its collar. With a kind firmness, she backed it away from the door, her free hand clutching a string of rosary beads. "Nai'ya said you might come."

My heart leapt. "Nai'ya was here?"

"Until two hours ago. *Señor*, I am so worried." She fingered her beads and looked up at me with moist eyes.

Maybe prayer was enough for her. It wasn't enough for my family, and it wasn't enough for me. I reached into my pocket and slid my finger along the barrel of my .38.

"*Casa!*" Pablita released her hold on the dog's neck. The animal moved straightaway to a rumpled blanket on the floor by the fireplace.

Though the old woman stood no more than four and a half feet tall, with thin arms and even thinner gray hair, she radiated inner strength and resolve. I might have felt reassured as well, except for what her eyes were saying. "Come. Sit." She pointed a bony hand toward a square wooden table in the middle of the room.

"Thank you, *Señora*, but I don't have time to talk right now. Nai'ya and my family are in danger."

She fixed me with a steely stare. "Let me tell you what happened."

I took the nearest chair and leaned my arms forward on the table. "Where are they?"

Pablita ignored the question. "A few hours ago, Nai'ya, Angelina, and Matty came to my door. Estefan sent them. Two strangers had entered the village, but Estefan had men watching. They recognized one of the strangers as Jacob Wallace. The man who is called Gray Wolf. Nai'ya told me he was after them."

"Where is she now? I have to find her."

"We all do what we can. I pray." Pablita rolled her beads in her hand. "Nai'ya and Angelina have gone to *Tsirege*. Estefan told them to hide there and wait."

"Puye?" I knew the cliff dwellings and mesa top well. The ancient ruins were about three miles south, back along Route 30, and five miles west along the tribal road. "Did they go by the main road or cross-country?" If they'd gone on foot, they would face more than six miles of rugged terrain. In the dark.

"They took the old trail. Nai'ya knows the way. I gave them some food and a blanket."

I thought of the plummeting temperature and the likelihood of more snow during the night ahead. "One blanket for the three of them?"

"Matty is too young. He's here—sleeping in my bed."

"Here?" My heart quickened. "May I see him?"

"You'll wake him up."

"I won't make a sound." I tiptoed to the only closed door. "In here?" My hand settled on the doorknob. My eyes looked for approval in the old woman's face. She nodded, but remained seated.

The knob squeaked, so I turned it less than an inch at a time. I paused inside the tiny room while my eyes adjusted to the darkness.

A small rustic bed sat flush against the exterior wall beneath a square, shuttered window. A shelf with several *santos* and unlit candles protruded from the wall above the bed.

Matty lay on the bed, his body covered by a blanket, his head resting on an overstuffed pillow. Light from the main room illuminated his face. I bent forward close enough to hear his breathing. His features were dark, with hair hanging down across one eye. Was I looking at him or trying to find something of myself in his face?

I kissed his forehead and blessed him with a sign of the cross. Buoyed by this first glimpse of my grandson, I turned and left the room, closing the door behind me.

"Keep him safe, Pablita. I'll be back with Nai'ya and Angelina as soon as I can."

She nodded without a word and continued her rosary.

I lifted the collar on my leather jacket and walked out into the cold. I hurried into the darkness and back to my car. Onion was standing there, his back still to the wind.

I huffed up to him. "I know where they are." I leaned against the Hudson's fender and sucked in a couple of deep breaths. "What did you find out?"

"Plenty." He pulled his notebook from inside his coat and thumbed through it. "Two guys Estefan had posted at the entrance to the Pueblo say Jacob Wallace and another man—Anglo, maybe thirty-five years old, five-six or seven—drove into the village about four this afternoon. The lookouts alerted Estefan by phone. He told them to find Sheriff Naranjo and bring him to the trailer. Naranjo was somewhere off Pueblo. It took more than an hour to find him. By the time the lookouts and the sheriff made it back to the trailer, well…you saw what happened there."

"Anything about my family?"

"A young woman says she saw three people, two women and a boy, run from Estefan's shortly after four o'clock and head for the other side of the village."

"That checks with what Pablita told me."

Onion continued, "I spoke with a paramedic and an EMT aide before they left for the nearest hospital." He squinted to read what he'd written. "Christus San…"

"Christus St. Vincent. It's in Santa Fe."

"Anyway, they said he's in real bad shape."

"What about Belana?"

"Who?"

"His wife."

"Oh. She came by about fifteen minutes ago and spoke with the sheriff. They both left the scene. Probably off to Santa Fe as well. I heard Naranjo tell one of his men he'd be back as soon as he could."

"Damn. I need him now."

"Why? What did you find out? Your family safe?"

"Nai'ya and Angelina are on foot, traveling cross-country to the Puye ruins."

"Where's that?"

"About six miles from here."

"How much of a head start do they have on us?"

I looked off to the west. "It's not their head start on *us* that matters. Jacob Wallace and that other guy are already following them. I have to find them first."

"What can I do?"

"Stay here and grab the sheriff as soon as he gets back. If I drive back to the Pueblo entrance and go south to Tribal Road 601, there's a chance I can be at the ruins by the time Nai'ya and Angelina arrive."

"What about the kid?"

"He's staying at Pablita's. He's safe for now."

"So you saw him?"

"Laying on the bed there. A little angel."

"Doesn't resemble you at all then?"

I let that pass. "Might have my blue eyes, couldn't tell. At least his nose is straight." I fingered my own, broken three times.

"Back to work, Brain."

"Remember. Corner Naranjo the minute he gets back. Tell him to meet me at Puye mesa top. He'll know where." I slid the .38 from my jacket pocket and checked all of the chambers. "If Wallace and his friend arrive, I'll hold them off until you get there."

"You sure?"

"It's our only chance." I started the Hudson and turned back down the Pueblo road. I kept one eye on traffic in the oncoming lane, in case the sheriff came along with Estefan's wife. There was no sign of them.

I doubled back and drove south to the westbound turnoff for Tribal Road 601. The first ruins were five or six miles away. The dashboard clock showed six-fifty. Not much daylight left.

One of the advanced features of the Hudson in its day was a low center of gravity, what they called its "step-down" design. Unfortunately, this meant I had a mere twelve inches of clearance between the bottom of my car and the road.

For the first three miles, it didn't matter. The gravel remained level. Only an occasional pothole that I swerved to avoid.

Then I had to slow up. Runoff from a recent storm had washed down the incline to my right and across the road. Deep furrows carved by the water crossed my path. I down-shifted and crawled ahead, praying I wouldn't bottom out among the fissures.

I cleared the damaged area at last and drove on to within a mile and a half of the first group of cliff dwellings and ruins. Even in the dusk, I could see how much the area had changed over the past thirty years. The massive Cerro Grande fire in 2000, and the mudslides that followed left fearful scars on this land.

About a mile on, I hit a second area of severe erosion, worse than the first. The creases across the road were two feet deep in places. The Hudson couldn't take me any farther.

"Fuck." I pulled over to the side of the gravel road and left the car there, keeping the roadway open. I figured Naranjo would have four-wheel drive.

I grabbed a flashlight from the driver's side glove compartment and stepped outside. Gusts of wind spilled down from the rocky plateau above me. The frigid air burned my cheeks. Large snowflakes were now sticking to the ground.

The faintest bit of daylight remained. I slipped the flashlight into a jacket pocket and hurried along the road, my .38 ready. I shifted the gun from hand to hand and tried to flex away the numbness in my fingers.

The sound of gravel beneath my feet and the howl of wind filled the air. A low ceiling of gray clouds slid toward the east and cast a dull cloak over a desolate expanse of road in front of me.

Then I heard it—carried on the wind—the cry of a woman's voice, faint and distant. Nai'ya's voice.

I froze in my tracks and tilted my head to determine the direction of her call. I couldn't. The wailing wind drowned out everything else. I ran on up the road.

CHAPTER THIRTY-THREE

I heard another faint voice—a man's, this time. Then a second one. Both came from the darkness in front of me. A sick feeling bubbled in my stomach. I gripped my gun and slid the flashlight out of my pocket with my left hand. I left it off for now and continued on.

Every twenty yards or so, I stopped to listen. The voices sounded louder, closer. Definitely two men. I shuddered and kept on up the gravel road as it angled to the right, hugging a tall, rocky outcrop. I edged around the corner. A dark green Range Rover sat in the middle of the road. The engine was off.

A hulking figure with a ponytail hanging down over a buckskin jacket stood with his back to me. He murmured to a shorter man in a brown bomber jacket, a wrap-around scarf, and tan khaki pants. The shorter man unfolded a piece of paper and stretched it out on the hood of the vehicle. They huddled over it, deep in quiet conversation. The taller man pointed twice in the direction of the Puye Cliffs.

I hung close to the rock wall and waited. A minute later, the shorter man folded the large paper and tossed it into the front seat of the Range Rover. Both men checked their guns. Then the taller man led the way off the road and across a small empty parking lot.

I crept along the edge of the wall, then darted out and knelt behind their vehicle, keeping the body of the Range Rover between us. The howling of the wind made it impossible to hear what they were saying. I scurried around to the driver's door.

The men paused at the base of a concrete stairway that lead up a slope to a familiar adobe building. I'd been here with a group of undergraduate students back in the early 1980s. It was an old Harvey House, now converted into a Visitors Center with a souvenir shop on the right side and tribal offices on the left.

A ten-foot wide passageway at the top of the stairs split the two halves of the building and allowed access to the Puye Cliffs about fifty yards in the distance beyond. A series of dim lamps lined the stairs and the path beyond as far as I could see.

The smaller man stepped aside. I got a brief, clear glimpse of the ponytailed man in buckskin—Jacob Wallace. The picture I'd given Estefan was a good likeness.

I had to make sure both men stayed here until my help arrived. I peered into the Range Rover. A set of keys hung from the ignition switch inside the car. I tried the door. Unlocked. When another howl of wind raised the dust at my feet, I inched the door open. The overhead light flashed on. I reached inside and stabbed at the keys. They wobbled and fell to the floor. I stretched and snagged the ring that held them, pulled my arm out and closed the door. The light blinked out. One more gentle push and the door lock clicked.

Bracing myself against the vehicle, I stood, extended my arms across the hood and took aim at the buckskin jacket. "Stop where you are, Wallace!"

Both men turned my way and froze.

"Sit on the steps. Don't try anything."

Wallace sat down first. The smaller man crouched down behind him. When they did so, they moved into shadow. I'd made a mistake.

"Don't shoot, Mister. There's been some kind of mix-up. My name isn't Wallace. It's Goodwin. Frank Goodwin." He brushed his ponytail aside and raised his hands.

I kept a steady bead on him with my .38. "Shut up. And you—little guy—move out where I can see you. Now."

A crack broke the sound of the winds. A gun flashed from behind Wallace's shoulder and a bullet ricocheted off the roof of the Range Rover. I ducked behind the left front fender. A second bullet buried itself in the gravel at my feet.

I swung to my left, peered around the front bumper and caught sight of the smaller man rolling to my right and off the steps into darkness. My first shot caromed off the metal railing. I shot into the darkness beneath it.

He cried out and staggered into the open, one hand clutching the side of his face. I aimed low with my third shot and caught his leg. He folded, sprawling across the steps, his head landing below the rest of his body.

There was a commotion farther up the stairway. Wallace had taken off, disappearing into the darkness on the far side of the Visitors Center. I'd deal with him next.

First, I approached the fallen man, edging toward him with my .38 fixed on his chest. His gun lay on one of the steps several feet below his body. I bent down and pocketed a 9mm Beretta.

Blood discolored the man's pants. I spent a moment examining his head wound. He appeared to be half-conscious and probably in shock. He groaned. I rolled him on his side and his hand fell from his face. My second shot had creased his cheek. One of his teeth stuck through the wound and dropped onto the concrete as his head swerved side to side.

He wasn't bleeding too much. I left his head wound alone. But I unwrapped a patterned scarf from around his neck and jerry-rigged a tourniquet six inches above the bullet wound in his knee.

His jacket was open. I felt around for an inside pocket and touched a wallet. In the dim lamplight, I opened it and turned my flashlight on the New Mexico driver's license it held. The photo matched the man's face. I checked his name—Charles Jepson. Then I read his address.

In that one moment, *everything* I thought I knew about recent events changed.

The wallet contained fifty-three dollars in mixed bills. I lifted them out and threw them to the winds. Only a folded piece of light green paper remained inside. I took it out and unfolded my bank check made out to cash in the amount of five hundred thousand dollars.

I ran back to the Range Rover and looked for anything inside that might help me take down Jacob Wallace. One of us would have to die tonight.

CHAPTER THIRTY-FOUR

I found nothing useful in the Rover except a mini-flashlight. It fit in the breast pocket of my shirt. The large folded paper in the front seat turned out to be a map of the Puye region, with the area of the nearest ruins circled—the very place Nai'ya and Angelina were heading. I reloaded my .38 and slipped it into my jacket pocket.

Charles Jepson lay still now. I moved around him on my way up the stairs, keeping to the edge and staying out of the light as best I could.

At the top of the stairway, I tested the doors to the souvenir shop and the tribal office. Both locked. I crept beyond the passageway and out along the path to the cliffs.

Dim solar lights marked both sides of the pathway. The cliffs stood fifty yards ahead of me. I took a parallel route, well to the side of the path, stepping with care through the rocks and thin vegetation. *Stay in the darkness, Gabe. Wallace could be anywhere.*

I paused at the base of the cliffs and listened. The wind swept down the wall of rock and whistled in my ears. I looked up just before a boulder crashed to the ground at my feet. Wallace might not be able to see me, but he knew I was coming after him. I stepped out from behind the rock and fired a shot up toward the edge of the cliff.

"It's no use, Wallace," I yelled into the wind. "The police are on their way. Come down now. Give yourself up."

Two more rocks cascaded down the cliffside in response and fell ten feet to my right. I took the large flashlight from my jacket and stood out from the wall. Holding the torch at arm's length, I aimed the beam toward the top of the cliff. Wallace hugged the edge, then slung his body over and disappeared from view. He'd reached the top of the mesa, less than a quarter mile from the ruins.

The cliff rose nearly one hundred feet at an angle about twenty degrees off the vertical. Somehow, Wallace had made it in the dark. I'd have to do the same.

I re-tied my hiking boots and unzipped my jacket for greater flexibility. One last sweep of my flashlight along the incline, searching for the path of ascent. After a couple of deep breaths and a short prayer, I started up the wall.

Very few loose stones along the narrow path. That was good. What wasn't good was the mere sliver of moon. The rock outlines were still clear, but depth was impossible to judge. One step at a time. I made a good thirty feet, moving on a diagonal, then stopped for breath and scanned the wall above for the first switchback.

Ten feet away and five feet up, a lone tree projected from the rock, its trunk a solid half foot at the base. If I could reach it, I might see a way to the top.

I inched as close as possible and stopped. The path dropped off between my foothold and the tree, the opening nearly five feet across. The pathway I'd remembered must have been washed away over the years. No way I could jump that without a long running start. No way at all.

My jacket scraped against the rock wall and I felt the flashlight in the jacket pocket. I grabbed it, flicked it on once more, and swept the wall above me.

That's when I saw them—a series of ancient, ascending hand and toe holds two feet behind me. They continued all the way up the rock face, as far as I could see. I'd been so fixated on the tree that I'd moved right past without noticing.

The holes were small, barely large enough for the toes of my boots. I'd need both hands and feet to make the climb and would have to feel my way. I turned off the flashlight, put it back into my jacket pocket, and took the mini-flash out of my shirt pocket. I turned it on, clamped it between my teeth with the beam turned away from my face, and bit down hard. It was the best I could do. Hand-over-hand, toe-over-toe, I edged up to within twenty feet of the top.

Then the wind shifted. It gusted down along the wall and swirled around me. I pressed my body to the rock as sand from above spilled down the embankment onto my head, into my face and nose. I felt the urge to sneeze. With no way to stifle it by hand, I buried my face into the shoulder of my jacket and let it come. My right knee buckled, my body wavered and the mini-flashlight fell from my mouth. It clanked against the rock wall several times before thudding to the ground at the base of the cliffs.

I opened my eyes. Nothing but a thin, gray haze all around. I blinked, but couldn't focus. I remembered Dr. Aguilera's warning about visual distortions and gripped the handholds as tightly as I could. Climbing blind, I scraped the rock with my boot for the next toehold. Despite the temperature, sweat streamed into my eyes. I blinked and blinked some more until the stinging abated and my sight cleared. The outline of the rim against the darkened sky spurred me on. I couldn't let Nai'ya and Angelina down.

Ten more feet to go. My left boot caught in the next toehold. I heaved myself upward and flailed with my right hand. *Got it.* I pulled and stabbed out with my right foot at the same time. A few feet closer. More sand in my face. Another sneeze. My left hand slipped. My fingers wildly fought to regain their hold. *Got it again. Hold on. Now once more...*

The next handhold was full of sand. I leaned into the wall once more and scraped out as much of it as I could. Another pull. Another toehold. I could see over the edge of the rim now, the mixed scent of sand and knapweed on the ground made a sweet perfume.

One final toehold to go. I paused for a deep breath. I had one shot. Make it over the rim, or plunge to my death.

I waited for a lull in the wind and pushed upward with my right leg. I felt for the toehold with my boot. My left hand felt along the top of the plateau. The sandy ground beneath my fingers slipped away over the ledge. With a final, desperate effort, I pushed and grunted and willed my way over the top.

Exhaustion made it impossible to stand. I laid out on my back and stared at the slight crescent moon off to the east.

For some crazy reason, I thought of the original inhabitants of this land. Had it been this hard for them as well? I forced the question from my mind. The only two people I cared about now huddled somewhere in the darkness ahead of me.

The one thousand partially restored rooms atop the mesa formed an adobe and sandstone maze, a vast grid of shadows under the faint starlight. At least the walls would provide Nai'ya and Angelina cover from Wallace's eyes and some measure of shelter from the bitter winds.

I had the large flashlight in my jacket pocket and a .38 in my hand. Enough. I crept ahead toward the outer rim of the ancient settlement's walls.

The adobe perimeter was uneven, four or even five feet high in some spots, little more than a single course of adobe brick elsewhere. I crouched behind one of the taller sections, afraid to lean against any wall lest it give way. I felt the urge to cry out and let the women know they were no longer alone. But I couldn't risk alerting Wallace.

I waited and listened. The wind rose. No other sound. I raised my head and looked around. A faint clang of metal against metal echoed from the center of the ruins. A hoarse, whispering voice broke through the darkness to my right. "Nai'ya, where are you?" It sounded too much like my own voice for comfort.

Nai'ya called back. "Gabe? Is that you?" She was nearby and off to my left.

The urge returned to call out in protest at my imposter. I caught myself. Better to approach in the darkness carrying the weapon of surprise.

"Do you have a light?" The man's voice to my right was closer now.

"I'll light our lantern. We're in the ceremonial room near the center. Hold on."

I gripped my flashlight, but kept it inside my coat pocket. With my .38 in my right hand, I felt along for a gap in the wall, easing myself over a low pile of fallen bricks. I edged forward in a crouch.

A spark of light twenty yards ahead grew and brightened. Brick walls took form as lantern light flooded the ruins.

Nai'ya and Angelina huddled against the back wall of a circular, roofless outdoor room. There was a sound of footsteps. The two women glanced off to my right.

Jacob Wallace leapt from the shadows into the lantern light. "At last," he purred in satisfaction, like a man about to devour a hot meal on a cold night.

Angelina screamed and buried her face in her mother's coat.

Nai'ya held her ground. "Leave us alone!"

Wallace approached, and with each step his shadow grew on the wall behind her. He held a gun in one hand and had a foot-long knife cinched in his belt.

"That's far enough, Wallace!" I shouted from the darkness.

He froze, still holding his gun on the two women. His eyes strained in my direction. Then, in a flash, he dashed behind them, using their bodies as his shield.

I knelt behind a section of adobe wall and took the flashlight from my pocket. I switched it on and hurled it as far as I could across the expanse of the ruins. It twirled and cut a crazy pattern of light, a drunken flare dancing through a black sky.

Wallace jerked his head toward the light and wasted a bullet on it in his momentary confusion. I scurried for twenty feet along the outline of the wall, then stopped.

Wallace turned back to my original position and fired off another angry shot. I had the angle on him now. I aimed for his head.

"Drop the gun!" I watched as he peered into the darkness again. "Do it now!"

He spun behind Nai'ya. "I don't think so, McKenna." Angelina staggered out from behind her mother. Wallace held her hair in his fist and jerked her out toward the lantern light, his gun pressed against the side of her head.

"I'll give you five seconds to come out where I can see you. Hands in the air. Or this young lady dies. It's your choice."

I stepped from darkness to shadow to light, hands above my head, my .38 still in my grasp. "Hear me out," I yelled.

"Drop the gun."

I flexed my legs, crouched, and placed the gun on the ground in front of me. Then I stood and stared back at him from twenty-five feet away. It wasn't easy to sound calm, but I did my best. "Don't be a fool, Wallace. Your partner is dead and the police are on their way."

Wallace jerked Angelina's head back and she cried out in pain. He sneered. "You're lying."

"I can prove it. But I need to reach into my pocket. Please."

Wallace just stared at me and pulled Angelina's head back again with a violent tug.

With my left hand held above my head, I inched my right hand into my jacket and fingered the bank check in my shirt pocket. I unfolded it ever so slowly and pulled it out. My gaze never left his face. I held the check out toward him.

"Let the women go, Wallace." I waved the piece of paper. "This is the bank check I took off your friend's body. It's yours. Half a million dollars. If you leave now, you can get away before the cops arrive."

Far off to my right, a police siren sounded. *Damn.* A flashing red light cut the darkness at the northern edge of the mesa.

Wallace shot. His bullet whistled through my leather jacket just under my right arm. Angelina screamed and tore away from her captor. Nai'ya reached out and grabbed her.

I dropped to the ground. My hand flew into my right side pocket and grabbed Jepson's Beretta. I dove flat-out onto the sand and fired a single shot. Wallace grabbed his chest, dropping his gun while he fell. He twitched once and lay writhing on his back. His hands flailed about for his weapons. He tried in vain to pull the knife from his belt. Then he lay still.

I scrambled to my feet and rushed forward. Both women recoiled as I drew near. I held the gun on Wallace and stood over his body. He stared at the sky until his face froze.

The image of Estefan's bloody face flashed through my mind. I took a slow, deliberate breath and shot out both of Jacob Wallace's eyes.

CHAPTER THIRTY-FIVE

The Beretta slipped from my fingers and landed in the sand at my feet. I felt my side and then my jacket. Wallace's shot would cost me a new coat.

I turned to the women. Angelina clung to Nai'ya, who stared at me with a wide-eyed mixture of disbelief and horror.

"It's over," I managed to say. "You're safe."

Neither one responded. They huddled closer. I felt an urge to move forward, yet I stepped back. This was not quite the introduction to my daughter I'd been hoping for.

The siren grew louder. A flashing red brightness danced along the walls of Puye ruins. I looked at the Beretta on the ground. My own gun lay a few feet off to my left. While the patrol car drew near, I gathered up my .38 and slipped it into my pocket.

A tribal police car skidded to a stop twenty-feet away, parallel to the nearest adobe wall. Onion jumped out first and raced to my side. He grabbed my arm and rested his other hand on the back of my neck. "You okay?"

I shrugged.

He looked at Wallace and then at the Beretta by my feet. "Jeezus." In one continuous motion, he snatched it up to his waist and rubbed his shirttail over the grip and barrel. He dropped it to the ground a moment before Naranjo and another officer arrived. "Don't worry," he whispered to me.

The sheriff turned his collar up and looked around. He knelt and checked out Wallace. He spotted the gun at my feet. He let it stay there. "Back away, McKenna."

I did just like he said.

"Orosco," Naranjo barked at his deputy, "shine the searchlight over here. Then look after the women. We'll take their statements after they've had a chance to calm down a bit." He edged closer to Onion and me. "Don't say a word to each other."

My legs felt unsteady. I'd never killed anyone before. "May I sit down?"

"Suit yourself." He pointed to Onion. "You go wait over by my patrol car. I'm gonna need to talk to you, too."

Onion walked to the car. I glanced over at Nai'ya and Angelina who huddled and cried about fifteen feet away.

Naranjo got on the police radio and ordered backup, an ambulance, and a medical investigator to come to the scene. When he finished calling in, he knelt next to the Beretta. "This yours?"

"No." I pointed to my pocket. "May I?"

Naranjo's hand moved toward his gun. "Go ahead."

"Mine's a .38, Sheriff. Fully loaded." I handed it to him, butt-first.

"You got a license?"

"In my wallet." I fished out my concealed-carry permit, unfolded it and handed it over. My hand shook.

Naranjo stood up, examined it and then put it in his pocket. "You won't be needing this for a while." He turned his back and slouched over the body. "You have any idea who this guy is?"

"Jacob Gray Wolf Wallace. He's wanted for questioning by APD and state police regarding three murders, a kidnapping, and an attempted murder. If you don't believe me, just ask Sam—"

"I'm aware of all that." He looked down at the body and then back at me. "Just didn't recognize him without his eyes. You say your gun is fully loaded? I count three bullet wounds here." He sniffed the barrel of my gun. "And your gun has been fired recently."

"Wallace's accomplice attacked me down by the Visitors Center." I pointed south, over the edge of the mesa. "We exchanged gunfire. He's down below on the tribal road."

"You claiming self-defense?"

"The guy's name is Charles Jepson. And yes, he shot at me first. Twice." I lifted up the side of my jacket and let him see the bullet hole.

Naranjo took hold of it and poked his finger through the ragged opening.

"I fired off three or four rounds," I continued. "One of them went through his cheek. My final shot caught his knee. I saw to his wounds. He was alive when I left him."

"We'll check on all that when we get down there. When did you reload?"

"Right after I shot him. Then I came up here."

Naranjo's eyes narrowed. "How the hell did you get to the top of the mesa?"

"I heard Nai'ya's voice above my head. I thought she and Angelina were in danger. I took the shortest route to the ruins I had. Up the rock wall."

Naranjo looked at me like my hair was on fire and shook his head. "That's crazy."

Over the sheriff's shoulder, I caught Officer Orosco leading Nai'ya and Angelina back to the squad car. When they passed by, Nai'ya looked my way, her tears glistening in the beam from the patrol car's searchlight.

I gave her a weak thumbs-up. She turned away and passed into shadow. Ten seconds later, car doors opened and closed.

Lights appeared in the north. A second squad car, an EMT vehicle, and another car with an unfamiliar insignia on its door came to a stop next to the sheriff's car.

Onion still stood nearby. He fidgeted and gave me a wave. I pointed to my eyes, then back to him and then toward Nai'ya and Angelina in the back seat of Naranjo's patrol car. He nodded in return. I knew he'd look after them if the cops gave him any room.

"Okay, McKenna." Naranjo's sharp tone snapped me back. "You and I are going down to check on that other guy." He turned to the second patrol car. "Sanchez!"

A diminutive officer stood by the second squad car. At the sheriff's call, he scuttled back in and drove over to us.

"Get in the back, McKenna. Wait for me," Naranjo snapped.

I slipped into the rear seat of the patrol car, staying close to the window and watching every move the sheriff made.

He conferred with the EMT personnel. One of them hurried off to check on Nai'ya and Angelina. Two others walked over to Wallace's body. A tall, gray-haired man in a white lab coat was already examining him. I figured it was a medical investigator, or coroner, or whoever handled that job around here.

After five minutes, Naranjo lumbered back to the car and swung in next to me. Sanchez leaned against the cage behind his headrest. "Where to?"

"Go out the service route the way we came. Hang a right at Puye Road." He looked at me. "Both you and the other guys drove right past 608."

"What's that?" I asked.

He laughed to himself. "The approach road to these mesa ruins. Ya'll could have saved yourselves the climb up and down that rock face."

Sanchez interrupted Naranjo's moment of satisfaction. "What should I do then, Sheriff?"

"Keep going west on Puye until you find a couple of cars. We're gonna check out McKenna's report of a wounded man down there."

The search and headlights helped Sanchez navigate the steep curves of the road as it twisted down the northern slope of the mesa. I felt events closing in on me. Too many things to explain and not enough answers.

Naranjo looked at me the way a cat looks at a half-dead mouse. "This should be interesting."

"What?" I asked, afraid of his answer.

"The ballistics tests on your gun and Wallace's. And that Beretta we found beside the body. We'll run the prints too. You have anything you wanna tell me now?"

"The Beretta belongs to Charles Jepson, the guy who fired at me on Puye Road. I shot him in self-defense. That's the truth, I swear."

"Explain how his gun gets up to the mesa."

My mind raced. "He dropped the gun after I shot him. I bound up his wound with his scarf and took his gun with me up to the ruins."

"Uh-huh."

"There he is, Sheriff." Sanchez pulled the squad car off to the edge of the gravel road.

Naranjo glowered at me. "Get out."

I slid out behind him and followed both cops to Charles Jepson. He lay on the stairs unconscious, right where I'd left him. His skin looked pale in the glare of the headlights.

An EMT van screeched to a halt behind us. Its crew bulled their way around us to Jepson. "Fuckin' busy night for you guys," Naranjo said after them.

The first paramedic, a short, round man with dark hair, grunted and motioned us out of his way. He and a second man who could have been his twin crouched over Jepson and conferred in Spanish. A third member of their team arrived from their vehicle carrying a stretcher and straps.

They tossed aside Jepson's scarf and applied proper sterile wrapping to the man's wounds.

I shivered, then reached down and lifted the scarf off the ground. My first impulse was to wrap it around my neck, but I stopped. The light from the vehicles made it easier to see its true colors.

Bingo.

With the attention of the police and medical personnel diverted by Jepson's condition, I snuck the scarf inside my jacket. "Sheriff, I have to get back to Albuquerque right away. A woman's life is at stake."

Naranjo walked over and leaned his face to within an inch of mine. "Not a chance, Galahad."

"I'm pleading with you."

"No."

"Let me call Sam Archuleta."

He flashed a cold smirk. "I'm thinking about all the things I already have to charge you with. You need to make a phone call? Call your lawyer."

I felt the muscles tighten in the back of my neck. "If that girl dies, I'll have your badge."

"You will, eh?" Naranjo gave me a glassy stare. "I'd be more likely to lose my badge if I let you go now. You're at *least* a person of interest in this mess. And I have jurisdiction here, *not* Sam Archuleta. This is sovereign tribal land. You get that?"

"Sheriff, please listen to me. What happened here tonight is connected to killings in Albuquerque, Northern New Mexico, and even New York City. The FBI is involved."

My words seemed to give Naranjo pause. "Really."

I pressed him. "Archuleta will vouch for everything I've said. You call him. Tell him Wallace is dead. It'll settle his stomach."

Naranjo made a guttural sound. "Wait here." He slouched back to the squad car, sat inside and talked for a while on the police radio. By the time he hung up, my stomach felt the way it had back at the hospital.

"Archuleta confirms what you said. Wants you to call him *pronto*. Wants everything that you know."

"See?"

"He also said that if I felt like holding you for a couple of days, he'd understand. Says you have a habit of going off half-cocked. Says you like to take things into your own hands."

"But Sheriff, I *have* to get back to Albuquerque. I've got to be the point man on this."

"So, now you're Mr. Indispensable?" Naranjo looked at Sanchez. Their laughter made me shake.

"Look," I said at last, "I give you my word. I'll be back here within twenty-four hours. Then you can arrest me, lock me up, and do whatever you want."

"Why should I believe you?"

I thought for a second and then reached into my wallet. I took out the bank check, unfolded it and handed it to Naranjo. "Here's half a million reasons. That's a bank check drawn on my personal account. Says it right on the bottom there."

He took out a flashlight and examined both sides of the check. "Is this real?"

"As real as you are. If I'm not back here in twenty-four hours, I'll forfeit that entire amount. The Pueblo can keep it for all I care. Satisfied?"

Naranjo's face soured. He scratched at his neck. "I dunno…"

"Let me go, Sheriff. Call Sam back. He knows all about the check."

He drew a line in the sand with the toe of his boot. "Okay, McKenna. Twenty-four hours. Then you get back here. Bring your lawyer. Try anything and your ass is mine."

CHAPTER THIRTY-SIX

I pulled onto the shoulder of the Interstate just south of Santa Fe and took out my phone. "Sam. It's Gabe."

"Where the hell are you and what have you been up to?"

"On my way back to Albuquerque. You and I are about to solve all of these killings."

"What?"

"Jacob Wallace is dead."

"Naranjo told me." Sam's lighter clicked.

"His partner Charles Jepson is now in custody."

"Where'd you find him? Never heard of the guy."

"You weren't supposed to. He's been a silent partner in this all along. But we have bigger fish to fry now. Meet me at my house in half an hour. I'll explain everything."

"You'd better. You managed to piss off Naranjo pretty good. I'm surprised he let you go."

"He'll be shaking my hand tomorrow. And you'll be getting a promotion."

"Terrific." He said it like I'd just promised him a root canal.

"Listen, I need you to do me one favor."

"You usually do."

"I need to be wired when we move in on the ring leader."

"Jeez, Gabe. Nobody wears a wire anymore. This is the digital age. Or haven't you heard?"

"Then get me whatever you use these days. If I can get them to let me in first, you won't need a search warrant. When this is all over, Sam Archuleta will be a household name."

"That's what I'm afraid of."

Two police cars clogged my driveway. I parked the Hudson on the street and bounded out. The chill wind from the Pueblo had followed me home. Archuleta and Darrell Jackson stepped out of their respective squad cars and intercepted me on my way to the front door. It was eleven-thirty.

"Inside." I opened the door. My breath was visible in the foyer, so I turned on the heat. My jacket stayed on, with Jepson's scarf tucked inside.

Sam opened a fresh pack and lit up. "Okay. Spill. What's going on? Why all this mystery?"

"Understand one thing," I said. "Nothing and nobody is going to stop me. This has been personal all along. My family disappeared. My old friend was murdered. Attempts were made on my life. And then Rebecca..."

At the mention of her name, Jackson flushed. "What can I do?"

Archuleta whirled toward him. "Hold it right there, Rookie. Remember who's calling the shots here?"

"Sorry, Sam, but I am." I poked myself in the chest. "It's my fault that Rebecca is in this mess. I'm the one who had her nosing into Klein and his affairs. She saved my life once. Now it's my turn."

"The police are trained for these situations," he said.

"I appreciate that. It's why I called you in on this, to back me up. Did you bring that recording device?"

He reached into his shirt pocket and handed me a pen. "Here you go, hero. Press the white button on top and every word it picks up becomes part of the police record."

I took the pen. "This is it? Amazing. I expected you would hide it in a pack of cigarettes, or something. Shows what I know."

Archuleta reached into his coat pocket and pulled out a second pack of Camels. He held it up and jiggled it back and forth. "Recorder's inside."

"Beautiful." I slipped the pen into my breast pocket. "Wait here a minute." I hustled in to my library and found a stack of index cards in the desk. Taking one off the top, I wrote an address on it and handed the card to Sam back at the front door. "In case you need to call for backup. No telling what might happen once I get inside."

He flipped the card around a couple of times with his fingers. Then he tapped it against his lips before shaking his head. "You really need to let us handle this."

"Damn it, Sam. Don't you get it? The minute a cop knocks on the door, Rebecca will be killed. Remember what the ransom note said? If I can get inside, we've got a better chance to save her. Assuming she's still alive."

"He's right, Lieutenant." Jackson's face burned a bright red.

Sam shot an amazed look at his subordinate. A long second passed. Then he melted.

I patted him on the back and pointed to the card. "Follow me to that address. Once we pull onto that street, cut your lights. We approach in silence. I go in first, by myself."

He flicked his cigarette out the front door and onto the porch. "You're going to get yourself killed."

"Maybe. I'm willing to put my life on the line for Rebecca. Are you?" I looked at Officer Jackson. He looked at Sam.

I continued, "Once I'm inside, you come up on the porch and listen. If you hear me in trouble, come in fast and furious."

"I can cover the back," Jackson offered.

"Just don't go inside on your own," I said.

Sam sighed and nodded. "We do what we have to do. Let's go."

The Hudson was still warm and started right up. The two police cars followed me to 4th Street, across to 2nd and then east on Paseo del Norte toward the mountains.

CHAPTER THIRTY-SEVEN

We turned onto Tennyson Street and drove north for half a mile. I flashed my right rear blinker as we approached the house. Archuleta and Jackson turned off their headlights. I coasted up the driveway of the upscale southwestern-style house and pulled up outside the front porch. As I climbed from my car, I pressed the button on top of the pen in my shirt pocket and checked the scarf inside my coat.

With attempted nonchalance, I took the front steps one at a time and rang the bell. Almost midnight. I studied the kaleidoscopic glow of a lamp through the etched glass of the front door.

I rang again. A shadowed figure approached the door. I took a deep breath as the porch light came on and the lock clicked. The door opened.

"Good evening, Mrs. Houseman."

"Mr. McKenna?"

"May I come in?"

"It's rather late—"

"It's important or I wouldn't have bothered you at this hour." Without waiting for a response, I elbowed my way into her living room. A standing lamp glowed behind a recliner to my left that was covered by a thin plaid blanket. More light streamed in from the hallway on the far side of the room.

"Really, Mr. McKenna, what is the—"

"I have something that belongs to you." Her expression darkened as I reached into my jacket. I inched out the black and gold scarf worn by Charles Jepson, the one I used to bind his gunshot wound—the scarf Elaine Houseman was knitting as she sat next to me on our flight back from New York.

Her voice sliced through me. "Where did you get that?"

"Don't worry, Mrs. Houseman. Or should I call you Mahatma?"

She froze.

"Charles is in custody and is receiving proper medical care. He may not walk for a while, but he's certainly able to talk. And the cops are taking down every word. Jacob Wallace, on the other hand, won't be talking to anyone, ever again."

She spoke through her teeth. "You need professional help."

"I have it. The police are covering all your doors."

She looked over my shoulder toward the front door, then back at me. "I feel a bit faint. I need to sit down." She shuffled to the couch and sat next to a round, wicker basket of knitting supplies.

"While you sit there, perhaps you can explain your role in all these crimes, starting with the killing at the Pueblo-66."

"Mr. McKenna, I know you're upset about your friend. I heard about that killing on the news—"

"How did you know Tommy O'Donnell was my friend? I never mentioned him to you. The only people who knew that are back in New York. Your Friends of Tammany."

"I don't know what you're talking about. You're impertinent. Get out of my house."

"Well, well..." I pointed to a four-by-six knitted piece in a gold frame that hung just to the right of the fireplace. It showed the same image of Chief Tammany I'd seen on all those damned rings. "Interesting wall-hanging behind you. Did you knit that too?" I turned back to the couch and found myself looking down the barrel of yet another Beretta. "Nice gun."

"Such a smart guy, McKenna. You think I'm going to let you ruin the money machine my associates and I have been working for more than forty years? If Nellie McKenna had left her estate to us as we told her to, I wouldn't have to kill you now."

The front door burst open. "Drop it, lady!" Sam yelled.

Mahatma turned and fired off three rounds. Two hit the door

and the other rained down plaster from the ceiling. Sam took time to aim before his gun answered. A single shot drove her back against the couch. She clutched her right hand as blood flowed into her lap. She'd never knit again.

A thunderous crash and the sound of breaking glass echoed from the hallway. Sam's gun never wavered from the bleeding old woman. "See what's going on with Jackson," he said.

I ran down the hallway and burst into the kitchen. With a final push, Officer Jackson barged the back door off its hinges and ended up on his knees in the middle of the room.

"I'll get the basement." He staggered to his feet. "You stay here and guard the door."

I backed over to where the hallway and kitchen met. From there I could see more of the first floor. Sam was on the phone with someone. I couldn't hear what he was saying.

"McKenna!" Jackson's voice carried up the basement steps. "Down here!"

I barreled down the stairs, grabbing the rail every fourth or fifth step. Mrs. Houseman's daughter sat rigid on a hard-backed chair. The handcuffs that secured her glinted in the overhead light. She snarled at me. "You again!" A baby cried in the distance.

Over in a corner, a blonde woman lay on a green army cot. She faced the wall, curled in a fetal position, naked except for a rope that bound her hands behind her back. Drug paraphernalia covered the top of a small table by the side of the cot. Jackson knelt at her side. His hands hovered, reluctant to touch her.

I crouched next to him. "Untie her."

He fumbled with the ropes. I helped him set Rebecca free and rolled her onto her back with great care. There was no way to tell how drugged she might be.

She made no sound and lay still. I leaned forward. Her breath was coming in shallow, irregular fits. "Find something to cover her and keep her warm. Then get an ambulance here, on the double." I kept the needle marks along her left forearm to myself for now.

Jackson flew up the stairs. I heard him talking in a frantic voice. The young woman in handcuffs stared at the floor. "Karen, isn't it? Karen Houseman Jepson?" I looked at the pile of vials and syringes.

214

"I suppose you're Rebecca's attending nurse?"

Her scalding eyes let go a couple of tears. "Where's my husband?"

I looked at Rebecca and spoke matter-of-factly. "I shot him." *Chew on that, lady.* I stood when Jackson came hurtling down the stairs with the plaid blanket from the living room recliner.

"Darrell, I'm going upstairs to talk with your boss. Cover her up. Don't try to shake her or bring her around. Let the EMTs handle that. Make sure the syringes and everything on the table aren't disturbed. They need to be analyzed for drugs and checked for prints."

Jackson's eyebrows rose. "You sound like a cop."

"No. Just a concerned parent, I guess. See you later." When I climbed the stairs, my legs ached on each step. The strain of the night had finally hit me.

Sam was still in the living room covering Mahatma. "How's Rebecca?"

"Drugged. Unconscious. I don't know what they were giving her, or how much, or for how long."

The front door opened. Three EMTs and two more cops entered the room.

Sam spoke to the medical personnel. "Downstairs." He looked at Mahatma, now white-faced on the couch. "One of you might want to check her out, too." He pointed to the two newly arrived cops. "Secure the area. The crime scene unit is on its way. They'll need to bag that gun over on the end table and that wicker basket with all its contents. I want the old lady's prints as soon as she gets medical attention. Then take her down to the station. Her daughter is downstairs. She goes too."

"Sam," I interrupted, "here's your pen back. Think we have enough?"

"That's up to the D.A. Off-hand, I think we have plenty to hold them both. Ultimately, it'll depend on what the FBI wants to do here and back in New York." A fresh cigarette made its way to Sam's lips.

"I need to ask a favor," I said.

"Of course you do. Now what?"

"I have to get back up to Santa Clara. Nai'ya and my family are waiting. Okay?"

Sam's official frown thawed. "Yeah, I guess so. But be back

tomorrow. I'm gonna need you here."

I smiled. "We'll all be back."

"I'm glad your family is safe, Gabe. I really am."

With a thumbs-up, I hurried out the front door. The night air felt fresh and invigorating. I cleared the porch steps and climbed into my car.

I had to pull off the driveway for a moment to let three more vehicles race up to the house. Once back on the street, I headed back to the Pueblo—less than two hours from my family.

CHAPTER THIRTY-EIGHT

I took Sheriff Naranjo at his word. Despite the hour, I called my lawyer before I crossed the Santa Fe County line.

You have reached the office of Erskine Pelfrey III, attorney-at-law. I am not available at the moment. Please leave a message at the tone and I shall return your call as soon as possible.

"Erskine, this is Gabe McKenna. I know you're there. If you don't pick up, I'll leave a sarcastic message."

He came to the phone in less than five seconds. "Professor, how nice of you to call. What time is it?"

"Time for you to start earning your sizeable retainer."

"Very well. Let me turn off this infomercial..." An angry cat hissed through the phone. "There, there, Buckminster. Now, Professor, what can I do for you?"

"Meet me at the sheriff's office on Santa Clara Pueblo at noon. You better allow yourself ninety minutes for the drive."

"Can you give me some background? I like to be prepared."

I filled him in on the details of the past twenty-four hours and painted a broad picture of my troubles over the past few weeks, both in New Mexico and back in the Big Apple. I told him about the bodies in my barn, about Nai'ya and my family, and about the attempts on my life.

"You should have contacted me earlier. But not to worry, I shall be there as you ask."

"I haven't committed any crime, but Sheriff Naranjo might not see it that way. I want you to make sure I get a fair shake under the law. I don't trust the guy."

"I shall be at your side every minute. You said it's a ninety-minute drive?"

"Give or take."

"Guess I had better eat something before I leave."

"Do that. And don't wear that old brown suit of yours, okay?"

"I shall wear my new one. See you at noon."

The bit of coffee remaining in my thermos was ice cold. Without a working heater, the Hudson was no warmer than the frigid outside air. I drew my collar up and called Onion to see what had gone down back at the Pueblo.

"Where are you?" From the sound of his voice, I wasn't the only one dog-tired.

"On my way back. I'll be there in an hour. How are Nai'ya and Angelina?"

"They're here at the community center. Your grandson, too. That old lady brought him over. They've put us up in a conference room. Gave us cots, blankets, and soup. We've been treated well."

"Have the women let on about what happened?"

"Naranjo interviewed them about two hours ago. They didn't say anything to me afterward. They're asleep now. At least your daughter and grandson are. Nai'ya's been nodding on and off."

"Is she up now?"

"Yeah, looks like she might be. But how the hell are you? Did you handle whatever took you back to Albuquerque?"

"Things couldn't be better, pal. I'll tell you about it when I arrive. We need to get our stories in sync."

"Understood. Naranjo questioned me only briefly. I played it straight, but didn't volunteer a thing. Far as he's concerned, I arrived in New Mexico yesterday and know less than he does."

"Good work. Put Nai'ya on. I need to talk to her."

"Hang on a minute."

My stomach did a flip as I waited for her to come to the phone. What must she think of me now?

"Gabe? Where are you? You okay?" I could barely hear her over the drone of the engine. Maybe she just woke up.

"I'm okay. I'm on my way back to the Pueblo. Everything is fine. Tell Angelina she doesn't have to worry anymore. The people who threatened her won't bother her ever again."

"Gabe..."

"Yes?"

"It's not going to be that easy. Watching you kill Jacob Wallace seems to have reinforced her fear. Then shooting out his eyes like that..." Her voice drifted off.

There was nothing I could say.

"Gabe? Are you still there?" Nai'ya said. "Seeing you do that shocked me, too. I realize there's a lot I still don't know about you. I've been mulling that over ever since."

I held my breath. *Was she about to walk away?* "And...?"

"When Sheriff Naranjo questioned me, he told me what those two men had done to Estefan, how they'd gouged his eye and tortured him...you did what had to be done."

I closed my eyes and exhaled. "Thank you. Thank you for understanding."

"I still love you, Gabe. But it's not easy."

"My epitaph. A couple of questions before I go—how's Estefan?"

"They say he'll make it. His other eye is fine. But I don't know what he and Belana will do. The fire wiped them out."

"I'll take care of them."

"You said a *couple* of questions."

"Did either you or Angelina tell Sheriff Naranjo you *saw* me shoot Jacob Wallace?"

"No. I told Angelina not to say anything. She was still too shocked to remember much. Naranjo spent most of the time questioning me."

"What did he ask you?"

"He wanted to know if we saw Jepson—is that the other man's name?"

"Yes."

"If we saw him shoot Wallace. I told him we heard shooting, but by the time we got to the mesa, Jepson must have left. I let him think Wallace was dead when we arrived. Was that okay?"

"God, yes. Do you think Angelina will go along with that?"

"She's hardly talking at all. This whole ordeal has been too traumatic for her. She's sleeping now."

"Good. Give her my love when she wakes up. Matty, too. He's a handsome boy."

"You *saw* him?"

"At Pablita's. I stopped by there looking for you. She's the one who told me where you'd gone. Matty was sleeping like an angel."

"I think he looks like you." I thought I heard a smile.

I wiped my face on my sleeve. "I've always wanted a family."

"You have one now."

"Nai'ya, you're my angel. Be there in less than an hour." I wanted to fly to her. Instead, I shivered all the way back to the Pueblo.

Onion met me at the door of the Community Center. "How you doin' Brain?"

"A bundle of joy. Listen…" I took him by the arm and led him to a dark corner where no one could hear us. "Did I see you wipe Jepson's Beretta clean?"

"You sure did," he said with obvious pride.

"Nuts."

"What do you mean?" He looked like I'd hurt his feelings.

"How do I explain the absence of my prints on Jepson's gun? Naranjo knows I brought it with me to the top of the mesa."

"Let me think." Onion made a fist and bit down hard on it. "Okay. Our story has to be that Jepson—"

I shook him off. "No. My story has to be that Jepson—who I shot in self-defense—killed Wallace before anyone else got to the mesa." I thought about that and shook my head. "Nah, I don't think—"

"That works," Onion said. "Sure…Jepson's dead, right?"

"No. He's alive."

"Shit. Then he'll deny it."

"Of course he will. But it's his word against mine. The law has him on so many other charges, I'll take that chance."

"Got it!" Onion's face lit up. He reached into his coat pockets and brought out a pair of gloves and held them out to me. "Here. You wore these when you climbed that rock wall. And when you left Jepson's gun by Wallace's body."

"New York move, Onion." I took the gloves and put them in my jacket pocket for Naranjo to find. "So, our story goes like this: Jepson and Wallace have a falling out. Jepson shoots Wallace and leaves him atop the mesa before the women arrive. Jepson returns to his Range Rover and he spots me. He shoots. I drop him in self-defense and disarm him. I call out for Nai'ya and she responds from up above me. I climb the wall and find her and Angelina next to Wallace's body. I drop Jepson's gun and keep my own pocketed. That's when you and Naranjo arrive."

Onion rubbed his chin and looked anxiously toward the door. "That could fly. But why does Jepson shoot Wallace?"

"Over my bank check—half a million negotiable dollars. Plenty of motive for murder."

"How do you prove they even knew about the check? Naranjo might think you brought it with you and—"

"Stop." I held up my hand to reassure him. "Archuleta will confirm that Wallace picked up the check at the post office in Albuquerque. That Mahatma tried to poison me. Sam's in possession of the note she sent me."

Nai'ya rose from her cot and smiled when I re-entered the conference room. We rushed to each other and embraced. I brushed the tears from her cheeks and kissed her.

"Think I'll go out for a while," Onion called after us. He turned and disappeared through the main door.

Nai'ya and I didn't say a word. It was enough just to feel her in my arms. I hoped she felt the same.

At last, she pulled back and studied my face. Her hand fluttered against my cheek. I held my breath and awaited her next words.

"You've smelled better, Gabe."

This was true. I sniffed a couple of times before we broke down in barely stifled laughter and embraced again.

"Where's the washroom in this place?"

"Go out the door you came in and turn left. End of the hallway. I'll set up a cot for you next to mine." She pointed toward a table in the corner of the large, dimly lit room. "There's snack food left over there, if you're hungry. Sandwiches, chips, bottled water."

I looked over her right shoulder toward the cots where Angelina and Matty lay.

Nai'ya put a finger to my lips, and whispered, "Let them sleep. Better we talk in the morning, don't you think?"

After planting a kiss on Nai'ya's forehead, I soft-shoed my way out of the room and spent ten ineffective minutes in the bathroom trying to humanize myself. Without razor or comb, there was only so much I could do. Anti-bacterial soap made for a tolerable deodorant and shampoo. It failed miserably as mouthwash. Still, the hot water did revive me. I used my undershirt as a washrag and tossed it in the trash on my way back to the dim light and quiet of the conference room.

Nai'ya had my cot set up touching hers. Angelina and Matty remained asleep in the corner of the room.

I fluffed the thin pillow and spread out both of the blankets. Then I leaned over and kissed Nai'ya good night. She beamed at me and stroked my cheek again before she closed her eyes. It was seventeen minutes to four.

CHAPTER THIRTY-NINE

I needed a few good hours of sleep, but didn't get them. My body collapsed, but my mind marched on, non-stop. Without a drink to restore order, all my inner voices were talking at once.

Around seven o'clock, the morning sun broke through half-drawn shades on the large window behind me. The room seemed bigger in this light, but felt colder than when I'd arrived. Our hosts had pushed a circular wooden table aside to make room for our sleeping area. The half sandwich and three bags of chips on the table held no appeal. I leaned back against my pillow and studied the patterns on the off-white fiberglass ceiling tiles.

Matty awoke first. He sat up and rubbed his six-year-old eyes. He bounced off his cot in a flash and headed toward the food table. He didn't notice me until he brushed against the foot of my bed. He stopped and stared at me, then looked back to his mother.

"It's okay," I said.

"Are you my grandpa? They told me my grandpa was coming."

"That's right, Matty. I'm your grandfather." I ached my way off the cot and extended my right hand. "My name is Gabe. It's short for Gabriel."

He looked at my hand and spoke matter-of-factly. "Can I call you Grandpa? That's what other kids do."

"Just don't call me late for dinner, okay?" My lousy joke confused him. I tried again. "Sure, you can call me Grandpa. Can I call you

Matty?"

"Everybody does."

I pointed to the conference table across the room. "Let's go over there and talk so we don't wake up your mom and Nai'ya."

"You mean Nana?"

"I guess I do." I shuffled across the thin carpet and plopped onto a gray fabric covered chair.

Matty made a detour to the food table on his way. "Here." He handed me a bag of chips and placed two other bags in front of him on the table.

"Thanks, just what I wanted." I looked at the bag and then put it aside. "I didn't know I even had a grandson until a couple of weeks ago."

He ripped open one of his bags and stuffed a fistful of chips into his mouth.

"Tell me about yourself." I watched him grab a second handful. "What do you like to do?"

He spoke through his food. "I like baseball. I want to be a baseball player when I grow up." His cheeks were so filled with chips by now, it looked like he had a major league-sized chaw of tobacco.

"Me, too. Since I was a kid."

"Did they have baseball back then?"

I laughed. "It was just getting started. So who's your favorite player?"

He answered without hesitation. "Jacoby Ellsbury."

"Ellsbury's a good player."

"He's Navajo. Visited his grandma on the rez when he was little."

"No kidding?"

"Yeah. He likes Teenage Mutant Ninja Turtles."

"Really?" I had no idea where this was going, but he had my attention. "Where'd you learn that?"

"On TV."

"Matty, come here!" Angelina called from her cot. Without a word, he grabbed both bags of chips and walked across the room. By now, Angelina and Nai'ya were both sitting up.

Angelina stood, put her hand behind Matty's head and guided him to Nai'ya's cot. "Stay here with Nana."

I inched up from my chair and she froze. I held still, except for a slight nod of my head. "It's okay, Angelina. Don't be afraid. I'm so happy to meet you after all these years."

She advanced a step at a time and stopped a few feet away. "Hello," she said, her voice barely a whisper.

I extended my hand. As she took it, I pointed toward the table with my head. "Let's talk."

My gaze never left her. She perched rigid in the chair next to mine. So much of Nai'ya in her face and bearing. She was her mother's five-two or three, slim, and with the same long, dark hair. But her face spoke of sadness. She seemed older than her twenty-six years.

"Will you be staying?" she said.

It wasn't the question I'd expected. "Yes. Of course. I live here in New Mexico now."

"Good. Matty already lost his father. I don't want him dragged through those emotions again."

"I'll do everything I can for him. And you."

"It may take time before Matty warms up to you. Since his father went missing, he's been more withdrawn around adults. I think it all confuses him."

"Nai'ya told me about your husband. I'm very sorry." I searched her face for something of my own. Nothing. Perhaps it would be in her smile.

"Matty was only two and a half when John disappeared in Afghanistan. He asks about his dad all the time. We pray for him every night."

I wanted her to understand. "I can imagine how it must feel. My wife died eighteen months ago."

She let out a gasp and looked away. "I had no idea."

"We were married twenty-three years."

"My mother never told me."

I shook my head. "She didn't know, not until recently." Strange, that my daughter and I would come together over our mutual sense of loss.

"Do you have other children?" Her head was down. She lifted her eyes.

"You're my one and only. You and Matty and Nai'ya are all the family I have."

Angelina sat back in her chair. She started to speak and then stopped, as if reconsidering what she was about to say. Her eyes searched my face in earnest. Maybe she wanted a look inside.

Her hand rested on the tabletop. I dared to place mine on hers. "Please, give me a chance. I may not be what you expected. I may never be what you hoped for." I cleared a slight catch in my throat and looked away for a moment. I took a deep breath and it shuddered out of my chest. "I'd rather look ahead to what could be, instead of back at what we missed. Can we try that? And maybe fill in all the blanks as we go along?"

"Why didn't Mom tell me about you?" Her eyes moistened. She gripped my hand tighter.

"Your mother has a fierce love for you, Angelina. She did what she thought best. What her elders urged her to do."

"But it wasn't fair to me." Tears rolled over her cheekbones.

"She never told me either," I said. "At first I was hurt and angry too. But I love your mother. Now we're together. I'd like the chance to love you and Matty."

She sniffled and blinked, unable to clear her tears.

I held on to her hand. "Let's go back to your mom and Matty. Would that be okay?"

She nodded. We made our way across the room hand-in-hand.

The next few hours were awkward, painful and beautiful. Nai'ya, Angelina, and I spoke of many things and asked some long-held questions. We took the first steps on a healing journey we all seemed to know would take time.

Angelina and I did most of the talking and asked most of the questions. We had so much to learn about each other and our respective lives.

Matty became animated when I spoke of my past as an amateur boxer. But he deflated a bit when told I'd never done mixed martial arts. He asked a few questions about my time in the army. Maybe this tied me to his father somehow.

Nai'ya mostly held my hand.

Around nine o'clock, an elderly woman in tribal dress arrived with coffee and donuts and a small cider for Matty. Two hours later,

Onion finally showed. I left my family for the moment to meet him at the door.

"Where the hell have you been?" I asked.

"I drove to Santa Fe. Figured you needed time with your family. Had breakfast with a friend and then drove back."

I looked at him the way an old friend looks at an old friend. "So did you give her back her eyelash?"

Onion laughed. "Never could fool you."

A gnomish figure nearly engulfed by an oversized briefcase entered the building at eleven-thirty. Erskine Pelfrey III looked as woebegone as when I'd last seem him, but his new suit was a step in the right direction. Too bad it didn't fit any better than his old one.

Onion and I greeted him. "Erskine," I said, "let me take your hat." I hadn't seen a boater in decades.

The three of us trooped over to the conference table for necessary and intense conversation. We went over what Onion and I had discussed a few hours before, just to get things straight. My account of the previous night's arrest of Mahatma back in Albuquerque brought them both up to speed on that as well.

"You have had a lot on your plate, Professor."

"Yeah, and I don't want to switch to jail food, which is why you're here."

Pelfrey sprung the lock on his gigantic briefcase the way a killer cocks his gun. The move looked more comical than dramatic.

I leaned forward and put a hand on his forearm. "Sheriff Naranjo may try to hold me on suspicion in the shooting death of Jacob Wallace. I assure you I did nothing illegal. Listen closely to his questions and stop him anytime he overreaches. And stop me if he gets me too riled up and I start to say something stupid."

"I shall do my best. Is there a men's room nearby?"

"Through that door and turn left. End of the hallway." When my lawyer disappeared, I turned to Onion. "I'm still worried Naranjo will want to know why my prints aren't on Jepson's gun. Let's hope your gloves do the trick."

He gave me a confident nod. "Don't say anything about them. Give the sheriff a chance to jump to his own conclusion."

I looked across the room to Nai'ya, gave her a reassuring wave and a thumbs-up. When Pelfrey returned, I told them both to go out to my car. I wanted some time with my family.

Nai'ya had her brave face on, but couldn't hide the concern in her eyes. I struck an upbeat pose.

"We'll be back as soon as the sheriff finishes his questions. Then we'll all go home." I looked down at Matty. "You like barbecue?"

"Yeah!"

"Well then, you're going to have the best in town tonight!" I tossed a wink to Angelina. "Nai'ya, maybe you can call C.J. and tell him to expect us?"

"Sounds like a plan."

I joined Onion and Pelfrey for the short ride across the Pueblo to Naranjo's office. Halfway there, I looked over at Onion in the passenger's seat with one final request. "When Naranjo starts putting together the sequence of last night's events, would you mind taking over and giving him your 'professional opinion' on it all? Clutter his mind."

Onion smiled. "I know just what to do."

Pelfrey piped up from the back seat. "And I shall be listening closely."

CHAPTER FORTY

Officer Sanchez told us to cool our heels in the lobby of the sheriff's office. We cooled our heels. We cooled everything else, too—the heat in the building wasn't working. Ten frigid minutes to soak up all the ambience inherent in pale green cinder block.

We had to step aside at one point. A pair of uniformed officers dragged in a disheveled teenager who yelled and cursed alternately in Spanish, Tewa, and English. A third officer pulled a muzzled, snarling Doberman after them across the lobby and down a connecting hallway. A fluorescent light fixture flickered overhead. Shouts drifted in from the hallway in counterpoint to the boy's screams.

The door to a side room off the lobby opened and Sheriff Naranjo leaned out. "Come in, gentlemen."

We took our places at a six by four rectangular table. I sat in the middle on one side with Onion to my right and Pelfrey to my left. Naranjo filled the other side all by himself. Sanchez stood by the door. Both cops had their coats on. Naranjo's breath was visible in the air, like a bull ready to charge.

"Sorry about the cold," he said. "Baseboard panel isn't working. We put a call in."

I took Onion's gloves out of my coat pocket, slipped them on, and rubbed my hands together. "Any chance of coffee?"

Naranjo shook his head. "The outlets aren't working either." The overhead light flickered again.

"Let's get this over with as quickly as possible." I pointed to my lawyer. "This is my attorney, Erskine Pelfrey III, from Albuquerque. You already know Mr. Gagnon, my detective friend from New York City."

"We've met." The sheriff placed a blue file folder on the desk and opened it.

Before he could begin, Pelfrey spoke up. "Sheriff, with the unreliable state of electricity here, it seems problematic for my client to give you a tape recorded statement. Perhaps you could give us a list of questions to respond to in writing."

"I'll run this show my own way." Naranjo looked at Pelfrey the way a man looks at something before he scrapes it off the bottom of his shoe. He took out a recorder and placed it on the table. The overhead light flickered yet again and blacked out. Naranjo stood and lumbered to the window blinds and opened them all the way. Then he sat down and focused on me.

"McKenna, I'll hear what you have to say. Afterward, if I think we need a recording, we'll relocate and you can make a recorded statement. For now, we have to stay here. We sent out the guns and blood samples last night for faster testing in Albuquerque. I'm expecting the results soon."

"That's reasonable," I said. "So what do you want to know?"

"I want you to go back to the beginning. Tell me everything you can about your involvement with Jepson and Wallace. And all other relevant details. I may have a few follow-up questions when you're done."

I breathed an inner sigh of relief. He was letting me control and frame the story.

Erskine slid his chair up close to mine and placed his right hand on the back of my shoulder. I figured he would nudge or pinch me unnoticed if I said anything that could be used against me.

I gave Naranjo fifteen minutes of non-stop narrative, beginning with the initial discovery of a body buried in my barn. I ended with a final flourish about how Archuleta and I rounded up Mahatma in Albuquerque the night before. Once finished, I sat back in my seat and rubbed my gloved hands together.

"Very impressive," Naranjo deadpanned. "Now let's focus on

what happened on the Pueblo last night. Two men shot, one killed. That's what I care about—what happened in my jurisdiction."

I swallowed and took a deep breath. "Well, I can tell you what I saw. Mr. Gagnon and I came here to find my family. We didn't know at that time that Wallace and Jepson were on the Pueblo."

"May I jump in here?" Onion leaned forward. "I have years of experience with N.Y.P.D. and in my own practice. I can give you my take on—"

"No." Naranjo spoke with a slow, firm voice. "Gagnon, I know what you saw on the mesa. We drove there together, remember? I don't need conjecture. I want to know what Mr. McKenna did and why."

"I did nothing illegal," I insisted.

Naranjo shot me an angry look. "Did you discharge a firearm on my Pueblo?"

"I returned fire at Jepson in self-defense. Ask him."

"We did. He admits shooting at you. Also in self-defense, he says. And he denies killing Wallace."

"Of course. He would. But that won't matter anyway. If you can't nail him for Wallace, Archuleta and the Feds have him on conspiracy and as an accessory in other shooting deaths, maybe as many as five, both here in New Mexico and back in New York." I prayed he wouldn't ask me directly if I shot at Wallace.

Naranjo held me off with a raised finger and answered his office phone. "Right. Hold on, I'll take this in another room." He left without a glance in my direction. Sanchez remained by the door.

Onion and I exchanged glances. Pelfrey let out a quiet "Shhh" under his breath. Onion shrugged. The sheriff didn't care what he had to say. I was on my own.

Five minutes later, Naranjo returned. He laid five or six fax pages on the table next to the blue folder. He stared at me. "That was Archuleta. They have the preliminary ballistics and fingerprint results."

The three of us leaned forward like we were welded together at the shoulders. "And?" I said.

Naranjo studied the topmost page. "Wallace's gun fired the shots that killed Klein and his two assistants. Wallace's blood type matches that found at the scene of your secretary's abduction. His fingerprints match those found there as well." He read farther down the page. "Jepson's gun—the one that killed Wallace—also fired the fatal bullet into a Mr. Thomas O'Donnell at the Pueblo-66 Casino."

I hadn't expected that. My money had been on Wallace or Klein. "Where is Jepson now?" I said.

"Archuleta said Jepson, his wife, and the old lady—Mahatma?"

I nodded. "That's her."

"They're all in FBI custody and will be flown to New York. The Feds have taken over everything. Guess the biggest fish are still caught in eastern waters. The Bureau says they are 'confident.' But then, they always are."

I let out a deep sigh. "Can I go now?"

Naranjo's face lowered the temperature in the room a few more degrees. "Not quite."

Pelfrey's back stiffened. "And why not?"

The sheriff casually turned to the second fax page. "Tests on Jepson's gun fail to show his prints. You want me to believe that he killed Wallace and shot at you, but left no prints?"

Suddenly the room felt warm. I held my breath.

"And you tell me you carried Jepson's Beretta all the way to the top of the mesa and your prints aren't on the gun either?"

I held my gloved hands out, palms up.

Naranjo didn't move. "So how did your prints get on your own gun?" He sat back, like he thought he had me. Of course, in one sense he did.

"After I fired at Jepson, I reloaded my gun. You can't do that wearing gloves. That's why it was fully loaded when you checked it."

He gave me the Cold Stare. "Go on."

"Sheriff, I don't remember all the details. I'd just been shot at, then shot a man in self-defense. I've never done that before, except in the army. I scaled the side of the mesa in the dark after I heard Nai'ya's voice above me. I was tired and freezing, and almost fell a couple of times. Then I reached the top of the mesa and found Wallace. I remember dropping Jepson's gun by Wallace's body. Then you and Mr. Gagnon and Officer Sanchez arrived." I felt Pelfrey's hand pat the back of my shoulder.

Naranjo leaned his head back and rubbed his temples. He let out a deep, tired lungful of air. He reached into the blue folder, pulled out my bank check and fingered it for a bit.

"McKenna, whether it happened that way or not, I don't have sufficient evidence to charge you with a crime. Unfortunately, the two women's eyewitness accounts were less than useless."

He leaned forward in his chair and we stared eye-to-eye. "So I can't hold you. But as far as I'm concerned, McKenna, you're bad news all day long. You brought violence and death to my Pueblo." He tossed my bank check carelessly in my direction. "Take your blood money and get the hell out of here."

I drew a deep, quiet breath through my nose. "Thank you, Sheriff. I'll go." I swept up the check and handed it to Pelfrey. "Hold this for me."

Naranjo and Sanchez left first. I shook hands with Onion as Pelfrey slapped my shoulder.

"Erskine, I want to split that money. Half of it goes to Estefan Alonso-Riley to cover his medical bills. And so he and Belana can get a new house and start over."

"Got it." He wrote the details in a small, spiral notebook. "And the other half?"

"The other two hundred and fifty grand goes to Santa Clara Pueblo anonymously. With the stipulation that it be used to repair damage from the Conchas Fire of 2000 and the subsequent flood. They still have some ways to go."

"I shall arrange everything. May take two or three days. No more."

"Naranjo is right, you know."

Pelfrey frowned. "About what?"

"It *is* blood money. All the money I inherited is. But I'm not doing this out of guilt. I'm doing it to honor Edgar Lee Hewitt, one of my heroes."

Onion rolled his eyes. "Who'd he kill?"

"Hewitt was an archeologist who worked to preserve the whole Pajarito Plateau." I turned to Erskine. "Inform the Pueblo governor of my intentions before you leave today. Keep my name out of it."

"Gabe," Onion said. "Naranjo will tell him it's from you."

"Then let him. Erskine, let me know if anything needs a signature.

I'll stop by your office whenever."

"Done." His notebook disappeared into his briefcase.

The lights came back on. The baseboard crackled along the exterior wall.

CHAPTER FORTY-ONE

Erskine drove us back to the Community Center where my family waited and where Onion and I had left our cars. We piled out and stood for a moment beside the lawyer's Grand Cherokee.

"I owe you both a debt of gratitude," I said. "These past few weeks have been hell. I couldn't have made it without your help." I shook hands with Pelfrey first.

"Just doing my job, Professor. Everything worked out."

"Gimme a call when those papers are ready."

"I shall. Goodbye, Mr. Gagnon. Safe travels back to New York." Erskine started his car on the third try and disappeared down the road.

I handed Onion his gloves. "Will you have dinner with us tonight?"

"Not a chance, Brain. Tonight is for you and your family."

"Will I see you before you leave?"

"I'm gonna try and get a late flight out tonight. If you're done eating early, we could meet at the airport."

"That's an idea. And when you get back to New York, don't forget to send me your bill. I owe you more than money can ever repay."

Onion gave me a fake shoulder punch. "There won't be any bill. We go back too far. You'd do the same for me."

"You're a true friend, Deke."

"Old friends are the best friends," he said. "See you tonight."

When his rental car was nothing but a speck in the distance, I turned and walked into the Community Center.

With coffee for the adults and hot chocolate for Matty keeping us warm, we talked about the future for the most part on our way back to Albuquerque. Angelina alone dwelt on the past. Her curiosity about the earlier years of my life surprised me.

"Tell you what," I said at last. "How about we spend Christmas in New York this year? I'll show you where I grew up, got in and out of trouble, and generally raised hell. You could get in some serious holiday shopping too."

"It's my birthday in two weeks. I'm going to be seven years old." Matty waggled his fingers at me in the rearview mirror. He bounced up and down despite the seat belt. I'd have to get a child's car seat, and soon.

"Seven is pretty exciting," I said. "When I was seven my dad took me to my first baseball game. I'll never forget it. It was July 6th in 1967. Mickey Mantle hit one out against the Tigers."

"Who's Mickey Mantle?" he said.

Ouch. I still had some history left to teach. "Maybe we need to go to the World Series next year."

"Yeah!"

"If your mother agrees," I said.

"We'll see," Angelina said. It was a start.

C.J. laid out an impressive spread for our mid-afternoon lunch. Charmaine was smiling, even. Matty ate enough for three kids his age. C.J. and I took him into the back office to show off my friend's collection of boxing trophies and memorabilia.

"Did you ever fight my grandpa?"

"Sure did." C.J winked at me. He knew what question would be next.

"Who won?"

Mischief flashed in my friend's eyes, then he seemed to soften. "I'd have to say we both did. Your grandpa was quite a fighter. In fact, he still is."

Matty beamed at me. "We're going to a baseball game for my birthday next year. And to the World Series!"

"You have to help me convince your mom," I said. "Work hard in school, keep your room clean, help with the dishes, go to bed when your mom says to."

His young face scrunched up like he was eating his first pickle. "All that?"

C.J. and I laughed. "All that," I said. "Now I need to talk with Mr. Jester for a few minutes. Why don't you go back to your mom and see if dessert is ready?"

"Okay!"

C.J. closed the door once Matty left and sat at his desk. "I got an update on Rebecca for you. Sit down." He motioned me to the chair across the desk.

"Hospital?"

"For a couple of days, at least," he said. "Those people gave her a bad mix of drugs, but she's gonna be okay. No visitors until tomorrow. The cops have someone outside her room twenty-four-seven. Just as a precaution, you understand."

"I'll visit her in the morning. Thanks for keeping an eye on things."

"One question, Gabe—you clear with the law?"

"Sure as hell hope so. I've got a lawyer here and one back in New York just in case."

"Good." C.J. drummed his fingers on the top of the desk. "Can I give you some advice as your friend?"

"Anytime. Whether or not I'll listen…"

"Slow down. Lay low. Don't go off half-cocked like you usually do. Relax and take some time to be with your family. They need you."

"Don't worry. That's exactly what I'm going to do."

Nai'ya and I agreed to meet for breakfast the next morning. I dropped her off at her place on Marquette. After stopping for a gallon of milk and incidentals, I drove Angelina and Matty to their townhouse in the northeast heights. After I parked, she opened the door and lifted a bag of groceries from the back seat.

"Will you be okay?" I said.

"I'll look for a new job in a few days. I've started over before."

"You don't need to do it alone, you know."

Angelina bent down and looked into the back. "Come along, Matty." She caught his hand as he spilled out of the car.

"Goodnight, Grandpa."

"Goodnight, kid."

I stayed at the curb and called Sam Archuleta.

"Welcome back," he said. "Had enough excitement?"

"Too much. Listen, how about meeting Nai'ya and me at the El Camino tomorrow morning around nine? I'm going to visit Rebecca in the hospital. We're having breakfast on my way there."

"I'm afraid I can't. Guess you didn't hear about Crawford."

"What did he do now?"

"It's not him, it's his daughter Jennifer. She died the day before yesterday. The leukemia. Her wake was today. The funeral is nine-thirty tomorrow morning. Such a waste. Seven years old."

"Nobody deserves that, not even Crawford."

"You do realize, you're a lucky man, don't you?"

More than I had any right to be.

A text message came in on my phone. It was Onion: *Scored 2 seats to NY on red eye. Dep. 11:45. C U at airport?*

It was now 7:30. I texted back that I'd be there by ten-thirty.

My house was dark and Otis greeted me with his hungry-angry voice. I kicked myself for not having brought home some leftover barbecue. "Sorry, Your Lordship," I said. "Your hard stuff will have to do." I filled his bowl and then filled a clean glass with my own hard stuff. I thought about a little nap. No, I might not wake in time to meet Onion.

I punted my shoes onto the rug and leaned back in the library desk chair. Onion had his faults and weaknesses all right, but he sure nailed it about old friends being the best.

One more phone call, this time to Sloppy in New York. Onion had already called him with a summary of what had happened over the past two days.

"Yeah, Brain, heard all about it. You have *any idea* how big this turned out to be?"

"What do you mean?" I let a healthy swallow of whiskey glide down my throat.

"Mahatma wasn't just the boss in New Mexico. She'd been coordinating everything with their east coast organization for more than thirty years."

"I'm not that surprised. There's an evil mind under all that gray hair."

"That son-in-law of hers has been singing like Caruso to the Feds. Check the online New York papers. It's the lead story today. Will be for days."

"Bottom line?"

"The Sons of Tammany are toast. The Feds swooped in this afternoon and rounded up all the ringleaders. Their Big Cheese turned out to be a Manhattan Federal District Court Judge, no less, guy named Quentin Kirschner. A real bastard. They also nabbed that Queens Assistant D.A. we wrestled with. Found Tommy's missing files right there in his office."

"Couldn't happen to a nicer fella."

"By the way, Tommy's boss at the *Daily News* finally found his *cojones*. He knew a lot more about Tommy's investigation than he let on to you. Must have been scared silent. He's cooperating fully with the investigation now."

I raised my glass. "You, me, Onion, and Tommy. Still undefeated."

"Damn right, Gabe."

"I'll be in the Big Apple for Christmas this year. Hoping to bring my family. Will I see you then?"

"Great," Sloppy said. "Maybe we can sing them some holiday carols."

"Don't push it. My daughter is easily frightened."

I arrived at the airport early. Maybe time enough for a parting drink with my old friend. The departures board said his flight would leave on time at 11:45. We'd have the better part of an hour for our goodbyes.

"You just get here?" The voice came from behind me.

I spun around. Onion and his *femme du jour* from the Santa Fe hotel looked at me. Hand-in-hand, no less.

"Juanita," I smiled. "We meet again." Both of her eyelashes were attached this time, but she still appeared off-balance. After a brief nod hello, she excused herself and did a stiletto-induced wobble to the ladies' room. I gawked until she disappeared, then turned to my friend. "Explain, please."

"It's like this, Gabe. My third wife and I—"

"The Greek one?"

"Yeah. Well, we didn't exactly part on friendly terms when I came out here."

"So you figured you'd bring Juanita back as a peace offering?"

"Hear me out, man. I'm going back to an empty apartment."

"And you don't want to let the other side of the bed go to waste."

Onion punched my shoulder. "I knew you'd understand. That's why we've been friends for so long."

I gave him a half-hearted shrug. "Guess the least I can do is buy you both an adult beverage and send you on your way. What does the lady drink?"

"Anything you put in front of her."

CHAPTER FORTY-TWO

My alarm rang at seven-thirty the following morning. I drank my first cup of coffee and checked the websites Sloppy mentioned the night before. He was right—large, splash headlines above photomontages of lawyers, judges, and politicos covering their faces, and FBI agents leading them off to justice, however delayed.

Their bloody scheme had been going on for more than four decades. Details were still incomplete, but the Bureau estimated more than thirty men of wealth and standing had bought into the false promise of getting a do-over on their lives. They'd all been killed of course, their fortunes stolen by the Sons of Tammany. I wondered, what other schemes had they pulled off over the years?

I couldn't ignore the probability that Aunt Nellie had played a role in these crimes. The fortune she'd willed to me made me feel dirty. I put such concerns aside for the time being. I had personal business to take care of first.

Breakfast was the house omelet at El Camino. Nai'ya just had coffee. We made promises about our family. I swore to go back on the wagon for good. Over our second cups, I asked to stay at her place that night. She gave me *That Look*. I kissed her hand and she left for UNM.

At a nearby florist shop, I bought a dozen yellow roses for Rebecca, my return of a thoughtful gesture she'd once made to me.

She was in a private room. I'd had C.J. see to that. As I strode to the elevator, the woman at the reception desk waved like she knew me. Once aboard, I fluffed the roses so they'd look their best. A gray haired woman in blue hospital garb flashed me a bemused smile before she stepped off one floor below Rebecca's.

I inquired at the nurses' station, where they directed me to a corner room down the hall and to my right. I stopped short in front of an empty chair that rested against the wall outside her door. *Where was the guard?* I knocked and poked my head inside. Rebecca sat propped up in bed watching the overhead television.

"Are you decent?" I said.

"Gabe!" She smiled and stretched out her arms.

I moved to embrace her but the roses got in my way. We shared a joyful, awkward moment before she took the flowers and plopped them in a water pitcher beside her bed.

"They're lovely, Gabe." She pulled one rose out of the bunch and fingered the stem before inhaling its fragrance.

"How are you? When will you be out of here? I was afraid I'd lost you."

"I'm not that easy to get rid of," she said. "You, of all people, should know that by now."

"I do. You're the strongest woman I know."

"Thanks. Unfortunately, it looks like I'll be here for another day or two at least. Still have a lousy headache. And my legs are a bit wobbly."

"If there's anything you need, just give me a call."

"Actually, I'm being looked after rather well…" The tone in her voice was suggestive.

"If you mean the cops, I should tell you that the chair in the hall is empty. I was told they'd be protecting you but—"

"They are," she interrupted. Rebecca looked beyond my right shoulder. "Come on in, Darrell. It's Gabe."

Officer Jackson entered with two slices of chocolate cake on a single plate and a cup of coffee. "Hello, Mr. McKenna. Nice of you to drop by." He put the food and drink on the bedside table next to my flowers.

His clothes were disheveled and he hadn't shaved in a while. Even his buzz-cut looked messy. "How long have you been here?" I snitched a finger of frosting from one of the cake slices.

"Ever since we brought Rebecca in. Except for when I drove home to change into my jeans and hoodie."

"He's using up his vacation days to stay with me. Isn't he sweet?"

"Well," I said, mostly to myself, "you two certainly surprised me. May I?" I pointed to the coffee.

"Sure," Rebecca said. "And we have another surprise for you."

"Oh? What's that?" I slurped the lukewarm brew.

"We're getting married."

I managed to swallow without choking, but all I could utter was a weak, "What?"

Rebecca laughed and looked at the blushing Jackson. "I told you he'd be shocked!"

"Well, well…" I bought a few seconds to regain my composure. "I wish you every happiness. You know that." I shook Jackson's hand. "Congratulations." Then I bent down and kissed Rebecca's cheek.

"Darrell," she said, "will you go get me a pitcher of water? Oh, and I've changed my mind. I think I'd like a Diet Pepsi with my cake instead of coffee."

"Anything you want, dear." Jackson disappeared down the corridor.

I turned to Rebecca. "Sounds like you've been married for years."

She brushed off my remark. "Gabe, I wanted a minute alone with you. I have a favor to ask."

"Anything."

"When Darrell and I get married, will you give me away at the altar? You're the closest thing I've got to a real father. Please?"

I sat down on the bed and took her hand in mine. "Nothing in this world would give me greater pleasure. And the honeymoon is on me."

Rebecca threw her arms around my neck and hugged me tight. We stayed like that and said nothing more. When I finally drew away, tears rolled down her cheeks. She kissed my hand.

My eyes welled up. I took a couple of deep breaths. "I should have worn my fucking shades." I turned toward the door just as Darrell reappeared with a can of Diet Pepsi and a silver water pitcher. "Come with me a second," I said, and backed him out into the hall.

"What is it?"

I stared at him and spoke in a forceful whisper. "You take good care of her. I'd hate to have to kill you."

"Yessir. I will, sir."

I got out of the elevator and headed outside. The late morning sun warmed the air. The frigid wind of the past few days lingered only in memory.

At my bank, however, Mr. Woolsey the Branch Manager was downright frosty when I informed him that the half million dollars would not be returning to my account.

Maria looked up in surprise when I walked into the El Camino diner just before noon.

"Did you forget something this morning, *Señor?*"

"No. I'm here for lunch." My smile spread to her face. "I've always believed that you can't get too much of a good thing. Is Lieutenant Archuleta here yet?"

"Your policeman friend?" She nodded to her left. "In the booth by the front window."

"Thanks, Maria." I slid in across from Sam and got right down to business. "So when do I get my car back?"

Sam pushed the menu across to me. "Oh yeah. I forgot that every couple of months you feel the need to total your Land Cruiser. Let me check on that and get back to you. Want your .38 back too, I suppose."

"Keep the gun."

"Smart."

"And I promise you, no more surprises from now on."

"That's good," Sam said. Then he paused. "Now I've got a surprise for you."

"This seems to be a day for surprises. Shoot."

"I've thought it over. I've decided to retire from APD."

He could have knocked me over with a single puff of smoke. "You? Retire? Why?"

"Mahatma. That old bag got off three rounds at me from close range. If she hadn't been such a pitiful shot, I would have retired right there on her living room rug."

"I saw what happened. You took an extra second to aim carefully so you could stop the old lady without killing her. That's commendable."

He clicked his lighter on and off; on and off. "That kind of soft-headed response will get me killed next time. I've lost my edge. I'm going out alive, my friend. And, if you read today's paper, I'm going out on top, too."

Sam referred to the front page of *The Albuquerque Journal,* where his tough-guy countenance appeared under the headline "Heroic Local Cop Cracks Nationwide Crime Ring." I wondered how many shades of red Carlson was wearing on his face today.

Maria came by. We ordered two combination plates and two beers. Sam added a side of *carne adovada.*

He put the lighter back in his coat pocket. "Just one thing…"

"What's that?"

"Loose ends. I don't like 'em."

"Oh."

"There's the not so little matter of—"

"Stop," I said. "Don't you think I've realized it too? My own aunt."

Sam held up a finger to stop me. Maria brought our beers and disappeared into the kitchen.

I took a chug and looked across the table. "That first body was Joseph Force Crater. Nellie had to be involved with him. All those weekly deposits—"

"That ended just about the time Dr. Holtzmann tells me Crater was killed."

"I know, Sam. Crater bought the farm and Nellie bought the house. Or somebody from Klein Associates gave it to her. Mahatma knew her, too. Any way you slice it, my great aunt was on the inside." I took another swallow of beer. "Hard to believe a member of my own family—"

"Relax, Gabe. We're going to close this case and let that float. What you do with all her money is up to you. Me, I'm going fishing."

"I'm going to miss you, Lieutenant."

"You think so?" he said. "I have this dreadful foreboding that our paths will cross again. And probably sooner, rather than later."

"That may be. Look, how about we get together one last time to celebrate your retirement? We could meet at one of those e-cig joints. You could vape while I nurse a club soda."

"In a pig's eye."

CHAPTER FORTY-THREE

The morning sky of December 12th cloaked Albuquerque in a mantle of unrelenting gray. Thirty-mile-per-hour wind gusts brought a chill to the air and a hint of an impending winter storm, our first of the season.

I came into my house through the front door and put down the mallet I'd used to post a "For Sale" sign out by the street. The library phone rang. I was expecting a call from my real estate agent. Nope. It was Carol Something-or-Other, my travel agent.

"Your airline tickets are in the mail. Three seats together in Row 4. The fourth seat is right across the aisle."

"Great." Matty could sit between his mom and his Nana. I'd have extra room for my legs.

"Your hotel reservation is all set. Two adjoining suites. I got you a limo from and to the airport. It'll all be in the envelope."

"Wonderful, Carol. I thank you."

"You should. You have any idea how hard it is to get good flights to New York and accommodations over Christmas? One last question, Professor."

"What's that?"

"How come you're not staying over for New Year's Eve? You know, Times Square, the ball, all that?"

I sighed and sat down in the chair. "This has been one hell of a year for me. I need to celebrate the end of it quietly. No excitement.

At home. Just me and my family."

I reached into the drawer for my checkbook and booted up my computer. The online banking page showed a balance of $24,236.16 in checking. Enough for our trip to New York and Rebecca's honeymoon. Enough to get me by after that. For a while, anyway.

I clicked on my savings account, where I kept the rest of the money I'd inherited from Aunt Nellie. The balance read $412,325.05. I did an online electronic transfer of the full amount into my checking. Then I picked up my Mont Blanc and wrote a check to the Children's Cancer Fund of New Mexico in the amount of $412,325.05 for leukemia research.

I slipped the check into an envelope, attached a stamp and bent down to lick the flap. I stopped. Let it sit there on my desktop for now. There'd be plenty of time to mail it on Monday morning when I went out to look for a job.

CHAPTER FORTY-FOUR

I drove downtown and stopped off at a bar for a quickie before heading to Nai'ya's place for the night.

It was the El Tapado, the same bar I'd visited the day I inherited Aunt Nellie's estate six months before. The place was just as cold today, just as unwelcoming. And just as on that day, there was only one other patron—a sinister hulk of a man seated off in the shadows at the far end of the bar, all the way down by the bathrooms.

I got the barkeep's attention and ordered a double Black Bush. I savored it, reflecting on the joy I felt for my family and Rebecca. And on all the misery and violence of the past ten days.

The giant at the end of the bar interrupted my reverie. "Bartender!" he snarled. "Another!"

It was Sergeant Crawford. I glanced at him, but made no other move. He gazed my way, all watery eyes and blank, puffy face. I don't think he even saw me. His massive frame and threatening bulk seemed to be receding, like a ripened grape shriveling into a raisin.

"Bartender," I said. "That man's next drink is on me." I looked at Crawford once more and tipped my glass.

"Get lost." He slugged down his drink and turned away toward the shadows.

ABOUT THE AUTHOR

Robert D Kidera's debut novel, "Red Gold" received the Tony Hillerman Award for Best Fiction of 2015, and won Best Mystery of 2015, and Best eBook at the New Mexico/Arizona Book Awards.

"Red Gold" is the first novel in the *Gabe McKenna Mystery* series from Suspense Publishing. Its sequel, "Get Lost," will be released on March 8, 2016. A third volume, "Cut.Print.Kill." will follow.

After an early fling in the motion picture industry and a long and successful career in academia, Kidera retired in 2010. With his desire to play major league baseball no longer a realistic dream, he chose to fulfill his other lifelong ambition and became a writer. He is a member of Southwest Writers, Sisters in Crime, and the International Thriller Writers organizations.

The author lives in Albuquerque, New Mexico with his wife Annette and two cats, Otis and Woody. He has two daughters, a grandson, and granddaughter.

PRAISE FOR "RED GOLD"
THE FIRST VOLUME IN THE *GABE MCKENNA MYSTERY* SERIES

"RED GOLD," the first *Gabe McKenna Mystery*, debuted in April of 2015 from Suspense Publishing. It was named winner of the Tony Hillerman Award for Best Fiction, Best Mystery, and Best eBook at the New Mexico/Arizona Book Awards for 2015.

Here's what noted authors have said about this award-winning mystery:

"Author Robert D. Kidera owes me big time. His debut novel in the promised *McKenna Mystery* series, 'Red Gold,' kept me up all night. Who can resist a good old-fashioned treasure hunt? 'Red Gold' is a thriller packed with deceit and danger but also compassion. McKenna is a damaged hero, but also one to root for."
—**Vincent Zandri**, *New York Times* and *USA Today* Bestselling Author of "Everything Burns," "The Remains," and "The Shroud Key"

"If you enjoy first-class suspense and an author with a unique voice and style, then you will love 'Red Gold.' This novel is a masterful blend of mystery, action, and love story, all wrapped up in a wonderful cast of characters and beautifully-described scenes of New Mexico. Robert Kidera's first novel is a real treat that will have readers demanding more."
—**Joseph Badal**, Award-winning Author of the *Danforth Saga*

"In his stunning debut novel, Robert Kidera takes readers on a wild ride through New Mexico as a troubled professor gets caught up in the search for lost gold. Filled with lush detail and packed with thrills, 'Red Gold' grabs the reader and refuses to let go. Fans will look forward to more books featuring widowed protagonist Gabe McKenna."
—**Steve Brewer**, Author of the *Bubba Mabry* Mysteries

"The often-told tale of lost gold, a treasure map, and various people attempting to find it, never grows old. And Kidera's 'Red Gold' mystery is no exception. Kidera's dialogue rings true and his descriptions allow readers to taste the dirt of a Southwest sandstorm, feel the prickly heat of late spring, relax in the cool of an adobe house. Gabe McKenna, laden with emotional baggage, arrives in Albuquerque from New York. In the process of settling his inherited estate, he discovers a map, hints of treasure and most importantly— himself. 'Red Gold' is a traditional story turned on its head and, oh so well written! Fast paced, plot twists at every turn, humor thrown in at just the right moments, Kidera's debut novel is one that keeps pages turning. "Red Gold" is a gem."

—**Melody Groves**, Award-winning Author of *The Colton Brothers Saga*

"Robert D. Kidera has written a winning mystery that incorporates the spirit of Raymond Chandler and his characters with an authentic feel for Albuquerque and many other places in New Mexico. Kidera has a native's eye for quirky details in characters, architecture, and natural features of the Land of Enchantment. The suspense begins to build in the first chapter and Kidera never takes his foot off the pedal. The search for 'Red Gold' will evoke comparisons to B. Traven's 'The Treasure of the Sierra Madre.' Be there for the exciting finish."

—**Robert Kresge**, Author of the *Warbonnet* Historical Mysteries and the Civil War Spy Thriller "Saving Lincoln" (Winner of the 2014 Tony Hillerman/Best Fiction Award)

Stay up-to-date with each new story by visiting http://www.robertkiderabooks.com/

Or follow the latest developments in this series at the online author page on Amazon: http://www.amazon.com/Robert-D.-Kidera/e/B00IP23642/ref=dp_byline_cont_book_1

6160963